CW00733686

DEATH'S REQUIEM

DAVID J. GATWARD

WEIRDSTONE PUBLISHING

Death's Requiem
By
David J. Gatward

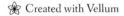

To Aled: you asked for it...

Grimm: nickname for a dour and forbidding individual, from Old High German grim [meaning] 'stern', 'severe'. From a Germanic personal name, Grima, [meaning] 'mask'.
(*www.ancestory.co.uk*)

CHAPTER ONE

THE CHILDREN KNEW WHAT THEY WERE DOING WAS naughty, that if their parents found out they'd be in for it, but in the end, that was what made it all so much more exciting.

The day had been a dark one, starting off warm, too warm by far, the threat of a storm ever-present on the horizon, only now it stretched itself across the sky, thick and bloated.

Early evening was around them, dressing them in its shadows. They were standing in the graveyard, all in a circle, after one dare too many had gone just a little too far.

'I don't like this.'

'Scaredy cat.'

'Am not!'

'It's spooky though, isn't it? So creepy...'

'It's supposed to be! It's a graveyard!'

'Graveyards aren't supposed to be spooky or creepy, they just are!'

One of the children let out an eerie moan and another

screamed. Then another. Soon, everyone was screaming. Well, almost.

'I'm going home!'

'You can't! Not yet! We haven't done it!'

'It's silly anyway. I don't like it.'

As one of the children turned to break from the circle, another of the group said, 'What about a sacrifice? We need one, don't we?'

'Why? I thought that was just a joke!'

''Cos that's what the Devil wants.'

'The Devil isn't real. This is stupid. I'm going home.'

'You've said that already!'

'Yeah, go home then, if you're chicken!'

'Don't you call me that!'

'Then don't be so stupid!'

'I'm not being stupid! You're the one being stupid! This wasn't my idea. It's just a stupid dare, that's all! A stupid, stupid dare!'

The argument would have continued for quite some time if one of the other kids hadn't stepped in to shush them, the one whose idea this all was in the first place, their own reasons for what they were doing a very big secret because if any of the others found out, they'd never shut up about it. And that would ruin everything.

'Sacrifice is everywhere, isn't it? Even in the Bible. It's what's needed when people do this stuff. And I've seen it in films, too.'

'You've not seen any of those films that you say you have.'

'I have, too!'

'No, you haven't!'

'Anyway, we've got that dead rabbit. That'll do, I'm sure it will. It's symbolic.'

The kid smiled, knowing that word would have everyone quiet because it sounded so grown up.

'Yuck. Just look at it.'

'That's so unfair. Poor thing.'

'Don't cry!'

'I'm not crying, I'm just sad!'

'I shot it this morning with my air rifle,' another kid said. 'Clean kill, too. I'm really good. Might join the army when I'm older.'

The rabbit was in the middle of the group, resting on top of a grave, the writing on the weathered stone at its head too worn to now be read.

The one who had boasted about shooting the rabbit said, 'Come on then, let's get this done. I'm getting hungry and Mum'll kill me if I'm too late back, like.'

A rustling of paper being unfolded had everyone quiet.

'I've got the instructions,' the one in charge said, checking through what was written on the paper to make sure that everything was right. 'It's a ritual.'

That was another grown-up word.

'So, why are we doing this, exactly?'

'We're making a deal, a pact.'

'A pact? Why?'

'So that we can get a wish granted, that's why! Don't you listen to anything ever?'

'And you really think it will work?'

'I read it in a book. Said it was based on a true story, so I guess so. We make a sacrifice and then our wish is granted!'

'What was the book, then? Is it here? Have you got it?'

'That poor little bunny.'

'I can't remember which book.'

A laugh.

'You made it up, then, didn't you?'

'I did not! It was one of my dad's books. A really big horror one with this creepy cover with a skull and a snake. You make a sacrifice and you get a wish! That's how it works!'

'Why don't we just pray for things, then?'

'We've all been doing that and nothing ever happens, does it?'

No answer.

'And God doesn't want you to be rich or to get what you want, does he? So that's why we're trying this. And it will work, I'm sure it will. And imagine if it does!'

'Prove it, then.'

'Right then, I will!'

'Good! Go on then!'

'Everyone needs to join hands!'

'What, hold hands? With her?'

The one in charge said, 'No, I'm holding hands with her!'

Someone giggled as a hand reached out for another and held it nervously, gently.

'Shut up! Now everyone do the same and hold hands. It's important!'

With that, everyone did as they were told and the one in charge, the one now holding the hand of the person this whole ritual was secretly about in the first place, started to read. And the words, which many of them didn't understand, and which had been pulled together not just from the book mentioned, but from lots of other books and comics and movies and even the Bible, seemed to some of them to turn the evening darker and the air still. But it also all sounded and felt familiar, because they were all of them used to a little ritual in their lives thanks to the building behind them, a church they all attended. Something which made this all feel like the naughtiest and most dangerous thing some of them had ever done.

'Someone has to stab the rabbit now.'

Gasps around the circle.

'What?'

'Someone has to stab it! That's what happens!'

'But look at it! It's already dead!'

'Stop talking about it and just stab it!'

The reader held out a large knife.

'Here. Use this.'

'Why me? Don't you want to do it?'

'I didn't say I didn't want to do it! I just said that it needs to be done! I'm the one doing the reading! Someone has to do the stabbing! I can't do everything!'

No one moved.

'Fine!'

A heartbeat later and the knife was brought down into the dead rabbit with a dull, wet thud.

'Yuck!'

'That's disgusting!'

'It stinks!'

'Shut up!'

'Poor rabbit.'

A hammering crack of thunder broke the sky, the sound so ancient and deep that it seemed to reach into the ground beneath the children and make it shudder, the windows in the church behind them rattling.

The one with the ritual grinned.

'See? I told you it would work! Didn't I tell you? Didn't I?'

A flash of lightning then, so bright, so violent, the world

was momentarily a negative, sharp black and white, devoid of colour.

Then the wind and the rain came, snatching the ritual from the hands that held it, slamming into the ground like bullets, and so thick that the wall of the graveyard disappeared from view.

The circle broke and everyone scattered, running home as the thunder rolled above them, the far off fells blasted with a thick white lance of the brightest lightning.

Well, almost everyone.

In the rain and the thunder, and alone now, the one who had been in charge spotted the written page of the ritual on the ground, dancing on the wind, picked it up, folded it and stuffed it into a pocket.

Then the knife was pulled free.

Knowing that the church would still be open, because the vicar wouldn't lock it until later that evening, the remaining child, with the dead rabbit cradled in gentle arms, walked through the thunder and the lightning and the rain towards the large building. Stepping into its shadow, the child knew that the best thing now was to lay the poor little bunny to rest, somewhere very safe, somewhere very secret, somewhere very special. And with it would go their own special secret, that one day the hand they had held only moments ago would be theirs.

Forever.

CHAPTER TWO

MUCH LIKE HIS TIME IN THE PARAS ALL THOSE YEARS ago now, Harry's life in the police force had presented him with numerous new and unique experiences which his training had never really had a chance to prepare him for. There was, after all, only so much that hall-room lectures, role-playing various scenarios, and going out onto the streets with real police officers, could do. And many of these experiences, he was sure, were barely covered by whatever job description it was that he had originally thought he'd been signing up to. And if they had been, if they had, for whatever reason, formed an essential part of some fancy new recruitment drive by the Government, then he probably would have thought twice about signing up for it in the first place.

As a soldier, Harry had been pushed to the very limit of his physical and mental endurance and beyond. It was the old adage of train hard, fight easy, and although the first was absolutely true, and clearly made all the difference when the bullets started to fly, fighting was never actually easy. In battle, he had experienced the kind of violence that even now, years later, had been so ferocious in the physical and mental wounds and scars that it had given him, that it would still wake him up at night in a sweat, the stench of it thick in the darkness.

There had been worse experiences than the heat and sweat and blood of battle, ones he told no one about, because to do so would be to relive them, and he'd done that more than enough times on various couches over the years, as therapists had done their level best to help him to come to terms, and deal, with not only what he had done to others, but what, in turn, others had done to him. Harry was fairly sure that no matter how thorough the therapy, or effective the coping strategies, memories not just of the IED which had so badly scarred him, but of capture, and the terror of interrogation, would always haunt him.

Then, as a police officer, Harry had seen yet further examples of the truly terrible things humans were capable of inflicting on their own kind, and more often than not it was usually just to earn some fast cash quickly spent. He'd arrested drug dealers and car thieves, dealt with gangs smuggling everything from alcohol and tobacco, to weapons and people and exotic pets. Though not exactly as exciting or ridiculous as the Samuel L. Jackson movie, *Snakes on a Plane*, Harry had, on one extra special day, had to deal with chinchillas on a bus.

He'd also dealt with knife crime, professional hits, organised gangs, and acts carried out by the most desperate of people just trying to get by. He'd been puked on by binge drinkers raging for a fight after a night on the lash and been spat and snarled at by attack dogs that were more rabid bear than pet.

One Halloween he'd even had to arrest an idiot dressed as a clown for what was now referred to as *public nuisance* and *outraging public decency*. And the guilty party had certainly managed to do both very well indeed, Harry recalled, with more than a little amusement. The first, by running through the streets squirting people with a water pistol filled with his own urine, and the second, by doing the whole thing in baggy trousers with the bottom cut out, a fox tail sticking out from where it shouldn't, jutting proudly from between his shiny white, jiggling buttocks.

However, of all the things that Harry had ever experienced and done over the years, and across these two high-stress, high-pressure, and sometimes life-threatening job roles, he had never, not even once, had to paint a sheep.

'And I just slap it on here, do I?' Harry asked, staring at a sheep and pointing at an area of its fleece just above its shoulders. The animal was eye-balling him from where it was pinned between two narrow lengths of fencing. He'd seen stares like that before, dead-eye stares, the kind that hid behind them the threat of relentless violence, even death. This was a sheep with murder on its mind, Harry was sure. By God, the thing looked evil.

'That's right,' said Jim, who wasn't just one of the local Police Community Support Officers, but also the son of a local farmer and still very much involved in the running of the family farm. He was standing just a few paces away to Harry's right, with his dog, Fly, sitting a little distance away from him, tail wagging, as it stared at the sheep. 'You just slap a dollop of that blue stuff onto the fleece there, right? Don't be shy with it either, like. I want this stuff in good and deep.'

In his hands Harry was holding a tub of a sticky, oily substance the colour of a raspberry slushy and a large, hefty paint brush with bristles stiff enough to turn sheet steel into ribbons. With Jim to his right, and the PCSO's dad, Eric, to his left, they were all hunkered down in a barn in the farm-yard. The rain that winter had not, as yet, decided to turn to snow, had welcomed Harry to his Thursday morning by turning his bedroom window into a solo any heavy metal drummer would be proud of, and was currently crashing against the metal roof above them.

A brutally cold wind was howling around outside, and although the walls of the building were keeping it at bay, it was still making good use of the gated openings, and every nook and cranny and gap that it could find, to slice and whip at them with seemingly relentless glee. At points, the building shook and rattled so hard, Harry was pretty sure it was only moments away from being ripped from its founda-tions and sent skyward. The barn itself was rich with the ripe stench of animals and straw. It wasn't unpleasant by any means, and Harry, who had once, not so long ago, been more used to the acrid air of a city or town, breathed it in, the life essence of the dales.

'Doesn't exactly look all that happy about it,' Harry said, reaching tentatively towards the sheep with the brush. 'By which I mean, I think the fluffy bugger wants to kill me.'

'Sheep always look like that,' Jim said.

'You mean, evil?'

'What? No!' Jim said. 'You're confusing sheep with goats.'

'Am I?' Harry asked. 'I'm pretty sure I know the difference.'

'You've obviously never been stared at by a goat.'

'Can't say that I have,' Harry said. 'Or, if I have, it's not an experience I've remembered.'

Harry, very aware of the eyes staring daggers at him, slapped a dollop of the blue stuff onto the sheep and smeared it around a bit, jabbing the brush deep into the fleece. The sheep continued to stare at him, with what looked like pure hatred in its eyes.

That done, Jim's dad, Eric, who was standing to Harry's left, then glued something into the fleece before releasing the sheep, allowing it to scoot forward through a small gate. Another sheep, shoved gently forwards by Jim from a larger pen filled with its friends, was now staring at Harry. It, too, didn't look all that happy about it. Word had clearly got around the flock that some west country idiot was here to ruin their lovely, warm fleeces.

'Hello there,' Harry said to the sheep, then turned to Jim. 'So, remind me how this works,' he said, reaching out with the blue stuff to anger another animal.

'It's called TecTracer,' Jim explained. 'It was originally developed to put on church roofs and stop folk hopping up there and nicking the lead. Bit of a problem round here a while back, until this was used.'

'It's microdots, right?' Harry said, daubing the sheep in front of him, its stare one of hot, unrelenting menace, as though its eyes were little more than glazed windows beyond which sat the fiery furnaces of Hell itself.

'Each one carries a code unique to whatever farm the sheep are from,' Jim explained. 'And all of that gets stored on a database. With the radio frequency identification tags that Dad's gluing in, it's the best anti-theft system around.'

'So, what did farmers use before?' Harry asked.

'Horn markings, mainly,' Eric said. 'And we still do that, like, along with electronic ear tags, but you can cut all that off right quick, can't you? Which is what those sheep rustling bastards do, isn't it? I tell you, if I ever get my hands on them ...'

Eric growled, the sound deep in his throat and mixed with curses that Harry couldn't quite make out, which was probably for the best, he thought. Eric wasn't exactly young, mid-fifties Harry guessed, but he'd lived a hard life, and the weather had carved its own tattoos and scars into the man's face, which resembled worn rock eroded by the harsh work of time passing. His skin, even now in the thick of winter, was brown, and his forearms were tight knots of roped muscle.

'It's clever stuff,' Jim said, shoving another sheep forward for Harry to paint. 'Any of this lot get stolen, an alert is sent out to not just the police, but auction marts and abattoirs. Means we can be one step ahead of the thieves. And maybe get our hands on the bastards who murdered Neil.'

Harry had been wondering when it would come up. It was barely a couple of months ago when Eric had lost fifty of his flock to sheep rustlers. And Jim had lost an old school friend, someone who it turned out had been involved in the whole thing from the off, not only leading the gang who did it to the farm, but keeping Jim away from the place while the theft was carried out. And then he'd ended up dead, a loose end that needed tying up, a chin that someone, somewhere, had obviously been very worried was going to wag. And Jim, understandably, hadn't taken it all that well.

'I wish we'd done this before,' Eric said, the words only just clear amongst the growls and grumbles. 'Then we'd have those buggers by the short and curlies, wouldn't we?'

As if to emphasise what he meant, the man reached out with his right hand and gripped what Harry assumed could only be an invisible ball sack, then twisted.

'I'd make the sods squeal, too, right I would.'

'So, you all sorted with the insurance?' Harry asked, moving on from Eric's rumbling urge for vengeance, fearing it wasn't going to do Jim any good to get all worked up about it. 'They paid up?'

'Yes, but only after a right load of old nonsense,' Eric said. 'To-ing and fro-ing, to prove what had happened, the usual bollocks.'

'That's insurance for you,' Harry said. 'You have to have it, then when you need it, they don't want to give it to you.'

'It's not the same, though, is it?' Eric said. 'Money, I mean? Because money is just money, isn't it? It can't replace what was taken from us.'

Harry heard the man's anger subside just enough to allow the faintest note of sadness through, a ripple on the sea's surface as the storm abated for a while.

'Covers the cost of the sheep, of course,' Eric continued, 'but there's nowt it can do to bring back the years of work we've put into breeding that flock. Prize winners, too, a lot of them. Good job they didn't take my tups. That would've been the end of me. But it's something, I suppose.'

At this, the conversation died, and the three men got on with the job in hand. As Harry stood there, daubing the beasts in front of him with technology's best hope for catching sheep rustlers, the whole scene before him took on an almost meditative atmosphere. Not that Harry was one for meditating, but the sounds, the smells of the place, what they were doing, it was altogether almost hypnotic. It gave him a sense as to what made people dedicate their lives to farming as a career, because it was more than that, or at least that's what he could see with Jim and his dad. It wasn't just a job, or indeed a vocation, it was a reason to be alive in the first place.

'Fly seems to be coming on,' Harry said, as they eventually drew to the end of the sheep they were sorting through. 'Not so much a puppy anymore, is he?'

'Don't let him fool you,' Jim said, a brightness in his voice again, talking about his dog. 'That dog's still daft. He's sharp, for sure, and keen, but he's just as happy to be lying on his back and having a tummy rub.'

'Who isn't?' Harry laughed, having developed a soft spot for the animal himself over the past few months.

'You should get yourself one,' Jim said. 'A dog I mean, not a tummy rub. Now that you're here permanent, like.'

'So people keep telling me,' Harry said. 'And by people, I mean mainly Gordy, though the rest of you seem fairly keen as well. Can't say I think it would be fair on any animal being put in my care.'

'I'll keep an eye out for you,' Jim said. 'A sheepdog might not be right, because they need to be out and about all the time. But a terrier maybe? No, they're a handful as well. Independently spirited little buggers.'

'A yappy dog?' Harry said, shaking his head.

'Just leave it with me,' Jim said.

'I didn't say I wanted one,' Harry said. 'In fact, I'm fairly sure that I've never actually said the words *I want to get a dog* in my entire life.'

'You didn't need to,' Jim replied, smiling. 'And seeing as you've given me responsibility for the dog-nappings, I certainly know what I'm talking about.'

'Please don't call it that,' Harry said, noting just a hint of sarcasm in Jim's voice. 'At least not in any reports you hand in. And it's not just dogs, remember?'

'Pet theft then,' Jim said. 'I'm just trying to make it sound more exciting. Honestly, you wouldn't believe the number of calls I've had about apparently stolen rabbits. Who'd steal a rabbit? Shall I tell you? No one! Because rabbits escape, bury, and nibble their way out of things, because that's just what they do! And don't get me started on mice and stick insects and hamsters!'

Harry stopped and stared at the PCSO. In all honesty, the reason he'd given the job to Jim a few weeks back was to help give him something else to focus on other than the loss of his friend. He wasn't really sure it was working, but time would tell.

'You know how much pets mean to people,' Harry said. 'And there's been a rise in the number being stolen across the country, particularly dogs. And someone like you, who owns a dog, would, I assume, understand just how devastating such a theft can be. Yes?'

No answer from Jim.

'But if it's too big a job for you, then I can always give it to Jadyn,' Harry said.

'What? No way!'

'I'm just saying,' Harry said. 'Just give me the word.'

'He'd never shut up about it!'

'No, you're right there, he wouldn't.'

'He'd turn himself into the pet detective!'

'I don't doubt it,' said Harry. 'Probably make himself a little badge, go around doing talks, do interviews on the local radio...'

Jim fell quiet for a moment before coming back with, 'It's fine. Really. I get why you've given it to me.'

'You sure?' Harry pressed again. 'I can give him a call now, if you want?'

'It's fine!' Jim said, and his voice was firm enough for Harry to back off.

When the work with the sheep came to an end, Jim walked away to the other end of the barn, Fly at his heel, leaving Harry with his dad.

'Thanks for helping out,' Eric said, as Harry turned to follow the young PCSO. 'Can't see many folk like you getting your hands dirty like this.'

'Nothing to thank me for,' Harry shrugged. 'Anyway, this whole thing is Jim's idea. Best I support him with it.'

'You mean all this?' Eric said, pointing at the sheep with the blue marks bright and proud on their faces.

'Of course,' Harry said. 'Rolling this out across the dales could make a huge difference to farmers. And leading by example is always more effective than just telling people what to do. He's a good PCSO, Jim. You should be proud.'

'He is,' Eric said, 'and I am. But that's not what I'm on about, now, is it?'

Harry knew what Eric was getting at. 'How's he doing?' he asked, his voice lowering a tone and growing quieter. 'After what happened.'

'Not great,' Eric said, shaking his head. 'Neil's death, well, it hit him hard. He feels responsible. Thinks he should be the one to find who did it. I get why you gave him the pet thing, I really do, and it's worked to a degree. Or it will do eventually, I'm sure.'

Harry thought back to what had happened, a month or so before Christmas, with Neil found in his car, a bullet lodged deep in his skull.

'There's nothing Jim could've done,' Harry said. 'There's no way he could've known that Neil was involved in what happened here, in the sheep rustling. He knows that.'

'Does he, though?' Eric said. 'It's because we had sheep stolen years ago that he became a PCSO in the first place. So, he blames himself for all of it, thinks he should've been able to stop it somehow.'

'Neil made his choices,' Harry said. 'Bad ones. You go getting involved in the kind of criminal gang that operates at the level the one that stole your animals clearly does, then there's never a happy ending. Ever. I've seen it often enough.'

Eric came to stand beside Harry. He was short, Harry noticed, but broad, with shoulders and arms that looked strong enough to juggle the bales of hay stored in another of the barns in the farmyard.

'I'm assuming there's nowt more on who was responsible, not just for the sheep, but for what happened to Neil, I mean?'

Harry shook his head, arms folded across his chest. He sensed his own muscles tensing at the thought of what had happened and how whoever had done it was still out there. 'Not a bloody thing,' he said. 'Which is enough to tell you that this isn't just some small-time criminals trying to make quick money. Neil's death, the way he was killed, it was professional. But don't take this as me saying I've given up. Trust me, that's not something I'm known for.'

'I can believe it,' Eric said.

A shout from the gate leading out of the barn and across the yard to the house interrupted the conversation.

'Away then, both of you,' Jim called over. 'You'll be needing a brew. Kettle's on and cake's plated up.'

'On our way,' Eric said. 'You get them poured, lad.'

Jim gave a nod and turned away to head back to the house. Eric made to follow, then swung around to look up at Grimm.

'Just keep an eye on him, will you?' he asked. 'He's all we've got, me and his mum, like.'

'You have my word,' Harry said, then followed Eric out of the barn and towards the house, his mind falling back to the moment when Jim had called him and his voice on the other end of the line had broken on the news of his friend's death.

CHAPTER THREE

Of all the ways to celebrate turning forty, Gareth Jones figured that launching a new solo album in a beautiful little church in Wensleydale, in the middle of winter, was certainly one of the most unique. And he couldn't help but smile, even though, deep down, pain still clawed at him like it wanted to draw blood. It hadn't been his idea, but he was very glad that he had listened.

Singing was where he felt, not only at his most rested, but also at his most confident and comfortable. Performing was his happy place. And happy was what he needed right now, more than anything, actually. It was, after all, why he had, after a hiatus of nearly three years, decided to launch a new album in the first place; to crack through the darkness with a light that, deep down, somewhere inside him, he was sure that he still had.

With everything in his life so broken, so completely in ruins, if his voice was still alive, then he had hope. Hope for what, exactly, he wasn't entirely sure, but he would think on that soon enough. And right there was another reason for doing the album now; it would give him the rest of the year to work out what exactly he wanted to do next, if anything. Because court cases and death certainly left their mark. And thanks to a certain record producer called Nicholas Hall, and his clearly mad as a March hare ex-wife, Cassie, those marks had been made all the deeper, hadn't they? His wounds had been deep enough, terribly so, but along they'd come and added their own. If he were honest, Gareth was more than a little surprised to have come out the other side of it with any shred of sanity left at all.

The church itself, which sat in the centre of the village of Askrigg, deep in the heart of the ancient landscape of Wensleydale, was nestled softly in the embrace of a graveyard, blanketed in the kind of quiet that could only come from the call of a solitary crow crying out on a north wind shaking bare trees. It was the end of the week, a blustery Friday that had started off cold and only grown colder. Gareth walked through the graveyard, hunched up in a thick jacket, his hands occasionally brushing the tops of the stones worn by weather now, more than grief, their inscriptions little more than memories of what had once been carved deep.

The day was dark and cold as iron, but that was to be expected, with the new year now fully underway. Gareth was pleased in pretty much every way possible that the worst of it all was over, though he had no doubt that the memories of it, and the scars caused by every moment, would be with him forever more. He'd even stayed up especially on New Year's Eve, to make sure that he could, albeit metaphorically, shut and lock the door on it and throw away the key, a symbolic gesture to make him feel that this new year was a new start in so many ways.

That particular evening had been one fuelled by ludicrously expensive champagne, 8os movies, pizza, and his own company. And he'd loved it. So much so, in fact, that at some point he'd even decided to video himself on his phone doing impressions of the various characters from the John Hughes film, *The Breakfast Club*.

The following day, in addition to the video which he'd forgotten he'd even recorded, he had also found a note on his fridge outlining an idea for another album, this one a collection of choral versions of hit songs from the 8os. At the time, and judging by the number of exclamation marks he had used, the idea had struck him as a truly tremendous one. However, even now, a few days later, he was still pretty unconvinced that what the world really needed was him singing *Ninety-Nine Red Balloons*, *Eye of The Tiger*, and *Come On Eileen*. Still, it would be fun, wouldn't it? he laughed.

At the end of the path, which led from the main door of the church and along to the small cobblestone marketplace, in the middle of which stood a stone cross, Gareth leaned for a moment on the wall which bordered the place. Just up and to his left stood the house made famous as Skeldale House Veterinary practice in the now-classic television series, *All Creatures Great and Small*. The reason Gareth actually knew this at all wasn't just because he had moved back to the area himself only a few months ago. No. It was because this place was home, and the church behind him was where his singing career had begun all those years ago.

The house he had grown up in was just on the outskirts of the village, an unassuming semi-detached cottage with a small garden, two tiny bedrooms, and a fireplace in the lounge large enough to roast a pig on. The house he had only recently purchased was also a small and unassuming place, because the last thing he wanted was to draw attention to himself, where he was, what he was doing. It was nestled in the tiny hamlet of Countersett, on the road up and out of Bainbridge, and just a walk away from the slate-grey Semer water Lake. It was a haven, a secret place, and his alone.

The move had been for the sake of his mind above all. It had certainly had little to do with practicality or investment. But he didn't miss London, indeed even thinking of his old life there was almost as though he was recalling stories told to him by someone else about another person entirely, someone he no longer was, perhaps had never, truly, even been.

Returning to the church, Gareth made his way back inside, through the panelled porch, and was aware immediately of the smell of the building, the tang of cold stone mixing with the sweet scent of varnished wood, of candles and books and history. He breathed deep, secretly hoping to take in some of the ancient peace that he always sensed buildings like this contained, as though they somehow saved up humanity's prayers, acting as great spiritual batteries where people could go to be recharged somehow.

Gareth walked across the flagstone floor, to his left was the door to the tower, and in that moment, he was no longer a man only recently on the other side of forty, but a young boy, singing in the local choir with his friends. He turned and strolled over to the tower, and pushed his way through the door, to find himself in a small, gloomy room, filled with scaffolding and timber, the walls hung with the pale blue uniform of the choir, one-piece gowns which were about as flattering and fashionable as sackcloth. From the space where the wooden ceiling should have been, which explained the scaffolding and the wood Gareth assumed, hung bell ropes, pulled out of the way behind hooks in the wall. The memories in this place were almost overwhelming, but Gareth soaked them up, pulling them down into him.

Gareth left the tower room, re-entering the church. At the far end, between the nave and the chancel, a small stage had been erected, and on it sat an electric piano, a number of chairs and a single microphone on a stand. Yes, he'd performed in some of the greatest venues in the world, from the Royal Albert Hall in London to the Sydney Opera House, but it was still the smaller venues that he loved the most. The intimate setting, that closeness with his audience, was simply unachievable in an auditorium designed to seat thousands. And there really was something quite special about singing in a church, Gareth thought, wondering then if somewhere above him the voices of those who had worshipped here over the centuries still drifted and would welcome his own to join them.

Gareth saw the microphone, and wings of butterflies fluttered in his stomach, making him smile, and in that moment he was every singer he had ever been, from the young chorister who found fame on a television talent show, the teenager with too much money and not enough sense, to the man he was now. He was, right then, and in every possible way, every good and bad decision he had ever made, every mistake, every treasured memory and all of those he wanted, and needed, to forget. Tonight he was going to make sure that when he sang, every bit of him, the very soul of what he was, would not just be behind every note, but alive in them. This wasn't about the money, about proving to the world that he still had breath in his lungs and was still relevant, but something more personal, more powerful, spiritual even. This was about him being alive to himself, coming back from the bleak

emptiness of death, and that was it. Nothing more, and absolutely nothing less.

Gareth walked down the nave, between the two rows of
pews, past the one his late parents had always occupied, and
stepped up onto the stage. He turned from the altar to face
back down the church, at the far end seeing again the small
door, which led through to the tower beyond. The emptiness
of the building, just for a moment, pressed in on him, and his
breath caught.

What if no one turned up? he thought. What if, for whatever reason, he was left to face the utter irrelevance of his
existence by launching an album to a world that just didn't
care? What then?

The creak of a door pulled Gareth from his self-doubt.

'Gareth?'

Gareth's eyes focused on the new arrival, a small
woman wrapped up in a bright yellow down jacket, her
head stuffed up tight inside a red-and-white striped woolly
hat on top of which sat the largest pom-pom he had ever
seen.

'Hi, Lisa!' he said, offering the smallest of waves to his
pianist, musical director, and old friend.

'You coming, or what? Lunch, remember?'

'Oh, right, yes.' Gareth nodded.

'It's a late one, but we've got ourselves a table down at
The King's Arms,' Lisa said, moving no further into the
church itself, 'and we won't have time later on for a proper
dinner I don't think, not with all the rehearsing we still need
to do before tomorrow.'

'Do we really have to do that much?' Gareth asked.
'We've gone through everything more than enough, right?'

Lisa shook her head.

'You may well be happy to stand up there and wing it, but I'm certainly not. And neither is anyone else.'

'That's not what I was saying,' Gareth said.

'I know,' Lisa replied, then smiled, and Gareth found himself wishing that he could love that smile as much as he knew Lisa wanted him to. But there was just no changing how he felt, was there? Sometimes, being friends was all you could ever be. Yes, there had been that one time, but they'd both regretted it, he was sure.

'Seems a little weird being back here after all these years, doesn't it?' Lisa said.

Gareth gave a nod then reached out and rested a hand on one of the huge pillars holding up one of the arches that lined each side of the nave.

'This was your idea, remember?'

Lisa's laugh was clear and bright and rang out through the church.

'You can't use that as an excuse to blame me if it all goes wrong!'

'I won't.' Gareth breathed in the cool air and tasted the cold stone of church on it.

'These stones hold so many special memories, don't they?' Lisa said. 'I bet if we listened, we could hear everything we ever said or thought or promised or prayed, stored in them forever.'

'You old romantic!'

'Nothing wrong with that.'

'No, you're right, there really isn't,' Gareth said, his voice cracking just a little as, deep inside, he found himself peering down into a hole he tried to avoid if he could.'

'You okay?'

Gareth smiled. 'Memories.'

'Karen?'

The mention of her name was enough and Gareth choked.

'It's three years now,' he said. 'But it still gets me.'

He watched Lisa walk over to him, rest a hand on his chest.

'It's going to,' she said. 'What happened, it was terrible.'

It was, thought Gareth, but he wasn't going to think about it because Karen wouldn't want that.

Neither spoke for a minute or two and Gareth slowly eased himself away from that hole.

Lisa said. 'My parents are coming, you know? And I think most of the old gang, too.'

'You mean they're all still alive?' Gareth replied, glad for the change of subject.

'We're not *that* old!' Lisa said. 'Anyway, I reckon there'll be loads of folk we know. There aren't many celebrities from around here.'

'I'm not a celebrity.'

'I hate to break it to you,' Lisa said, 'but yes, you are. And if you don't believe me, just check out the number of followers you have on Twitter.'

'I hate Twitter,' Gareth said.

'You've half a million followers,' Lisa said. 'Half a million! So, you may hate it, but it clearly loves you.'

'What does any of that actually mean?' Gareth asked. 'Oh, yes, that's right, nothing! It's nonsense!'

'You're hopeless, you know that, right?' Lisa said. 'This very concert itself has been announced on Twitter, on your account!'

'Fascinating,' Gareth said. 'That'll be my assistant being far too efficient.'

'I'd suggest announcing it with a ring of the bells as well, but they're being taken down for maintenance I think,' Lisa said.

'That would explain the scaffolding in the tower then,' said Gareth.

Lisa moved back to the door. 'Anyway, fun though this is, get a move on, will you? We've already got the beers in!'

Gareth laughed. 'You know as well as I do that I don't drink when I'm singing or on tour.'

'Who said they were for you?' Lisa chuckled, the sound fluttering around the church like a bird trying to escape.

As Lisa turned to leave, Gareth said, 'This is a good idea, right? All of this I mean, the album, the concert tomorrow? Us being here, of all places?'

Gareth saw Lisa pause before speaking again.

'No, it's a terrible idea,' she said at last. 'Awful, in fact! Considering who thought of it, how could it be anything else? But you knew that already. Fancy coming home to launch a new album. No story there at all, is there? Absolutely not the kind of thing the press and media will latch onto.'

'There is that,' Gareth said.

'And I doubt anyone will come,' Lisa continued. 'But we're all set up now, aren't we, so we may as well make the best of it, don't you think?'

Gareth stepped down from the stage and walked down the nave to join Lisa.

'You've always been so good at the motivational speeches,' he said.

'It's a gift,' Lisa shrugged. 'You've put on weight, by the way. That massive belly of yours is going to stick out something terrible when you pull on your tight, posh performing pants and get up on that stage.'

'The lighting will be kind,' Gareth said.

'No, it won't,' Lisa said. 'It never is.'

'No, you're right, it won't,' agreed Gareth, stepping past Lisa to the door and opening it. 'After you.'

'Thanks, Fatty,' Lisa said, shuffling past.

Outside, Gareth turned and shut the door behind them, then chased off after Lisa, who despite her size, walked with a speed most people would only ever achieve by running.

As they left the grounds of the church and headed off towards the pub, Gareth knew, deep down, that when he climbed up to stand on that stage tomorrow evening, it was going to be a night to remember. Whether anyone turned up to witness it, well, that was another matter entirely.

As to Lisa mentioning that the old gang would be there, too, he doubted it. He could barely remember that time anyway, it was so long ago. But it didn't matter because as far as he was concerned, he was going to be on fire! Right now, though? Right now, he needed to eat, so he caught up with Lisa and together they made their way along the quiet main street of Askrigg to the pub.

CHAPTER FOUR

THE ROMAN ROAD, WHICH LAY ABOVE HAWES, AND which stretched itself in a straight line across the feet of Wether Fell, was, Harry knew, a historic and evocative place. That it still existed at all was in itself quite the feat, he thought, because really there was no real reason he could think of for it to still be a thoroughfare. It didn't really join one place to another anymore, though whatever those places had originally been back in the mists of time, Harry hadn't the faintest idea. It was just an old track, bordered on either side by drystone walls, and whatever stories it had to tell had faded long ago. What baffled Harry the most, though, was why the hell he was traipsing along it early enough in the morning for it to still be dark, the air cold enough to freeze his bones, and his way forward only visible in the wobbling light being chucked out by the headtorch pulled on over the woolly hat he was wearing.

Harry's relationship with running, indeed fitness in general, was a fractious one. He understood its importance, the difference it had made not only to his ability to run up flights of stairs without sounding like he was in his nineties, but to his waistline and chin. But sometimes, just the effort of it seemed too much. And right now, his own behaviour had shocked him, because not only had he managed to heave himself out of bed and into the outside world before it had even fully woken, but jumped into his car and driven up through Burtersett to park where the road intersected the considerably older Roman one. From there, he had headed off on an early morning run, one he had done a few other times, but in considerably nicer weather and in daylight.

Now, though, it was dark as a coal bunker, the wind was bringing with it rain that clearly wanted to be snow, and the great silhouette of Wether Fell to his left was, to be frank, terrifying. It loomed over him, a vast and ancient beast, daring him to continue on, to sink deeper into its clutches.

Harry had never been one for having an over-active imagination, but right now, and with the wind snatching at him like the lustful claws of a witch, it seemed to be making up for lost time. Shadows grew and pulsed, stretching out towards him as he ran past. The wind carried with it voices that called to him, laughed. And the echo of his own massive feet slapping down onto the puddle-bedecked track beneath him soon morphed into the sound of someone, or some*thing* making chase.

This run needs to be over, Harry thought. And soon. Which was when, just ahead, he caught sight of a vehicle parked up, no lights on, except for inside the vehicle itself.

Harry slowed down, stopped, worked hard to control his breathing as he stared ahead through the darkness at what he could now see was a Land Rover facing away from him. The sensible part of his brain told him it was just a farmer out on the hills, because that was the most sensible and obvious explanation. But the suspicious part was also making its views known, and Harry couldn't help but reach up to switch off his headtorch as he edged slowly towards whoever was sitting inside.

With only a few metres to go, Harry could see now that the person inside the vehicle was busy shuffling through papers or files. This struck him as a rather strange activity for a farmer to be doing, not only at this time of the morning, but in a Land Rover on a lonely Roman road. He wasn't about to jump to the conclusion that such an activity was criminal, but it certainly seemed out of the ordinary.

Harry edged closer only to hear the door click open and then see the driver step out into the eerily dark morning.

'Jim?'

The figure jumped.

'Harry? That you? What the hell are you doing up here, then, and at this hour of the morning?'

'I was about to ask you the same question!' Harry said.

The PCSO remained where he was as Harry walked over to meet him.

'You've picked a proper rough morning for it,' Jim said.

'Apparently it's bracing,' Harry said. 'Well, that's what Jen says, anyway. I'm not convinced. But she can be very persuasive.'

'Yes, but she's part mountain goat, isn't she?' Jim said.

Harry laughed, because that really was the best description of Jenny Blades, one of two police constables on his team. If she wasn't working, then she was training, and if she wasn't doing either of those, then she was probably somewhere taking part in a race that involved far too many hills, and distances usually travelled on four wheels instead of two feet.

'So ...' Harry began, stretching a little and hunkering down close to the Land Rover to get out of the wind. But then he lost track of what he wanted to ask because really, this was Jim, so whatever he was up to, it was obviously nothing to worry about. Or was it? he thought, when over the top of Jim's shoulder, he saw into the Land Rover and spotted the files open on the seat.

'I'm, er, I'm just up here checking up on things,' Jim said. 'Always need to keep an eye on walls and whatnot. Holes need to be filled, that kind of thing.'

'Oh, yes, absolutely,' Harry said, 'and I've always found that looking for holes is easier when it's dark. Sometimes I even go wondering around blindfolded just to make absolutely sure that the task is as easy as it could possibly be!'

The smile on Jim's face faltered just enough.

'The files,' Harry said, nodding past Jim. 'I'm assuming that you've signed them out?'

'I'm not an idiot,' Jim snapped back.

'Wasn't suggesting that you are,' Harry replied, noting Jim's response but not reacting to it, because for a while now the lad hadn't seemed his usual, happy, positive self. Not since the murder of his old school friend, Neil. But then, that kind of thing would stick to you for a while, wouldn't it? Harry thought. And if anyone knew what that was like, it was him. Not that it was something he talked about much. Not anymore.

Keeping his voice calm, Harry said, 'I'd like an explanation though, as to why you're reading them out here, at this time, and in this weather, if that's okay? It would help me understand a little more, I think, don't you?'

'About what?'

'About a lot of things, Jim,' Harry said, and the rough

edge of his voice was filed off by the concern in his words. 'Everyone's noticed, you know, and we're all worried. About you. How you are, how you've been, since Neil. It's not easy. Trust me, I know.'

Jim was silent for a moment, then said, 'I couldn't sleep. Went for a drive. Ended up here. It's quiet.'

Harry said nothing, just waited for Jim to continue.

'Jump in,' Jim said. 'It's warmer.'

Harry walked around to open the passenger side door only to be attacked by a creature that seemed to be comprised of little more than fur and a tongue.

'Down, Fly!' Jim shouted. 'Get yourself down! Now!'

Harry climbed up into the Land Rover and pulled the door shut behind him. Fly jumped up onto his knees and tried to consume his face.

'You're no real help, you know that, don't you?' Jim said, as Harry ruffled the dog's head then gave its tummy a rub. 'All my work ruined by you being soft with him.'

'Don't you listen to him,' Harry said to Fly, holding the dog's head in his hands and staring into his eyes. 'He's just a grumpy bugger, that's all.'

'Coming from you, that's a compliment,' Jim said, and Harry was happy to see a smile dare to edge its way into the corners of his mouth.

Fly quickly calmed down, curling into a ball on Harry's lap. Harry reached for the file as Jim sat up in the driver's seat.

'Your dad's worried about you,' Harry said. 'We all are, if I'm being honest, as you're aware, I'm sure.'

'He doesn't need to be,' Jim replied. 'None of you do. I'm fine.'

The word *fine* had the air of a grumpy teenager about it, Harry noticed.

'Need has nowt to do with it,' Harry said, increasingly unaware now of how he was replacing the word *nothing* with the northern alternative more and more. 'He's your dad. And, as your boss, I'm worried as well. Comes with the job.'

Jim said nothing, just stared out through the windscreen, his hands gripping the steering wheel.

'We're doing everything we can,' Harry said. 'Not just here, but over in Darlington, too, where whatever gang Neil had got himself mixed up in is most likely based.'

'I know,' Jim said and reached his left hand out to stroke Fly's head. 'It's just ...'

'It's just what?'

'They shot him!' Jim said, turning his head to face Harry. 'And for what? Sheep? Who does that, Harry? Who? It's ...' Jim's voice faltered. 'I just can't get my head around it. Why they did it. How they've got away with it.'

'The sheep rustling at your dad's farm, it's bigger than that,' Harry said. 'It's not just a local thing. It's on a national, possibly even international scale. Stealing stock, illegal meat. There's even a suggestion that there are links with bush meat.' He held up the files. 'It's all in here. Everything we've got. Which isn't much, I know, but it's something.'

'And yet I'm supposed to be focusing on pet theft, right?'

Harry said nothing.

'Whoever did it ...' Jim began, and Harry heard the rage-driven threat in the PCSO's voice.

'Whoever did it,' Harry said, 'made damned sure that Neil wasn't just dealt with, but that the way it was done was a message.' He'd seen the same thing with other gang murders, where the death was almost more about making sure no one else made the same mistake, as it was about shutting someone up for good. 'Unfortunately for us, sometimes people can get away with murder. But that doesn't mean we stop looking.'

The PCSO's eyes were glassy and Harry could see that Jim was really fighting to control his emotions.

'But we don't even know enough, do we?' Jim argued. 'We've no idea who actually did it, who this gang is, anything! He's just dead and we've got no answers! Not a sodding thing! And I'm not going to find one either, am I, going out to speak to a little girl whose rabbit's sodded off somewhere!'

Harry waited for a moment before he spoke again.

'Police work, it takes time,' he said. 'You can't spend your entire life focusing on just one thing, running around the dales talking to farmers, checking every damned flock you see just in case one of them is your dad's, in the vain hope you'll get a lead on Neil's killer.'

'And I can't do nothing either, can I?' Jim said. 'I can't! I'll go mad!'

Harry gave Fly a soft tap and sent the dog over to Jim.

'Whoever killed Neil didn't want any blowback,' Harry explained. 'I've seen professional hits before, and that's what this was, Jim. Professional. And no, I don't mean that this was a hired assassin dressed in black and paid a fortune.'

'Then what are you saying?'

'Just what you already know,' Harry said. 'That whoever it is we're dealing with, they're dangerous. And I can't have you, through no fault of your own I might add, bar being a tenacious little sod, going off and putting yourself in harm's way.'

'I won't.'

'Jim, you won't know until it's too late,' Harry said. 'For all we know, you already have. Which is why I'm not ordering you to stop, I'm asking you. As your boss, yes, but also as a friend. And that's a word I do not throw around lightly. Because, as you know—'

'You don't like people?'

'Exactly,' Harry said. 'I've always maintained that the people I work with—'

'Are not your friends,' Jim said, finishing Harry's sentence once again.

'But since moving here,' Harry continued, 'to Wensleydale, it seems that you and the rest of the team have ruined that for me, haven't you? Not sure I'll ever be able to forgive you for that, but there we go.'

'Sorry about that,' Jim said. 'We'll try harder if you want?'

'God, no,' Harry said, shaking his head. 'Can you imagine what that would do to Jadyn's brain?'

Jim laughed and rested his chin on Fly's head. The dog nuzzled in close to his master and best friend.

'Neil only went to Darlington to be a DJ,' Jim said, and Harry heard the darkness in his voice, a deep echo of something Harry knew well—a mix of helplessness and the need for revenge. 'His parents,' Jim continued, 'well, I can't see them ever getting over it, can you?'

'No, I can't say that I can,' Harry said. 'And your parents would be the same.'

'I'm hardly going to get myself killed, am I?' Jim said.

'Which is, I'm sure, what Neil thought, right up until those last moments of his life,' Harry said. 'Because no one ever does. And I'm speaking from experience here, Jim, remember that. I've lost friends. Mates, I was speaking to just moments before they were gone.' Harry clicked his fingers.

'It's that quick, Jim. That quick! Neil wouldn't have even known. He'd have been sitting in his car, minding his own business, then nothing. Out like a light. Switched off.'

Jim breathed deep and sunk back deeper into his seat as he exhaled.

'But in over two months we're no closer,' he said. 'I just don't see how that's even possible. We must have missed something. We must have!'

Harry picked up the file and thonked Jim on the head with it just hard enough to make him flinch.

'Well, if we have, then it isn't in here, is it?'

As he spoke, Harry noticed a buzzing from one of the pockets of the supposed wind and waterproof running top he was wearing. He unzipped it and pulled out his phone.

'Grimm,' he said, answering without looking at the screen to see who was calling him.

'Boss? It's Matt.'

'You do know what time it is, right?' Harry asked.

'It's Joan,' Matt said.

'What is?' Harry asked.

'We're on our way to hospital,' Matt replied. 'She's been a bit off-colour for a day or so, and considering her condition, I've called an ambulance.'

'What condition are you talking about? What's up with Joan?' Harry asked. 'Anything I can do?'

'Yes,' Matt said. 'You're on bacon butty duty.'

CHAPTER FIVE

HARRY WAS FINISHING OFF A MUG OF TEA IN THE kitchen area of his flat when his younger brother Ben came through from his bedroom ready for work. Ben had now been living with Harry for a couple of months having left prison on probation. And, so far, things were looking good.

'You were up early.' Ben yawned, walking over to put on some toast, before opening the fridge to pull out a block of Stilton and some slices of ham for some sandwiches. Except, Harry noticed, that he didn't just stop there. Out came a jar of gherkins, an onion, and a chilli.

'Went for a run,' Harry said as Ben started to make his lunch, first spreading peanut butter on some bread, before piling it high with the ingredients he'd taken from the fridge.

Ben stared at his older brother. 'Bollocks you did!' he said, then glanced outside through the window in the lounge area of the open-plan living space. 'In that?'

Harry followed Ben's line of sight.

'Well, it wasn't snowing when I was out,' he said. 'It was just raining a bit, though that did start to change to a sort of slush. And it was dark. Cold though. Really bitter, like it was trying to cut into me and peel off my skin.'

'You're mad,' said Ben, sandwich made and wrapped up for lunch and now spreading his toast with the peanut butter.

'And you're going to have that sandwich for lunch, are you?' Harry asked.

'It's the king of sandwiches,' Ben replied. 'I'm not going to just eat it, I'm going to inhale it. Want one?'

'I'd rather eat my own legs,' Harry said, shaking his head. He then rinsed out his mug, grabbed his jacket, and made for the front door.

'Oh, while I remember,' Ben said, calling after Harry, 'I'm out tonight, so don't worry about me for dinner.'

Harry stopped, turned, stared at his brother.

'Out? Where?'

'Just in town,' Ben replied. 'Meeting up with someone.'

Harry didn't read so much in the words Ben said, as in the way he said them. That he'd referred to Hawes as a town made him smile.

'A date? But you've only been here three months, if that!'

Ben shrugged. 'If you've got it, you've got it. And you sound jealous!'

'Who is she, then?' Harry asked, ignoring the dig. 'What's she like?'

'Because I'm going to tell you that, aren't I?' Ben laughed. 'No, wait, I'm not. Sorry, Bro'.'

Harry resisted the urge to dive into full-on older brother mode and instead opened the front door.

'Have a good one, then,' he said, with a nod at Ben. 'And I'll see you later, if not, then tomorrow, right? Oh, by which I mean, well, I'm not saying that you'll ... I ... ah, bollocks ...' Harry stalled, his words crumbling in his mouth, so he finished with a short wave and a, 'Bye, then!' and was gone.

When it came to relationships, he was almost as bad at talking about them as he was at having them. But then, how many years was it? he thought, rubbing his face as he tried to sift back through his memories. Then he realised that he didn't need to, because the scars were reminder enough. It really had been that long ago since he'd been properly involved with anyone. Not just years, a lifetime almost.

Now outside, Harry closed a door on his memories and stepped out into some of the worst weather he'd seen in years. Greeting him was an apocalyptic mix of snow, wind, and a sky dark enough to make him think that night had arrived twelve hours early and invited along a few other midnights to join in the fun.

The last time Harry had experienced snow was so long ago now that he could barely remember it. In fact, he was pretty sure that the memory he was currently conjuring up wasn't a real memory at all, but an amalgamation of various other memories, all combining to give him some frame of reference for what was now attacking him as he made his way to work.

Head down and walking near sideways against the wind in a poor attempt to streamline himself somehow, Harry didn't so much stride off through town as shuffle crab-like along the pavement. The snow was wet, the flakes huge things coming at him like angry flecks of soggy royal icing, driven by a wind chucking itself along Hawes marketplace with all the wild abandon of stampeding horses. The snow was coming down so thick that it was almost impossible for Harry to see more than a few metres in front of him, and at his feet, the ground had already turned itself into a thick, grey mush, which seeped in through his shoes to freeze his feet. He could already hear Matt berating him for not wearing his Wellington boots and he nearly turned back to get them, but it was already too late, the damage was done.

When Harry eventually made it to the Community Centre, which contained the offices used by the local police force, water seemed to just pour off him and onto the floor, as though some fragment of the storm outside had followed him in to create a tiny shimmering lake at his feet.

'Dear God, man, you're drookit!'

Harry looked up to find himself under the befuddled gaze of Detective Inspector Gordanian Haig.

'Drookit?' Harry said, raising an eyebrow in confusion. 'Nope, no idea.'

'Soaked, like a cat dragged from a canal,' Gordy said, her soft Highlands accent curling its way through her words like wisps of smoke through charred logs. 'Which on a dreich day like this one, is no surprise, now, is it? And you didn't think of putting on a decent jacket, then, or your boots? Are you mad?'

Harry looked down at himself.

'But this *is* a decent jacket,' he said. 'It certainly cost me enough.'

'No, it's your *only* jacket,' Gordy said, shaking her head. 'You've lived here long enough now, surely, to know that you need something a little more, shall we say, robust?'

Harry pulled the jacket off and shook the water off. His feet were so cold that he couldn't actually feel them at all.

'Everyone here, then?'

Gordy shook her head. 'Not yet, no.'

'But you travel the furthest,' Harry said. 'To be honest, I wasn't expecting to see you today.'

Gordy's face fell just enough to tell Harry something was up.

'Stayed over with a couple of friends,' Gordy said, clearly battling to sound all fine and dandy. 'We were having an early Burns Night, seeing as they're going to be away on the twenty-fifth.'

'Sounds good,' Harry said, not really having any frame of reference for what to talk about when it came to Burns Night. He'd managed to get his head around the apparent Yorkshire delicacy of cheese and cake, thanks to a war of attrition, waged by his team, though mostly Matt. The detective sergeant had seemingly seen Harry's education of all things Yorkshire as a personal mission. But haggis? He really didn't understand that at all. Not that he'd ever tried it, but the list of ingredients had always been enough to put him off.

'It was better than good,' Gordy replied and Harry noticed a faint wistful look in the DI's eyes. 'After the food, came the whisky and a wee cracker of a movie; *I Know Where I'm Going*! It was my Grandma's favourite. Oh, and we scoffed down a few packets of snowballs as well. And some teacakes.'

'I'll be honest,' Harry said, still working on the pointless task of shaking himself dry, 'I've no idea what you're talking about at all, what with drookit and dreich and now snowballs?'

'Never had them?'

Harry shook his head.

'Well, that needs rectifying,' Gordy said. 'And I've the movie on DVD if you want,' she offered. 'Throw in some Irn Bru and you can have the full Scottish experience all to yourself!'

'Sounds interesting, I'll give it that,' Harry said. 'But back to what I said, about me not expecting you over here today. You going to give me a reason, or give me clues so that I have to guess and win a prize?'

Gordy's face fractured a little as she forced a smile. Then, as she was about to speak the main door to the Community Centre burst open and in its place stood Jim and a man in handcuffs. Both men looked not just sodden, but mucky, like they'd been rolling around on the ground in an attempt to pick up as much dirt as possible.

'You've been busy, I see,' Harry said, flashing a look over to Gordy who was also eyeing the PCSO with immediate concern.

'This bastard just tried to nick Fly!' Jim said, anger setting fire to the words as he spat them out.

'What?'

'I left him in my Land Rover while I nipped over to Spar to grab something for lunch, and when I came back, there he was, halfway out of the passenger door with Fly in his arms!'

'I want m' phone call,' the man in cuffs spat, his accent a vibrant mix of Scottish twisted into something almost incomprehensible thanks to half of his teeth being missing. When he spoke, what teeth he did have peered out from between his lips like broken gravestones tossed in a cave.

'And I want a ticket to the moon, pal, but we can't all have what we want now, can we?' Harry said, but his attention was still on Jim, whose eyes were wide with rage.

'I can't imagine Fly being too happy,' Gordy said. 'Where is he, by the way?'

Jim gestured to the door behind him. 'Liz has him,' he said. 'She's just taken him to the vets for me for a check over.'

Harry allowed his eyes to slide from Jim and focus on the man the PCSO had arrested.

'So,' he growled, leaning in just enough to cast his shadow over the man's face, 'you're not only partial to stealing dogs, you like to smack them around a bit, too, is that right? A proper tough guy, is that it?'

'I want m' fuckin' phone call,' the man repeated, his accent even thicker, his eyes focusing on something so far in the distance it was probably in another dimension, Harry thought.

'Quite the mouth on him, this one,' Gordy observed. 'From Glasgow I think, judging by the accent.'

'How's Fly?' Harry asked, trying to ignore the man, who was still staring at nothing.

'He's alright, I think,' Jim said, 'but when I caught him, he threw Fly at me and tried to run. So, you know, just making sure by having him away to the vets, like.'

There was a muttering from the man and Harry heard just enough to get his blood up.

'I'm sorry, PCSO Metcalf, but I think Mr Dog Napper here has something to say, am I right?'

'I didn't say nothin', man,' the man said, shaking his head, his eyes still not on Harry. 'Nothin', alright?'

'That's a double negative,' Gordy observed. 'If you didn't say nothing, then you said something, isn't that right, Detective Chief Inspector?'

'It is,' Harry agreed. 'So, if you didn't say nothing, then what did you say?'

The man rolled his head to bring it round to look at Harry for the first time since Jim had brought him in. As he did so, Harry watched his expression change from cocky contempt to confusion to finally land on something that was a mix of both horror and terror.

'Your face! What the hell happened to it?'

Harry leaned in real slow and real close.

'You need to answer my question,' he said, each word a section of cliff crumbling to crush the man in front of him. 'Before I show you.'

Harry was trying hard to stay calm, but there was something about crimes like this that really turned his stomach. The strong picking on the weak was like red to a bull for him. Harry clenched and unclenched his fists. One time, that would've been a precursor to a fight. Now though, it served to keep him calm. Just.

The man muttered under his breath once again.

'Didn't quite catch that,' Harry said. 'Did you, Detective Inspector Haig?'

Gordy shook her head. 'Nope, not a thing.'

'What about you, PCSO Metcalf?'

Jim said nothing, just shook his head, slowly.

'You're not doing yourself any favours,' Harry said. 'So... ?'

The man sighed heavily.

'It's just ...'

'What's just?' Harry asked.

'The dog!' the man blurted out, flecks of spit on his lips. 'It's just a bloody dog, innit?'

'Is it, now?' Harry said, his voice louder now, indignation setting alight. 'Just a dog? Well, I'm going to let you in on something. A little secret between you, me, and my two fellow officers here.'

The man managed to hold Harry's stare, but it soon faded.

'First of all,' Harry said, 'there's no such thing as "*just a*" when it comes to any animal or person or anything else you think is yours for the taking. Do you understand that? The world is not some enormous pick 'n' mix for you to just go a wandering around to help yourself to.'

'Pick 'n' mix?' the man said. 'What are you on about? Where's m' phone call?'

Harry ignored him. 'And second? Well, it just so happens that Fly is a member of my team. A very important member of my team, actually. One of the best. And going after that dog is no different to you going after one of my police officers. Do you understand?'

'I ... I was going to put it back,' the man said.

Harry laughed, but the sound was joyless and burning with deep, dark anger.

'So, you were borrowing it, were you?' Harry said. 'A dog? Like the world is your library and you can just help yourself to anything you want, is that it? Just thought you'd break into someone's car to cuddle their dog?'

'I thought you said it was a pick 'n' mix,' the man began, but Harry shut him down.

'PCSO Metcalf, take him to the interview room. DI Haig, I'll leave this in your capable hands.'

Gordy grinned, her eyes wide.

'It would be my pleasure!'

As Jim marched the man away, the front door to the Community Centre opened and in walked PCSO Liz Coates. In her arms, she was carrying Fly, who for once was rather subdued.

Harry reached over and scratched behind the dog's ears.

'He's fine,' Liz said. 'Vet checked him over and there's nowt broken. He's just a bit spooked I think, aren't you, lad?'

Fly's tail wagged just a little, but his ears were down.

Harry cast a look over to where Gordy had just followed Jim and the worst dog-napper in history.

'I hear Matt's not in,' Liz said.

'Called you, too, then,' said Harry.

'He did,' Liz said, 'but only to tell me that he'd already given you responsibility for the butties this morning. So, where are they? I'm proper hungry. Weather like this doesn't half bring on an appetite.'

Harry shook his head in mock despair.

'Right then,' he said, 'you get yourself and Fly into the office, and I'll head out and do my detective sergeant's bidding.'

'Will do,' Liz said. 'Oh, and while you're at Cockett's, can see if they've a bone for Fly here to nibble on? Reckon he could do with something to cheer him up.'

Harry made for the main door but hesitated before opening it.

'Forgotten something?' Liz asked.

'Yeah,' Harry said, 'my Wellies.' Then he pulled his collar up and stepped back out into the wintery maelstrom and strode off to find food.

CHAPTER SIX

GORDY SAT HERSELF DOWN BESIDE JIM, THE MAN HE HAD arrested sitting on the other side of the table. The room was dark, even with the lights on, and through the window she could see that the day was sticking to its guns and going all out with the wintery storm it had mustered up.

'So,' she said, pointing at the recording equipment front and centre, 'welcome to our interview room. Are you comfortable?'

'I want m' phone call,' the man said. 'Do none of you listen, is that it?'

'This isn't a TV show,' said Jim. 'You do know that, right?'

Gordy said, 'You have every right to a solicitor, and indeed I was just about to ask you about your legal representation. So, who is it?'

'What?'

'Your solicitor? What's their name? Perhaps the name of the company? Then we can arrange for a visit, can't we?'

The man's eyes flickered from Gordy to Jim then back to Gordy. 'You want a name? The name of my solicitor?'

'Yes,' Gordy said. 'I can't just pick up the phone and expect some kind of magic to happen now, can I? Well, I could try, but I'm not sure it would work. I don't think solicitors are like faeries and just a wish away.'

'What?'

'Magic,' Gordy said. 'You know, all that Harry Potter stuff. I pick up the phone and with the power of my mind and some weird words, somehow manage to whistle up a call to your appointed legal representative!'

'I can't remember his name,' the man said, sitting back, arms folded.

'Well then,' Gordy said, 'shall we start with the easy questions first, just to get you relaxed, and see how we do from there? Maybe that'll jog your memory. What do you say?'

She then flashed a smile, leant forward, and started the recording equipment which was sat in the middle of the table.

'I suppose so, yes,' the man said.

'Right then, that's great,' Gordy said. 'Isn't it, PCSO Metcalf?'

'It is,' Jim agreed.

Gordy said the date and the time, then asked, 'Now, let's start off by introducing ourselves, shall we? I'm Detective Inspector Haig, and this young man here is PCSO Metcalf, and you are?'

'Tim,' the man said. 'Tim Renton.'

'Thank you, Timothy,' Gordy said, her face breaking into a broad smile.

'Tim!' Timothy snapped back. 'It's Tim, okay? Tim. I don't like Timothy. No one calls me that. No one. I'm Tim.'

'Then why is it your name?' Jim asked.

'I don't know, do I?' Timothy said. 'My parents called me it. Do I even look like a Timothy?'

'No idea,' Jim said, shaking his head. 'Is there a specific look to Timothies, then?'

'What?'

'A look? Are you saying that all Timothies look the same and you don't fit that image?'

'What are you on about?'

'I'm just saying,' Jim said, 'that I can't commit to saying you do or don't look like a Timothy if I haven't got a frame of reference. What other Timothies could I compare you to?'

'Tim Rice,' Gordy said. 'No, he's a Tim. Timmy Mallet?'

'That's Timmy, not Timothy.'

'Fair point,' Jim said.

'Stop it!' Timothy blurted out. 'It doesn't matter! Call me whatever you want!'

'Okay then, Tim,' Gordy said, with great emphasis on the shortened name. 'So why don't you take us through your version of events. How does that sound? Just tell us what happened and we'll go from there. Something about wanting to hug a dog, if I'm correct.'

'I still want m' phone call,' Timothy said.

Gordy breathed deep.

'And you can have it,' she said, 'but let's not beat around the bush here, Timothy–'

'Tim!'

'Yes, of course, sorry,' Gordy said. 'Anyway, as I was saying, Tim, you were caught red-handed, by a PCSO no less, trying to steal his dog. So, not a good start, is it? Of all the people in all the world, am I right? And I can guarantee that he already has a number of witnesses to interview about what happened, don't you, PCSO Metcalf?'

'I do,' Jim said. 'A very long list, actually.'

'Now then, Tim, if you want, we can delay this, find your supposedly nameless solicitor, or provide you with legal representation. But that will take time, I'm afraid.'

'Time?' Timothy said. 'How much? I've got stuff to do, you see, and–'

'Hard to say,' Gordy said, furrowing her brow thoughtfully. 'But definitely a day or two.'

'What? Because I tried to nick a dog? Two days for that? You're having a laugh, right?'

'Is that a confession?' Gordy asked, amazed and relieved to have Tim blurt something out so quickly. 'And, just so we are all aware, I'm most definitely not laughing.'

'A confession?' Timothy said. 'No, of course, it isn't! I didn't confess to anything!'

'I think it was, don't you, PCSO Metcalf?'

'He definitely admitted to trying to nick a dog,' Jim said. 'My dog, actually. In fact, those were his actual words, "*because I tried to nick a dog.*" Which sounds very much like a confession to me.'

'And you know what?' Gordy said, turning her eyes back to Timothy, 'Admitting you've done something is the first step on the road to rehabilitation, so well done, Timothy!'

Gordy applauded.

'It's Tim!'

'Yes, of course it is.'

Timothy's agitation was clearly visible now in his body language. He was fidgeting in his seat as though it was either alive with static or his pants were filled with itching powder.

'Mind if I smoke?'

'Yes, I do mind,' Gordy said, and pointed to a *No Smoking* sign on the wall. Timothy, though, already had his cigarettes out and was tapping his pockets in search of a lighter.

'Just one though,' Timothy said, flopping the packet onto the table as he placed a fag between his lips. 'Calms me down, you see? Means I can think straight.'

Gordy leaned over, removed the cigarette, slipped it back into the packet, then handed the packet to Jim.

'Let's get back to your confession,' she said. 'Can you explain to me why you wanted to nick the dog in the first place?'

Timothy shrugged. 'Money,' he said. 'Fetch a couple of grand, a dog like that, easy money.' Then he smiled and leaned forward. 'But you see, the thing is, I wasn't trying to nick it, was I? No. That's not what I did. I'm just saying that if that's what I had been doing, then money would be why, wouldn't it? But that's not what I was doing.'

'Then what were you doing?' Gordy said.

'I was rescuing it,' Timothy said, leaning back in his chair with a snarky little grin on his face, the kind usually reserved for cheeky kids at the back of a geography lesson. 'Dogs die in cars, don't they? And I saw that little pooch on its own and I felt sorry for it and I thought, well, that's not good! That poor dog there might suffocate, over-heat, die even! So, I did the only thing any decent person would do, I rescued it! Yes, that's what I did! It was a good deed I was doing, and then this PCSO here came and attacked me!'

Gordy allowed Timothy's tale just enough silence to have him wondering if she was taking him seriously, then said, 'Take a look out of that window behind you, Timothy. Sorry! Tim ...'

Timothy turned his head.

'What do you see?'

'Snow,' Timothy said.

'Indeed you do,' Gordy said. 'Snow! And can you tell me what is one of the main characteristics of snow? By which I mean, one of its main defining features? You know, the one thing that really makes snow *snow*?'

'It's cold?' Timothy said, somewhat hesitantly.

'Bravo!' Gordy said, clapping her hands together loud enough to make Timothy flinch. 'Yes, that's it! Snow is cold! Well done! Hasn't he done well, PCSO Metcalf?'

Jim didn't reply. Gordy noticed that he was staring rather intently at the packet of cigarettes in his hand.

'So, perhaps you can explain, then,' Gordy continued, 'how a PCSO's dog was overheating in what looks to me like the worst winter weather we've had around here in over five years?'

'The heating was on,' Timothy said. 'Yeah, that was it. The heating was on and the dog was all hot and bothered. It was a good job I was there. You should be thanking me!'

'And we all know how effective Land Rover heating is, don't we?' Gordy said.

'I'm telling you, that's what happened,' Timothy said, leaning forward and jabbing a finger down on the table to emphasise his point. 'I saw the dog and I rescued it. You can't prove that I didn't either!'

'A question,' Jim asked, cutting in before Gordy was able to speak.

'What?' Timothy said.

Jim held up the cigarettes.

'Where did you get these?'

'What?'

'These cigarettes,' Jim said. 'The ones I'm holding in my hand. You can see them, right? These ones, right here?'

'Yes, I can see the cigarettes!' Timothy snapped back. 'Of course, I can see them! You're holding them, aren't you?'

'So, where did you get them?'

Timothy shrugged. 'No idea.'

'What, so they just appeared in your life out of nowhere, like, did they?' Jim asked.

Timothy's mouth fell open but no reply rolled out.

'Where did you get them?' Jim asked once again. 'It's a simple question so there has to be a simple answer.'

'What's this got to do with the dog?' Timothy asked. 'They're just cigarettes!'

'Except they're not, are they?' Jim said, and he held them up a little higher. 'These are Gauloises, right?'

'I guess,' Timothy said.

'Well, don't guess,' Jim said. 'Read the packet. There? See? Gauloises. They're French. Not something you find in your average, everyday newsagent. So, you clearly didn't buy them on the high street, right?'

'I suppose,' Timothy said. 'Where's this going? What are you talkin' about?'

Gordy wasn't sure where Jim was going with this, so she just sat back for a moment and let him continue.

'Which leads me back to my original question,' Jim said. 'Where did you get them? And I'm asking, as you don't strike me as the kind of person who would be all that keen on paying over the odds for cigarettes you can't really find in this country, from a specialist tobacconist shop, or a website, right?'

'Yes, I mean no, I mean, I ... what was the question again?'

Timothy stalled, Jim pressed on.

'What I think is that you got these cheap. Smuggled, I'm guessing. By whom though, that's what I want to know. Friends of yours, perhaps?'

'I don't know!' Timothy said. 'Stop asking me about my cigarettes!'

A knock came at the door, but no one answered.

'Then just answer the bloody question!' Jim snapped back, and then he was on his feet. 'Where did you get them, Tim? Where? Tell me! Tell me where you got them or I'll—'

Gordy was taken aback by the outburst from Jim and reached out a hand to gently ease him back into his chair. The knock at the door came again.

'Is there something I need to know?' Gordy asked.

Jim, back in his chair, kept his stare burning deep into Timothy before at last turning to face Gordy.

'Well?' she asked. 'Is there?'

Jim held up the cigarettes. 'These are the same brand of cigarettes we found at my dad's farm,' he said, standing up now to answer the door. 'And in Neil's car, when he was murdered.'

Gordy paused the interview and the recording device as Jim opened the door to find Liz staring at him.

'There's a call come in,' she said.

'For me?' Jim asked.

Liz shook her head and her eyes turned to Timothy.

'It's for him,' she said. 'It's his solicitor.'

Jim slowly turned his head to stare at Timothy, who was waving at him with his mobile phone.

'Told you I wanted my phone call.' He grinned.

CHAPTER SEVEN

Shrouded in a thick blanket of white, the church and graveyard in Askrigg looked so astonishingly picturesque that to Lisa it was as though she was walking through a world created in fairy tales. The kind she'd read about in the books she had devoured by torchlight under the covers of her bed as a kid. Either that or she was now on the lid of a Christmas biscuit tin.

The snow, bright under the floodlights which glared up at the church, was so fresh and perfect that it reminded her of meringue, the surface just crisp enough to crack because of the cold wind whipping its way through the late afternoon, down from the fells above. And that thought made her briefly recall her favourite of all of her mum's desserts, that being her homemade lemon meringue pie. God, what she wouldn't do for a slice of that right now, she thought. Maybe she'd ask her for some later, seeing as her parents were going to be at the concert in just a couple of hours.

It had been a good while since she'd last seen them, and they'd always had a soft spot for Gareth, hadn't they? Which didn't really help with her own feelings in the slightest. And there was no doubt in her mind that they would be asking her *how things were*, in the way only parents ever can, that being to mean, *have you finally got together with him, then?* Which was mildly inappropriate to say the least, considering what Gareth had just gone through these past few years with the loss of his wife, the court case with that other couple blaming him for everything, but then, to her mum, that was probably just an opportunity, wasn't it? An open door?

The thing was though, she'd seen it as one herself, too, hadn't she? But Gareth hadn't really taken the hint, not even that night eighteen months ago when she'd gone over to cheer him up and they'd got drunk together and then things had ended up going a little too far, and she'd said things, hadn't she? In the heat of the moment? Not just naughty sexy things either, but important things. About what she felt, how she had always felt, and how she would do anything for him, and no she hadn't just meant in the bedroom either, but in life. Because she'd always loved him, since they'd been kids and he'd been the eldest and found her annoying, and she'd been the youngest in the choir and barely able to sing a note in tune, and really the only reason she had been there at all was to just stare at him and ...

Lisa's breath stuck in her throat for a moment and she was sure that her heart had stopped, the memories of that night, of every moment she'd been with him, of being a starry-eyed seven-year-old in the choir, a teenager with a crush on a rising star, an adult chasing a music career not just for herself but to follow him, all the time wishing that there was more to it all than just being friends. But there wasn't and there never would be.

That was all in the past. It had to be, for her own sake, for her own heart. It was the only way to move on with who she was and with what she wanted. Well, not everything she wanted, clearly, because that wasn't happening, was it? And now there was this thing with Mick, who really was one of the greatest classical guitarists she had ever heard in her life. Kind, too, and romantic. He had that rakish look, like he'd just been pulled from a novel about the life and times of someone making his way through the early nineteenth century as a worker on a canal barge. But he wasn't Gareth, and Lisa knew full well that he never would be.

Lisa started to hum, 'If you can't love the one you want, love the one you're with ...' as she then thought about how she was going to introduce Mick to her parents and convince them that she really meant it this time, that he was the one.

Mick would be fine, she was sure of that. She had already prewarned him about them, their love of Gareth, the vast and almost terrifying array of horse brasses on the wall above the fireplace in the lounge, her father's oddly large collection of books about cheese, and her mum's all-consuming passion for quilting. Quite how they'd managed to sire a professional pianist had baffled everyone, not least Lisa, and the memories of her childhood made her smile as she walked out of the chill air and into the dusty warmth of the church.

Inside, the place was already abuzz and Lisa breathed in deeply the sense of full circle that this concert was giving her, and no doubt Gareth, too, she thought. They had grown up here, and it had been Gareth's springboard to stardom, this pretty little church in the dales. One she'd tried to follow him on as best she could.

At the front of the church, the stage was set and the various musicians and sound engineers were all doing their thing, which Lisa knew all too well was as much about making themselves look and feel important as it was about ensuring everything was right for the concert. Musicians were performers and if there was an opportunity to show off a bit, to sit or stand with their instrument and work that space like a peacock, then they would. Throw in a sound-check or two, some other musicians to talk shop with, and they were in heaven. As was she.

An arm slipped around Lisa's waist and a man came to stand behind her.

'We're all set,' he said. 'And if Gareth's head was big beforehand, I reckon it's going to be positively moon-sized by the end of this. It'll have its own gravitational pull. You can feel it now, actually, if you concentrate.'

Lisa looked up into Mick's eyes, shaking her head, then he nudged her a little towards the stage.

'Did you feel that? It's started already! Run! Run for your life!'

Lisa shook her head, smiled, pushed Mick away.

'He's not big-headed,' she said. 'He's just, well, proud of what he's done, isn't he?'

'Yes, and that's all he talks about.' Mick sighed. 'And I do mean, all. It's endless. I don't think he can manage a normal conversation without name-dropping or telling you he had a number one when he was eleven.'

'He's harmless.'

'He's a knob.'

'Mick!'

'He is though, isn't he?' Mick said. 'I mean, I know he's had a rough time of it and all, with his wife and the court stuff, and he's fine to work with, really, he is, but I just can't work out what you ever saw in him.'

'I never saw anything in him,' Lisa said, hoping to God

she wasn't blushing. 'We're old friends. That's all. And you should be a little more grateful. There are plenty of guitarists out there who would jump at this.'

'Yes, but none of them are as good as me, are they?'

Lisa kissed Mick and he returned it warmly.

'You don't need to be jealous, you know.'

'Of what?'

'Come on, Mick!' Lisa said. 'You know what I mean!'

'I'm not jealous at all,' Mick said. 'But you've still got a soft spot for him, haven't you? And I don't have to like him, do I? There's no law about it.'

'He's a friend,'

Mick *hmphed*.

Lisa pushed herself up onto her tiptoes and kissed him once again.

'You need to be a little more concerned about meeting my parents,' she said. 'And all my old friends.'

'Let me guess, they wish you were with Gareth,' Mick said.

Lisa dropped back down to her heels.

'You're impossible.'

A shout from the stage caught Lisa's attention and she turned to see Gareth waving to them both.

And even though she really wished it wouldn't, her heart skipped a beat. Deep down, she wondered if it always would.

Lisa felt Mick pull her closer as Gareth jumped down to come over and meet them. As he drew near, Lisa saw in him then every reason her parents had so desperately wanted her to marry him, even though they had never actually even been an item, because sometimes life just didn't work out the way you wanted it to, did it? She also saw everything he would always be that Mick would never, ever match up to, and quickly pushed that all down inside her to be ignored.

Gareth was tall, still wore that look of boyish charm, which had always been his calling card, and seemed to be almost supernaturally gifted at making people just feel better about who and what they were. He hadn't always been like that, for sure, Lisa thought, certainly not as a child or teenager, but she'd always seen the real him, and here it was now, for all to see.

His smile was genuine and as Lisa returned it, she could have been that kid again, calling to her childhood friend and crush, the boy who would then grow up to be the man before her now, bedecked in a life of fame and more than a little fortune, but still that boy at heart, she was sure. And one she had been pretty much obsessed with her whole life.

'We really don't need to be doing another soundcheck,' Gareth said, coming to stand at her side. 'but you know what our sound engineer is like. That man is obsessed, wouldn't you agree, Mick?'

'That's why he's so good at his job,' Mick said. 'It's all in the detail.'

'You're as bad as he is!' Gareth laughed.

'Just trying to make sure this album launch goes as well as you want it to,' Mick said. 'And on that, I'd best get back up there to keep an eye on things.'

With a kiss on Lisa's cheek, Mick strode off down the church.

'He doesn't like me,' Gareth said.

Lisa watched as Mick strode away, trying to ignore the scent of Gareth that she'd caught as he'd come to stand next to her.

'He's just nervous around you, that's all,' she lied. 'How are you feeling?'

'About the concert? Amazing!' Gareth replied. 'Can't wait! Love an album launch. I've done loads, but this is the best yet by far. Best thing to happen to me in the last three years, actually!'

Except for that night we had together, Lisa thought, but kept the sentiment buried deep and hidden behind her smile, though she was sure it was cracking through her armour.

'Mum and Dad are coming,' Lisa said.

'To meet Mick?' Gareth asked, looking back to Mick, who was now busy up on the stage with the rest of the musicians.

'Yes,' Lisa said.

'That's great to hear!' Gareth said, and Lisa could tell that he meant it, which only made her feel worse about the whole thing, about what the hell was wrong with her, and why she couldn't see how lucky she truly was.

Gareth glanced at his watch.

'So, we've got a couple of hours, then,' he said. 'Fancy warming up those fingers and running through a few things?'

Like you wouldn't believe, Lisa thought, but said, 'I think I know a tune or two that you can sing along to.'

And with that, Lisa walked down the aisle with the one man she knew that she would never walk down the aisle with for real, towards another who she fully suspected would, sooner rather than later, ask her if she would do him the honour of doing exactly that.

WHEN THE CONCERT FINALLY STARTED, and Mick —with Gareth, Lisa, and the rest of the musicians—stepped from the makeshift green room in the base of the tower and out into the church, the thrill of another performance sent a jolt of electricity through him so sharp that he felt it in his fingertips. It was as though he was charged with the stuff and that, at any moment, he would earth and the sparks of energy would explode from him like lightning.

Yes, he had a massive problem with Gareth, not least the fact that everyone else seemed to love him, but Lisa's seemingly undying obsession with the man, even if it was just a friendship, was still galling. Was there really such a thing as a friendship between a man and a woman? Really? The success of the man didn't help, either, Mick thought, as they made their way to the stage, everyone applauding, because it was Gareth they were there to see, not anyone else.

Jealousy was a difficult animal to tame, and Mick's version of it could get out of hand now and again. As it once had, but not for a long time now. God, he was pleased Lisa had never met his ex. It was a good while ago now, true, but she'd have said things that could easily have made all this happiness go away. But he had that under control now, had been to some really great counselling sessions, and everyone was safe from it, he was sure of that.

On stage and looking around the church, Mick saw that every pew was full, and not a seat was left in the additional seating at the back of the church either. If Gareth had wanted any confirmation as to his popularity, then this was it. Not that he needed any, that was for sure. Yes, it was a small event, but the press was here, the whole thing was going to be on film, the world would know that Gareth wasn't just still alive, he was still up there with the best. Lucky, lucky Gareth...

About halfway through the concert, however, everything

went to shit, and Mick was pretty sure that for the rest of his life he would never forget what happened, or that he would ever want to.

Gareth had been in the middle of one of his classics, a track he wasn't much of a fan of himself, but which had become a Christmas favourite thanks to numerous advertisements using it to help them sell more stuff, when the back door of the church had crashed open with such a thunderous crack that every single musician had stopped playing at the same time, and one of Mick's nails, which weren't exactly cheap, pinged off across the stage.

Necks had craned, people had stared, and then in had walked two men, one with long black hair, the other bald as a cue ball and clearly filming everything that was happening on his phone, both dressed in an eclectic collection of things you can do with black, red, and chains but probably shouldn't. It was a style Mick had never really understood, the look of the heavy metal musician. Assuming that's what they were. Or was heavy metal an old term now? Was that the 8os? He really wasn't sure, and neither did he care. But this was certainly turning the evening into something a little more entertaining, that was for sure.

Neither of the men said a word as they walked across the rear of the church then down the central aisle.

Gareth had broken the silence with the immortal words, 'Choir practise is tomorrow, lads.'

Laughter had then jumped and bounced around the audience, but the two men had simply remained standing, staring, and in their hands, Mick had noticed beer cans. He had also noticed then, that their faces were painted with strange symbols in white paint. Mick had half wondered if this was all part of the act, because he'd been to some weird concerts in his time, but no, this clearly had nothing to do with Gareth, that much was obvious from the look on the man's face, which was a rather entertaining mix of bafflement and anger.

When the laughter had eventually died, impaled on the creepy vision of these two strange men standing in the aisle, the one with the long hair had raised his beer can up into the air before pouring it onto the floor with the kind of laugh reserved for the cheesiest of horror movies. Mick liked horror movies and could easily see what was transpiring now as the opening scene in something a bit rubbish, but perfect for popcorn and a good fondle on the sofa.

A woman in her eighties, who was sitting to Mick's left, had then stood up and poked the long-haired man with her walking stick.

'Whoever you are, young man, can I suggest that you leave before I run you out of here, with a sore backside?'

She took a swing with her stick, but the man with the bald head snatched it out of the air, snapping it over his knee, his face stern, eyes wide. He then threw it at Gareth who dodged it with remarkable ease, surprising Mick and disappointing him at the same time.

'I claim this church in the name of Satan!' the one with long hair shouted. 'All hail Asmodeus, Lord Lucifer!'

It was between the snatching of the old lady's walking stick, and the mention of Satan, that from one of the pews a large shadow rose to its feet to cast itself over the men from behind.

And growled.

CHAPTER EIGHT

'Out!' the shadow had commanded. 'Now!'

The two men had turned to find themselves facing a man with a physique which more closely resembled a bull, Mick thought, a man who clearly spent a good amount of time and money on chiselling himself into a proper specimen of humanity. Mick also caught Lisa staring at the man, her eyes a little too wide he noted. And she really shouldn't have been staring like that, should she? Because she was there with him and he was there to meet her parents and that was all that should've been on her mind. Not this bull.

The two men faced the bull and the bald man threw his beer can at the bull's head.

You could've heard a pin drop when the beer can was caught mid-flight.

'I've asked you politely,' the bull had said, his voice frighteningly calm, the beer can in his hand, crushed, 'and as this is a place of worship, I'd prefer it if you left quietly and respectfully. However, if you decide against this, I will be more than happy to—'

The man with the long hair had then, for reasons known only to him, jumped at the bull, who had stepped to one side to then hoof him one up the backside and help him on his way as he flew past. Then the one with the shiny head had thrown a punch, which the bull had dodged and turned the man's momentum to his advantage, spinning him on the spot and into a chokehold.

With the help of a few more volunteers, including to his own surprise, himself, the two men were finally escorted out of the church and to huge applause, led by Gareth, they, and most notably the bull, had sat back down.

Back on stage, Mick again noticed how Lisa was staring at the bull.

AFTER THE INTERRUPTION by the two strangely dressed men, the strangest that Lisa had ever experienced in her life, the concert itself was then over far too quickly. And yet, every moment of it had seemed to her to be a thing of such vibrance and wonder, that every note she played didn't so much come from her years of practise, her muscle memory, her passion, but from another place entirely, some-where beyond who and what she was, a place where her soul called out to her. And the response from the audience had been electric, the cheers and applause lifting the roof on the wings of the stone-carved angels holding up the eaves. It was an evening she would remember for the rest of her life, and as she stood between Gareth and Mick, the lover she would never have and the lover she had but even now knew would never quite match up to what she really wanted and needed, she knew that no matter what happened, she would always and forever have her music.

Walking down from the stage, the applause finally fading to allow Gareth to head to the front of the church and do his famous thing, chatting and signing and taking photographs, Lisa made her way over to her parents and found them sitting with another face of old.

'Well if it isn't little Lisa Shaw!'

It took Lisa a few moments to realise that the man talking to her wasn't just the well-muscled eye candy who had dealt with the two gatecrashers earlier, but a very old friend indeed.

'Chris?' she said. 'Christopher Middleton? No way! It can't be, can it?'

'I know, right?' Christopher said, and Lisa noticed that he seemed almost shy. Though, with biceps like his, it was hard to imagine why. 'I've changed a bit.'

'A bit?' Lisa said, staring at the man's physique up close. 'What the hell happened? Did you eat Arnold Schwarzenegger?'

Christopher laughed.

'Not exactly, no, but I kind of got into the whole fitness thing, you know? Opened a gym as well, just down the road, like, on the way over to Bainbridge. And I can't exactly run a place like that if I look like all I do is eat doughnuts.'

'But that *was* all you used to eat!' Lisa laughed, remembering the chubby kid Christopher had been once upon a time. 'It's been years, Chris, how are you? Is anyone else here, any of the old gang, I mean? Oh, and what you did earlier? That was amazing. I've never seen anything like that in my life. I don't think anyone has! The way you just ... well, it was ...'

Lisa noticed a hand on her arm.

'Don't forget us, Love!'

Lisa looked down to see her mum staring up at her. The woman was small, yes, but she seemed smaller, as though every time Lisa came home, she had shrunk just enough for it to be noticeable.

'Mum!' Lisa said and threw her arms around her mother.

'It was wonderful,' said a man next to Lisa's mum, and Lisa looked up to see her dad staring back at her with love and pride in his eyes.

'Thanks, Dad,' Lisa said.

'Now, where's this Mick chap you're so keen for us to meet?'

'He's a bit busy at the moment,' Lisa said.

'No, I'm not!'

As if summoned by the mere mention of his name, Mick was at Lisa's side. Lisa noticed a steeling look in his eye as he turned his smile from her parents and onto Christopher, like a searchlight coming to rest on something it really didn't want to find.

'Mick Johnson,' Mick said, introducing himself. 'A pleasure to meet you both.' He shook Lisa's dad's hand before kissing her mum lightly on the cheek. 'Lisa has told me so much about you both. And most of it is actually pretty good!'

Lisa's dad laughed and her mum tittered before looking to Lisa.

'You're round to ours for dinner tomorrow, yes? Both of you?'

'As promised,' Lisa said.

'I've been told you do an excellent roast,' Mick said.

'It's a team effort,' Lisa's mum said.

'It is indeed,' her dad agreed. 'I do all the work, and you drink far too much tea!'

Christopher leaned in and said, 'If you'll excuse me, I

think I'll go and have a catch up with Gareth. And I'll grab the others as well if I can, though they said they'd meet us down the pub anyway.'

'So, they're here?'

Christopher gave a nod. 'Oh, they weren't going to miss the prodigal son's return now, were they? None of us were!'

Lisa punched Christopher gently on the arm. 'That's unfair,' she said. 'And you know it!'

Christopher just smiled at Lisa.

'I'll join you,' Lisa said, desperate to get away from the charm offensive both Mick and her parents were putting on for each other.

'So, will I,' Mick added.

'No, you chat with Mum and Dad,' Lisa said. 'I won't be long.'

Slipping away and doing her best to ignore how the conversation had, courtesy of her dad, already dropped a gear and accelerated full-on into the best way to roast beef and what joint to use, Lisa and Chris headed off to find Gareth.

'You're kidding me!' Gareth said as they came to stand in front of him. 'Chris? Really? It's you? It can't be! I mean, well, just look at you! You're enormous! But in a completely different way, obviously!'

'Those choir days are years ago, right?' Christopher said. 'And to think, I was head boy!'

'But you were, well, you were—'

'A bit on the chubby side?' Christopher said, finishing off what Gareth had clearly been about to say. 'Which reminds me, have you seen the photos yet?'

CHAPTER NINE

'What photos?'

Christopher pointed to his left.

'Those ones under that window over there.'

Gareth and Lisa looked over to see a collection of fading photographs framed and screwed to the wall, demonstrating someone's pride for the chosen subject more so than their talent for putting together a display that was in any way pleasing to the eye.

'Come on, they're worth a look, for sure! You'll love them!' Christopher said, then led the way. 'I think they just wanted to commemorate the fact that you, Mr Fame, started here of all places. And all those years ago, too. Nice really, don't you think? That they remember that?'

Lisa couldn't believe what she was looking at. The photographs were of half a dozen children, three boys and three girls. Gareth and Christopher were there, the oldest and tallest in the group. And there were four others, one boy and three girls, one girl being clearly the smallest and youngest of the group by just enough years to make a difference.

'Bloody hell, look at my hair!' Lisa said, leaning in to stare at herself right at the front of one of the photographs.

'Your hair?' Gareth said. 'Look at my teeth!'

'Now there's a sign of fame,' Christopher said, 'when you notice your teeth! How much did they cost you, by the way? And I really was chubby, wasn't I? Horrendous!'

'You don't want to know,' Gareth said.

'What, how chubby I was?'

'No,' Gareth said and pointed to his teeth. 'Shameful, to be honest.'

Lisa continued to stare at the same photo, taking in the date, her own face all those years ago, then moved on to others, memories jostling for place at the front of her mind.

'So, why's this display on the wall, then?' Gareth asked. 'Other than what you said, I mean, because there are dozens of photos, I'm sure, from back then when we were all kids. Why are these so special?'

'You don't remember, do you?'

'Should I?'

'It's the concert!' Christopher explained. 'The one we were spotted at for a certain competition? Well, not all of them are from that, and there's an album, too, but the main ones here, that's why they were put up on display.'

'What competition?'

The question was from Mick who had come over to join them.

'Mum and Dad okay?' Lisa asked.

'I think they like me,' Mick said, wrapping his arm around Lisa a little too tightly, she noticed. 'At least I hope they do. But anyway, what competition? No, wait, you mean, this is from back then? Really?'

'It is,' Gareth nodded, then pointed at the photograph. 'That's me, that's Lisa, and that's Christopher.'

'What about the other three?'

'That's Andrew, Penny, and Claire,' Christopher said. 'They're here, too.'

'This is a proper reunion, then,' Mick said.

Gareth tapped a knuckle on the photograph. 'If it hadn't been for this, I wouldn't be here now doing this.'

'Very true,' said Christopher. 'It's where it all began isn't it?'

Lisa was about to say something about how much all of their lives had changed since that night all those years ago, when she saw someone in among the crowds still hanging around in the church. Everyone was enjoying the refreshments Gareth had insisted on providing, buying CDs, chatting, but the person she'd just spotted, well, she was pretty sure that they weren't here for any of that at all. They just couldn't be.

'I'll be back in a minute,' Lisa said, breaking away from Gareth, Mick, and Christopher, who were so engrossed in reliving old memories to even notice. Well, Gareth and Christopher were, for sure, and Mick was doing his best to look and sound interested. His eyes weren't in it though, Lisa could tell.

Walking across the church, Lisa really hoped that the person she had seen wasn't actually the person she had seen. She knew how that sounded in her own head, like complete gibberish, but she knew what she meant, and that was all that mattered. But if it was, then the only reason he was here at all was to cause trouble, and that got her thinking back to the two idiots who had turned up halfway through. Had he arranged that as well? It had seemed a little too random, hadn't it? She wouldn't put it past him, that was for sure. And if it was him, then what else was he planning?

In the crowd, Lisa saw him again and started to push through to reach him. Part of her wondered why she was so bothered. After all, Gareth had had a fling with the man's wife, hadn't he? Yes, it had been a decade and a half ago now, but it was the news of it, that it had happened at all, which had served so well to derail Gareth's life even more than it already was, after the tragic loss of his wife, Karen. The tabloids had loved it, the whole story of Mr Nice, Mr Church Choirboy, having an affair. It was gold! It sold papers! And it destroyed lives and trampled on those already in ruins.

Lisa was approaching the edge of the crowd now and just ahead she saw the man she was after leaving through the main door. Well, she wasn't about to let him bugger off without an explanation now, was she? Not a chance in hell! So, she pushed through a couple who were busy discussing Gareth's concert over champagne and the tiniest of sandwiches and followed him outside.

The cold bit into her with teeth as sharp as razors and it was only when she slipped and fell on her arse that she realised just how much of a hurry she had been in to catch him up. The snow had cushioned her fall just enough but thumping down on the ground had still caused her to let out a cry of shock and pain.

Ahead, Lisa saw the figure she was chasing stop, turn around, and stare.

It was him alright. And to think that he was still mad and angry enough to travel all this way, from London, just to get one over on Gareth!

The man turned away and Lisa struggled to her feet.

'You!' she called. 'Stop! I need you to stop!'

But it was already too late and the man was gone.

Back inside the church, now soaking wet and a little bruised, Lisa made her way back over to Gareth and Christopher. Mick was still with them, and they were all clearly getting on well. At least, that's how it looked; it was always hard to tell with Mick.

Regardless of the fact that Gareth really only knew Mick from rehearsals, Mick didn't know Chris at all, and Gareth and Chris had last seen each other back when they were barely old enough to even grow a moustache each. Plus there was the issue of Mick feeling a little bit off about how Lisa was so friendly with Gareth, but he'd just have to get used to it, wouldn't he? She wasn't about to change her friends for anyone, couldn't see why she should.

'What happened to you?' Mick asked, reaching out for Lisa, again so tightly with that arm of his around her waist.

'Yeah, why did you dash off like that?' Chris asked. 'Just got a text from Andrew. They're at the pub already.'

'Thought I saw someone,' Lisa said.

'Who?' Gareth asked.

She wanted to tell him, to let him know that the mad and now ex-husband of a woman he'd had the briefest of flings with years ago, had been at the concert, that the only reason for him to be here at all was surely to be up to no good, but she couldn't. He looked so happy, like this had been the best day of his life, and who was she to ruin it? All she wanted to do, really, was make it better.

'No one,' Lisa said, then added, 'No one at all. So, pub, then?'

.   .   .

GARETH SUNK his first pint so quickly that it barely touched the sides. The liquid was cool, not cold, refreshing, and swept through his system on a tumbling wave of hops.

'Thirsty?' Christopher asked, slumping a hefty arm across Gareth's shoulders. 'You want another?'

Gareth thunked his glass down onto the bar top half wondering why he'd waited so long to come back, to return home.

'Sounds like you've already had a few!' Gareth laughed.

'Loads!' Chris roared back, his face a huge smile. 'Actually, not really, it's just that I don't really drink, being all massive and muscly and running a gym. Doesn't go with the image.'

'I can see that,' Gareth said.

'Goes right to my head!'

'And it really has, hasn't it?'

Chris laughed again, even louder this time, then ordered a couple of pints from the bar.

'You deserve this,' Christopher said, once the beers had arrived. 'It was a cracker of a concert. Loved it! You were amazing! Like, wow!'

'He's not wrong, mate.'

The other voice belonged to Andrew Firth, who was sipping on a large double malt. He had less hair than the last time Gareth had seen him, but he certainly seemed happy. He had his arm around Penny, whose smile was as bouncy as her ponytail. So, they'd finally ended up together then. Had he really lost touch with them that much?

'It's really good of you all to come,' Gareth said. 'I'm amazed to see you, truly I am.'

'We made a pact, remember?' said another voice, this one belonging to another woman, shorter than Penny, but a smidge above Lisa. 'No way that we were ever going to miss out on this!'

Her dark hair was cut in a bob and she was wearing an expensive pair of boots more suited to riding horses, thought Gareth. But that was no surprise, because Claire Sykes had always been obsessed with the animals, something he'd never really understood.

Everyone laughed at Claire's words and Gareth tried to take it all in, his eyes casting around this group of old, old friends, who had all come out to support him. It meant so much that when he tried to speak again, to say thank you, his voice caught in his throat.

'Oh, look, he's getting all emotional!' Lisa said, and Gareth felt her hand on his arm, then a slight squeeze of her fingers through the material of his jacket.

'It just seems so long ago,' Gareth said. 'All of it.'

'That's probably because it is,' Andrew said. 'And you've not exactly been around since it all took off, have you?'

'Not really, no,' Gareth said. 'The time's flown.'

'It really has,' Christopher agreed with an exaggerated nod. 'Woosh!'

Claire asked, 'So, what's it like then, being famous?'

'Don't forget rich,' Penny added, and Gareth caught the wink she sent his way, except the wink seemed to go through him, too, like it was sent to the others as well.

'No one likes talking about money,' Gareth said. 'But I've done okay. It's been good. Well, most of it has.'

Christopher then said, 'You were only... you were only...'

'Only what?' Gareth asked, wondering just how much more booze Christopher could actually handle.

'Thirteen!' Chris bellowed. 'And you had a number one

in the charts! I mean, wow, right? Just wow! You got every-thing you dreamed of!'

'Impossible to forget really,' Gareth laughed, 'seeing as I'm reminded of it every bloody Christmas!'

At this, everyone laughed and before he knew what he was doing Gareth had ordered everyone another round of drinks.

'It really is great to see you all,' he said, as he handed out the round. 'And I'm sorry that it's taken this long to come back. I mean, I've visited, but I've never really had the time to stay.'

'But that's all changed now, right?' said Andrew.

'Oh, yes,' Penny said. 'With the house, right? Up at Countersett?'

At this, Gareth's smile faltered just a touch.

'Yes, yes it is,' he said.

'Word gets around you see,' said Claire, smiling, and reaching out to squeeze Gareth's arm just a little.

'No secrets in the dales,' added Chris.

'And like I said before, we made a pact,' said Penny.

A memory hit Gareth then, of a churchyard and a storm and a group of children playing what his father would have undoubtedly called *silly buggers.*

'Bloody hell, I'd forgotten that!'

Chris laughed, shaking his head.

'That thunderstorm, right? Where the hell did that come from? Crashing and booming all around us!'

'Oh, we summoned it, surely!' said Andrew.

'The words did that, I think,' Penny said. 'The poetry of it all!'

Chris roared with laughter once more, the sound of it tumbling off through the bar like a barrel kicked down a hill.

'The things you do when you're young,' Gareth said, shaking his head.

'How do you mean?' Mick asked, talking for the first time since Gareth had stepped into the pub.

Gareth was pretty sure that the man didn't like him. Or Chris for that matter. Was it jealousy? Of what, his friendship with Lisa? There was nothing there, for goodness sake! Still, it wasn't his problem. So long as Lisa was happy, that was what mattered, wasn't it?

And so the drinks continued to be ordered and the conversation rolled ever onward, as old friends explored old memories, reliving them as best they could. Not all of them could remember everything, but by the end of it, most everything had been remembered by them all. Though some of the stories had grown, Gareth was sure, time serving to magnify the daring-do, the risks, the laughs.

When the evening drew to a close, and Gareth got a nod from the bar that his taxi was waiting, he sunk the remains of his last pint, and with smiles and thank-you's, he turned to leave.

'Told you it would work ...'

The words were a whisper, and who had said them, Gareth wasn't sure, but he turned and stared at his old friends.

'Pardon?'

Each one of them looked back at him, giving nothing away.

'You should see your eyes!' Andrew said.

'I thought someone said something,' Gareth said.

His friends looked at each other, shook their heads. Mick just stared.

'Hearing things as well, it seems.' Gareth smiled, then with a shrug and a wave, he left the pub.

Outside, the wind was getting up again. The moon was bright and the snow covering Askrigg seemed to glow with its light.

'You okay?'

Gareth turned to see Lisa standing at his side.

'Absolutely!' he said, noticing how loud his voice was and how little he could do to change the volume. 'Great idea coming here, you know! Well done to the person who thought of it! Ha!'

Lisa laughed and Gareth liked the laugh and her smile and wondered why she was with someone like Mick.

'He doesn't like me,' Gareth said. 'Mick. Stares at me. I think he's jealous.'

'Does he need to be?' Lisa asked.

The question took Gareth a little by surprise.

'No, I don't think so,' he replied.

Lisa was close then, really close, her hand on his chest, and he could smell the sweet warmth of the alcohol on her breath.

'I just want you to be happy,' Lisa said. 'You know that, don't you?'

'Yes, I do,' Gareth said, his voice firm, but his temperature rising.

'Mick's lovely, but...'

Gareth stared down as Lisa's face turned upwards to look at him, her mouth open just enough.

'Lisa...'

Lisa moved in and Gareth was suddenly hit by memory upon memory upon memory and he couldn't do it, he just couldn't, even though he wanted to, needed to, but it was wrong. It had been wrong that last and only time, too.

Gareth stepped back, knocking into the taxi.

'I'm sorry, Lisa,' Gareth said. 'No. I can't. You can't.'

Lisa stood staring at him.

'We could try?'

'No, we couldn't,' Gareth replied, firmer now.

'But the last time...'

'It can't happen again,' Gareth said. 'You're wonderful, you really are, but I can't. I'm sorry.'

Climbing into the taxi, Gareth slumped against the door, his head resting against the cool glass. The church slipped past a moment later, the tower poking out from behind the trees at the gate, and he closed his eyes, the alcohol in his system winning out over his urge to stay awake and watch the world drift by.

Then sleep.

CHAPTER TEN

HARRY LIFTED THE PINT OF BLACKSTONE STOUT AND took a sip, which quickly turned into a hefty glug. The liquid itself was the colour of tar and though not usually one for the darker beers, it had seemed the only appropriate drink to have on a wintery day such as this.

Since moving up north to Wensleydale from his old stomping ground of Somerset and Bristol, Harry had found himself becoming strangely changed by the place, as though to be in the dales too long was to become a part of it. He wasn't a hard cider drinker by any means, but it had been his usual drink of choice up until he'd arrived in Hawes all those months ago now. The pubs served cider, of course they did, but it wasn't the good stuff, more like fizzy pop for teenagers. So he'd drifted over to beer and now, here he was, taking a deep dive into the world of stouts. But there was no denying it, Harry thought as he eyed the pint in his hand, this was a proper tasty beer, smooth to drink and with a distant hint of vanilla. He took another deep swig and sat the glass back down.

'You're enjoying that, then?'

Across the table from Harry sat Gordy. They were both scooched up in a corner of the public bar of the Fountain Hotel in Hawes, Harry relaxing perhaps a little too much into the embrace of a wing-backed leather armchair, Gordy perched on a stool. To Harry's right an open fire blazed, the red flickering light dancing across the worn wooden floorboards. Outside, a bright sky gave the impression of warmth, but a biting wind was the death of any such promise, and its murderous intent was not only clear but something to be avoided for a good few days yet, according to the weather forecast.

'I am, indeed,' Harry said. 'As much to my own surprise as anyone's I think. How's your orange juice?'

'Orangey,' Gordy shrugged. 'Which is a relief.'

Harry rested his hand around his pint glass, turning it left, then right, and imprinting a damp ring mark onto the beermat on which it sat.

'So, do I need to ask what's up, or can I just assume that at some point you'll let me know?' Harry asked, then held up a small bag. 'Pork scratching?'

Gordy shook her head. 'Not with orange juice,' she said. 'Or anything, actually, if I'm honest. How can you eat those things?'

'Says the woman who had haggis this week, if I remember correctly.'

'You do,' Gordy nodded. 'But you can hardly compare the national dish of my homeland with a bag of deep-fried salty pig skin bits, can you?'

'Oh, I think I can,' Harry said and popped a scratching into his mouth. 'Yum!'

Gordy shook her head, folded her arms, sighed.

'I'll tell Jen and then you'll be in trouble.'

Harry laughed. Police Constable Jenny Coates had seemingly made it her life mission to get him healthy. He blamed her for the fact that he was now running almost regularly and had lost probably a stone in weight since moving to the dales.

'Well, come on, then!' Harry said. 'Out with it!'

'How's Jim?' Gordy asked.

'Swift change of subject there,' Harry said. 'He's okay. Need to keep an eye on him, though. He was hit hard by what happened to his old schoolmate. And after what you told me, about how he was when you were interviewing that dognapper? It's a concern, let's put it that way. He's clutching at straws.'

'The cigarettes you mean?'

Harry gave a nod.

'It was a bit odd, that'd he'd be smoking that particular brand.'

'Not really,' Harry said. 'Forensics found nothing from them last time. And he was pretty wired anyway having Fly almost nicked.'

'And none of it was helped by that solicitor,' Gordy said.

Harry shook his head. 'No, I can see that being a bit of an issue.'

'Didn't really strike me as the type to have such representation,' Gordy said. 'Which is a red flag in my book.'

'And mine,' Harry nodded, taking another gulp from his pint glass. 'Not much we can do about that, though, is there? And it all checked out.'

'Do you think there's a link, though?' Gordy asked.

'Between what?'

'Fly's attempted kidnapping and the sheep theft,' said Gordy.

'No, I don't,' Harry said. 'I've sent the cigarettes off for testing to see if there's any connection between them and the ones from before, though I doubt that'll come to anything. They're the same brand, yes, but the link is tenuous, to say the least. To be honest, I did it more out of respect for Jim than anything else.'

'Always best to be sure,' Gordy agreed. 'Did you get anything else on the man we questioned?'

'Well, brushing over how much of a complete delight Tim was,' Harry said, 'the best way to describe him is as an old acquaintance of the police.'

'So, not just dog theft, then?'

Harry shook his head. 'Not exactly, no. Been in and out of prison most of his life by the looks of things. And judging by the solicitor thing, he's probably managed to get himself into the very, very outer circle of something just big enough to make him feel important.'

'But still nothing on the murder?'

Harry shook his head.

'Not a damned thing.'

'It's not like it is in the movies, is it, this police stuff?' Gordy said, chasing the moisture running down her glass with her fingertips. 'I mean, there's always some evidence, isn't there? A link? A nice conclusion where the criminals are caught.'

'Except in the real world, it's just not that simple, sadly,' Harry said. 'And a murder like Neil's? They happen. And sometimes, whoever did it, just gets away with it. And that's the awful truth of it.'

'That got dark quickly.' Gordy sighed.

'Then best you get on and tell me what this is all about,' Harry said, lifting his pint to stare expectantly over the top of the glass at Gordy. 'But as I'm a generous soul, I'll give you a moment to prepare whatever it is you want to say by grabbing myself another one of these.'

Harry finished his pint, took to his feet, then squeezed out past Gordy and headed over to the bar. Drink ordered, he glanced back at the detective inspector. She was staring out of the window and Harry could see that something was off, in the way she was sitting, the way her hands were together, but fidgeting.

Back at the table, Harry placed his pint down, threw onto the table a couple of bags of Seabrook Crisps, then eased back into the armchair. He opened both packets fully and placed them in the centre of the table.

'Ready when you are,' he said, helping himself to the snacks provided. 'By which I mean, start talking. Because whatever it is that's bothering you, it's better said than not, right? So...' Harry splayed his hands as though offering the floor to Gordy.

Gordy nodded and smiled thinly, her eyes not exactly joining in.

'I... well, I miss home.'

'Scotland?'

'Aye,' Gordy said. 'Scotland. I've not lived there in years, you know? Not since before I graduated actually, but it's always there, calling me back.'

'Can't say that it ever had that effect on me,' Harry said. 'Visited a few times, courtesy of various all-expenses-paid trips back when I was in the Paras. Came back covered in midge bites and an almost pathological hatred of rain. I mean, it never stopped. No, I lie, it did, but only to snow. Not that we could see the snow because of the fog.'

Gordy laughed. 'You see, I miss all of that, too!'

'How?'

A shrug.

'Home's home, I guess,' Gordy said. 'Not much I can do to change it. I think last night, that early Burns supper I had, it kind of brought it all back, made me homesick.'

'You sound like you're in need of a holiday, then.' Harry said. 'Is that what this is about? Because really, you only have to put in a holiday request form, or whatever pointless paper-work is required. You don't have to do this, sit here and ruin my afternoon.'

'I think I might be needing more than a holiday,' Gordy said. 'A lot more. I mean, I'm not decided or anything, but I just thought it best to mention it, chat it through.'

'What about a sabbatical, then?' Harry suggested, knowing full well he should probably take one as well but never would. 'I've no idea how that works, but I can look into it,' he offered. 'I'll even have a word with Swift, and that's something I generally try to avoid doing if I can.'

'No, it's not that,' Gordy said, then reached for her orange juice to take a sip, only to return the glass, the drink untouched, back to the table.

Meanwhile, Harry's gut was starting to tell him that something was up. Gordy was a solid member of the team. She ran things down dale, yes, but she seemed to have a soft spot for Hawes, and Harry rather enjoyed having her around. They all did. So, what exactly was she getting at? Why ask to meet up on a Saturday to talk about being a little homesick? Harry had a horrible feeling that he knew, but he didn't want to voice it. That was down to Gordy. The words needed to come from her.

'I'm thinking about transferring,' Gordy said at last, confirming what Harry had started to suspect, and at the same time dropping a hefty stone into the pit of his stomach. He coughed, hoping to dislodge it. It didn't work.

'To Police Scotland?' Harry asked. 'That's quite a decision.'

Gordy gave a short, shallow nod.

'And you're sure a holiday wouldn't help?'

'Tried that, remember?' Gordy said. 'And like I said, I'm only thinking about it. I'm not decided by any means.'

Harry did remember. It was a while ago now, and he remembered it because he had missed having the detective inspector around to help during a case over in Swaledale.

Harry allowed silence to sit with them for a while as he took in what Gordy had just said.

'So, whereabouts, in Scotland, I mean?' Harry asked, working hard to sound encouraging rather than gutted. 'Edinburgh? Glasgow? Somewhere with a bit more excitement than the dales?'

'Well, I grew up in Glencoe,' Gordy said. 'Not in the valley itself, mind. The wee village at the far end. There's a station there, run by the team based in the Fort.'

'There's a fort?' Harry asked. 'Didn't realise things were so bad up there that the police had to have a fort! Do you get bows and arrows, too?'

'Fort William,' Gordy said, shaking her head, a smile curling the corners of her mouth. 'There's a good team there, really good, actually. Not sure there's space for someone like me, but there are other places, too, like Oban, maybe.'

'Oban?'

'On the west coast,' Gordy said. 'You can catch a ferry there out to the islands. It's a nice place. Not exactly cosmopolitan, but still, worth considering.'

Harry took a mouthful from his pint glass, but the beer didn't taste the same, not after the bombshell Gordy had just dropped.

'So, what next, then?' he asked. 'What do you need me to do?'

'Nothing yet,' Gordy said. 'But thanks for taking this so well.'

'Can't say I won't miss you, if you do decide to go,' Harry said. 'The whole team will. But there's no point staying if you're unhappy.'

'Oh, I'm not unhappy,' Gordy said. 'Not a bit I love it here. Always have. The countryside, the people. How could I not?'

Harry couldn't agree more. In the few months he'd lived in the area he had found himself slowly becoming so comfortable with the hills and the inhabitants that even in such a short time the place seemed more like home to him now than anywhere he had lived before in his whole life.

'No, it's not unhappiness. It's more that I just fancy heading home, and sooner rather than later, maybe. The Highlands, they're in my blood, and that's just the way it is.'

'Well, you just let me know, okay?' Harry said.

'I might not even go,' Gordy said, then shrugged. 'I'm just dipping my toe in the water as it were, seeing if it's an idea I really want to follow through with, you know?'

'So, you've basically got me all worried for nothing, then?'

Gordy winked, which was something Harry had never before seen her do.

'I'll see how something else goes first,' she said.

Harry perked up.

'Something else? What do you mean by something else? That's a bit mysterious, isn't it?'

A smile crept onto Gordy's face.

'Had a date, earlier in the week,' she said, and Harry watched the smile grow to a wide, happy grin. 'A friend of a friend of a friend kind of thing, Went well, actually.'

'Well, now, that's something to drink to!' Harry said, raising his glass. 'Great news! A date and Burns Night in one week? You've been busy!'

'It's someone from this end of the dale rather than down the other end,' Gordy said. 'And no, I'm not going to tell you who it is. Not that you'd know, but word gets a round.'

'Don't you trust me?' Harry attempted to look hurt.

'You, yes, but the rest of the team? Not a chance of it!' Gordy said.

A while later, when Gordy pulled herself away from the wonders of talking to Harry, Harry sat back in his chair and stared at his empty pint glass, the heat from the fire threatening to send him to sleep. As he pondered the pros and cons of ordering another drink, he couldn't help but think that, as ways to start a new job went, losing one of his team within the first couple of months wasn't the best. And in some ways, he envied Gordy, because she knew where her home was and wanted to be there. His last home had been Bristol, though he had never truly settled, despite being born and bred in Somerset. He knew that had a lot to do with his life as a soldier, but it also had a great deal to do with what had happened at home. None of which made for a place that Harry hankered for.

Hawes, though, Harry thought, could this be home? It

was for now at least, and there was no doubt that the dales, the people, had welcomed him. It wasn't perfect, in fact, as he'd gotten to know it more, he'd seen beyond the picture-postcard image and seen its flaws, its scars. But to Harry, that made it more interesting, more real. And perhaps that was what made him already feel so at home beneath the shadow of the fells, that the place, like he himself, carried its scars proudly.

Harry pushed himself to his feet, walked over to the bar to return his glass, then pushed his way out into the ice-laden wind of the night. When the cold hit him, he smiled. Yes, he thought, as places to call home went, this would do. And he trudged off through the snow, back to his flat.

CHAPTER ELEVEN

GARETH CRASHED THROUGH HIS FRONT DOOR WITH ALL the grace of a dancing hippo, tripping over his own feet as he went, then pirouetting in the hall, before stumbling sideways into the wall and knocking a mirror to the floor. After a brief pause to allow the world to stop spinning just enough for him to work out where to aim himself next, he then threaded himself through the lounge door, a task which was rather more difficult than he had expected it to be, the door somehow considerably narrower than it had been a few hours ago when last he'd negotiated it and been somewhat more sober. He was thankful that he'd had the sense to pre-book a taxi, knowing full well that such a thing in the dales was in short supply. After all, Askrigg on a Saturday night, regardless of how jumping the pubs were, was hardly Piccadilly Circus.

In the lounge, he navigated his way across a floor bereft of carpet, the floorboards covered in various old sheets held down with paint cans, and over to an as-yet unpacked box of goodness knows what, though he did catch sight of a frame which he assumed held a gold or silver record or something. He had so many of the damned things that he'd lost count.

He spied another box behind it, and dropping to his knees, he tore it open and cheered. More booze! Brilliant! And it was only just gone midnight so the night was still very young. Reaching in, Gareth pulled out a half-full bottle of single malt, decided against it, and after a bit of searching, managed to find some port. Perfect!

Back on his feet, Gareth headed back out of the lounge and into the kitchen diner, a room he was living in for the moment as he decorated the rest of the downstairs. Not that decorating was his thing at all, and he was fairly sure that his colour scheme was the wrong side of what-the-hell-were-you-thinking, but this was his new home and he was going to make it his own.

In the kitchen, he managed to find a glass tumbler, then dropped it, smashing it on the floor. With a shrug, he reached for a mug on the draining board by the sink, avoided walking on the broken glass, and slumped down on one of the chairs tucked under the dining table. Then, pouring a somewhat overly generous mug of port, he raised the sweet, ruby liquid to his mouth, and took a gulp.

What he needed now was something decent to watch, a classic movie or something, and he scrambled around for his laptop to stream something that had to be one of two things: funny, or violent. Both would be good, but then he saw *The Equalizer*, starring the legend that was Denzel Washington—someone he'd bumped into at a party once—and decided on that with a toast and more booze. Reaching forward, he clicked play, which was exactly when there came a knock at the front door.

The sound of the knock at such an odd time of night

caught Gareth with enough surprise to have him cough, sending a shocking spray of vibrant fortified wine not just across the table in front of him, but up the wall as well. Wiping his mouth, he wondered for a moment if the sound hadn't actually come from the front door at all, that perhaps it was just a vehicle bouncing past, or maybe a bird exploding. He had no idea where the thought of an exploding bird had come from, though the spray of port on the wall certainly looked like the remnants of just such an event.

The knock at the door came again. Gareth leaned forwarded and paused the movie, poured some more port, slowly clambered to his feet, and then with port in hand, made his way back out of the kitchen and down the hall to the front of the house. Reaching for the door, he took a slow sip of the port, enjoying its sweet taste and laughing quietly to himself about just how drunk he was, then dropped to his knees and knocked open the letterbox.

'Yes? Who is it?'

No answer came, just another knock, this time harder than before.

It wasn't Lisa, was it? Gareth thought. No, it couldn't be. She was sensible enough to know that he'd meant what he'd said. And anyway, it had surely been the alcohol talking, because she was with Mick, and he seemed okay, and had now even met the parents. No, it couldn't be Lisa. And even if it was, Gareth knew there was little else to say. He had too much going on, too much to do to get back to himself after these past few years, and he wasn't going to derail the train of recovery. He also needed to make sure.

'Lisa? Is that you?'

Another knock.

'Lisa, if it is you, and I don't think it is, but if it is, then I think you should head home to Mick. He seems good. Bit jealous maybe, but certainly has eyes only for you. Oh, and if it isn't you, then please go away because I need to get a bit more drunkerer.'

Knock-knock-knock.

'Did you not hear me?' Gareth said. 'I've been singing, you see. Launched a new album! How cool is that? Never grows old, you know. It's always exciting! Do you like port? I like port. Love it, actually. Though I did just redecorate my kitchen with it because your knock scared me. Anyway, I'm hungry. Oh, and I'm watching a movie, so whatever this is about, I'm not in. Well, I am, clearly, but I'm not, if you know what I mean.' Gareth laughed then, his chuckle more of a childish giggle, as he said, somewhat robotically, 'This is an answering machine. Gareth isn't home right now. Please leave a message after the—'

Gareth burped.

Gareth laughed.

Another knock, though this was less knuckle and more fist, Gareth noticed, the sound of it deeper, firmer, more violent. Definitely not Lisa.

'Look,' Gareth said, leaning so far into the letterbox that his lips were basically inside his front door, 'whoever you are, and whatever this is about, can you come back tomorrow? By which I mean Monday, not like later today, because it's Sunday now, isn't it? And Sunday is a day of rest, and I think I will most definitely be needing to rest. A lot. I'm not used to being up so late. Did I tell you I'm drunk? Ooh, look, port!'

Gareth took another gulp from his mug and rose to his feet.

'Bye, then!' he called back, and wiggled his fingers at the door in a weak attempt at a wave.

The next knock at the door, Gareth was sure, almost took it off its hinges.

'Hey! Whoever you are, pack it in, okay? Just go home. I don't know who you are and I don't care either. Just sod off!'

Another knock, a kick, and before Gareth knew what he was doing or why he was doing it, he was at the door and ripping it open.

'Right! That's it!'

In the space that had been occupied by the door a portion of the night stepped in from out of the cold.

'Hello, Gareth.'

Gareth wasn't just angry now, he was livid.

'Nicholas?'

The man at his front door stood there, staring at him, eyes wreathed in shadow, silent.

'What the hell are you doing here? And how did you find out where I live?'

The man didn't move, didn't speak, just stared, and Gareth could almost smell the heat of the rage in his eyes. Not that he cared. All of that was over, so whatever this was, he wasn't having any of it.

'What do you want? What? I'll call the police! No, actually, I *am* calling the police, Nick. Right now!'

As Gareth patted his pockets for his phone the man in front of him stepped a little closer.

'I was at the concert.'

'Were you, Nick? Well, thanks for the support. Thought you'd try and persuade me to sign to your label, is that it?' Gareth laughed at this, the utter nonsense of the idea so completely wrong on every level suddenly the most hysterical thing he'd ever said or heard.

Gareth lifted his phone up and placed it in front of the intruder's face. 'See? Nine-nine-nine. And I'm dialling.'

The intruder didn't budge.

'Seems you're doing okay for yourself, despite everything. And don't call me Nick. My name's Nicholas.'

Gareth couldn't believe what he was hearing.

'Despite everything, Nick? Really? You have got to be kidding me! You're here just to say that? Well, now, let me see which I prefer... Is it Nick or is it Nicholas? No, you're definitely a Nick. Rhymes with how you're a massive pri—'

'Shut up!' Nick roared. 'Please, just shut up! Your affair with my wife—'

'It wasn't a bloody affair! How many times do you need to be told?'

'So, you sleeping with my wife isn't an affair, then? And how would you describe it, Gareth? What was it exactly?'

Gareth rubbed his eyes with his thumbs, spilling a little of the port.

'Firstly, and as you well know because it was mentioned more than enough times in court, I'm sure, it was ten years ago, Nick. Ten! Have you ever counted them?'

'It's Nicholas ...'

'Ten! Years!' Gareth repeated. 'Here, tell you what, I'll count that out for you!' He raised up his left hand, his right busy with the mug of port, and flashed it palm first twice in front of Nicholas's face. 'Five plus five is ten! Ten years! It wasn't an affair! It was a mistake, one I regret and will do for the rest of my life, and I'm sorry.'

'Don't think that quite cuts it, Gareth,' Nicholas said.

'Blame me all you want,' Gareth replied, 'but I was just an excuse, and you know it. If Cassie was that unhappy all those years ago to have a fling with me, then God knows how she managed to stay with you for so long after it had happened!'

'She wasn't unhappy!' Nicholas snapped back, his voice rising. 'I gave her everything! Everything!'

'I don't care, Nick! I just don't!' Gareth bit back.

'It's Nicholas!'

'I didn't even know she was married, or have you forgotten that bit? Oh, yes, of course, you have, because it was a hell of a lot more convenient to do so when she filed for divorce and you thought you could hold something over her, right?'

'You slept with her, slept with my wife!' Nicholas said, his voice a seething, spital-fuelled thing of hatred.

'What did you want, exactly, Nick?' Gareth asked. 'Her to stay with you? Was that all that mattered to you? What about her happiness? You ever thought about that? No, of course not, because it's all about you, isn't it? I mean, I don't even know you, Nick, by which I mean at *all*, or actually want to, and yet here you are, at my door, invading my privacy! And you know what? Based on what you put me through, and your little display right now? I reckon that I already know you better than I would ever actually want to!'

'Shut up, Gareth ...'

But Gareth wasn't about to shut up. Not a chance in hell of that happening, fuelled as he was by adrenaline and booze and a fair smattering of righteous indignation.

'I was a pawn in whatever mad, sick game you two were playing as you tried to screw each other over for money! You both used me, Nick, you and Cassie, to make your divorce something so terrible that in the end, neither of you came out of it on top, am I right?'

'Seriously, shut up ...'

'Yes, yes I am. I'm so completely right and that's what really eats away at you, isn't it? And *still* you blame me! But there was never a thought about what you did to my life, was there? And there still isn't, demonstrated by you being here right now. No, because that would be too much to ask.'

'I'm warning you...'

'I was chewed up by the press, Nick. They mangled me! I was devoured by those bloodthirsty bastards! My image, my whole life, was put on display for the world to see, then hanged, drawn, and quartered! And all so that you and Cassie could rip each other's lives apart in the hope of emptying the other's bank account. And, in the process, you managed to completely ruin my life, which as I'm sure you'll remember, wasn't exactly in the best state of affairs seeing as I was still trying to come to terms with the death of my wife! Bravo, oh yes, very well done, mate, very well done indeed!'

Gareth applauded Nicholas, his hands millimetres from the end of the man's nose.

'Gareth...'

'What, the applause isn't loud enough? Here, let me see to that for you!'

Gareth's hands swept wide and the clapping grew even more frantic and wild.

'Better?'

'Please, Gareth...'

But Gareth really wasn't listening.

'You know what, Nick? I don't have to take this! You've done enough to ruin me as it is, not that you'll ever see it, so struck are you by your own self-importance. So, I'm going to call the police now. I'm going to call them, tell them who you are, and have you arrested. And then I'm going to call the press. On you. Because this, they will love,

Nick. And trust me, it's a love you really, truly do not want! But by God, I'm going to enjoy watching them ruin you!'

When the punch struck, Gareth neither saw it coming nor really felt it. He saw a great splash of light, sparks lighting up the inside of his skull. He sensed that his head was moving in a way that he was pretty sure he hadn't decided that it should. And then the wall had crashed into him from behind and Nick's fingers were around his throat.

The sensation of his windpipe being crushed was both alien and terrifying and Gareth's first response was to do nothing at all except panic and struggle pathetically against his attacker. He roared, he screamed, except the roar and the scream were spluttering coughs as the hands tightened like a rope around his throat.

Then, in a moment of clarity, Nick came into focus in front of him, and Gareth saw the wild eyes of the man who had gone to great lengths to use him, his celebrity status, his wealth, to destroy his own wife in the courts. Before Gareth knew what he was doing, he had sent his left knee crashing into the man's bollocks with such force that Nick was lifted into the air. When he landed, his legs gave way and he collapsed on the floor of the hall, moaning and trying to desperately suck in oxygen.

'You ... you hit me,' Gareth choked, his voice a dried, broken thing of shattered glass scratched with wet sand. 'You hit me and then you tried to strangle me! You actually tried to strangle me!'

Nicholas wasn't listening. He was writhing on the floor, his hands between his legs, tucked up into a foetal position and crying.

Gareth rubbed his neck and coughed.

'What the hell were you thinking, Nick? What? Did you come out here to kill me, is that what this was about?'

Nicholas coughed, whispered, 'Bastard...'

'And why did you come to the concert? Are you spying on me now, is that it? What the hell is wrong with you? What?'

Another cough, a whimper, the sound of it something which belonged more to the deep, dark hidden shadows of a forest, than a house.

A thought broke its way through the surface of the pain in Gareth's mind.

'Were those two gatecrashers your idea?' he asked, thinking back to what had happened at the concert. 'Is that why you were there, Nick? To see my attempt to try and get my life back on track, after everything that you did to ruin it, fall apart? I bet it was, wasn't it? You were there to gloat! Unbelievable!'

Nicholas rolled over onto his knees, his forehead resting on the floor. Gareth pulled out his phone.

'You'll be hearing from my solicitor in the morning,' Gareth said, opening the camera on his phone. 'And the police, no doubt. Because right now I'm taking a lot of photos of the bruises on my neck to add to the one I'm taking of you right now to send to her.'

Nicholas moaned again, but Gareth wasn't listening.

'And my guess is that she will have a lot to say about it all, which will then be put in a letter and sent to you and your solicitor, after which, unless by some miracle we decide to forget everything that's happened—and I absolutely won't, you can bet your house on that, pal—I'll undoubtedly see you in court charged with something pretty horrific. And the end result of that will be you paying me a disgusting amount of money and maybe even some jail time. Who knows? But it's going to be exciting finding out, isn't it?'

Nicholas had managed to pull himself up onto his knees now, but only just. So, Gareth reached down and half dragged, half lifted him up and onto his feet and back over the threshold of his front door, where the man tripped and fell down hard onto the snow-covered path.

'You're a pathetic man, Nick,' Gareth said, grabbing the door as he stepped back into his house. 'Now, if you would be so kind as to just go ahead and fuck off, I've this port to finish.'

Gareth slammed the door.

For the next few minutes, he listened to the sound of Nicholas dragging himself down the path to his car. He heard a door open, slam shut, an engine start, then the vehicle driving away.

Draining his mug of the port, Gareth headed back through to the kitchen, left the mug in the sink, then headed upstairs. In the bathroom, he checked his neck, his face, and took photos of the welts already showing, not just around his throat, but across his right cheek and eye. Photos taken, he stumbled along to his bedroom and fell into bed, deciding against getting changed, because really, it was just too much effort by far and he needed to sleep.

Closing his eyes, Gareth thought back to what had just happened, wondered if he would actually get any sleep at all now that his face was so sore, then nothing. He was gone.

GARETH WOKE WITH A START, mouth dry, head thumping, face in so much pain he felt like he'd been beaten up. Then he remembered that was exactly what had happened as a wave of nausea swept through him with enough force to have him running and stumbling along to the bathroom to stuff his head down the toilet.

God, I feel rough, Gareth thought, as his stomach emptied, burning his throat and mouth with stomach acid and bile. And that was probably what had woken him, wasn't it, a mix of dehydration and pain? Then a crash raked its way through the house and Gareth, despite now feeling like he'd been trampled on by a horse, felt himself burn with anger.

That bastard ...

Gareth went to his bedroom and pulled back the curtains to stare down at the front of his house to see that there, in front of his door, was a shadow.

That complete and total bastard ...

Wiping his mouth on his sleeve, Gareth marched out of his room and back downstairs. Grabbing an umbrella, which had been leaning up against the wall, brandishing it like a sword, as he opened the front door.

'You asked for this!' Gareth said, moving to lift the umbrella above his head.

Only it didn't even get to his chin as a cloth bag was pulled over his head and his world went dark.

Disorientated and panicked, Gareth stumbled, tripped, and fell backwards into the wall. The sparks came again, then nothing, nothing at all.

CHAPTER TWELVE

When Gareth came to, it was a deeply horrible experience. Instead of waking up slowly in bed, blurry with sleep and with the distant echo of a future hangover charging towards him with relentless enthusiasm, he was dragged out of whatever darkness he had been swimming in by a shock of the coldest water he had ever felt dropped over his head. The sensation was one of being dunked in ice. Then came a slap to the face which stung like a thousand wasps, setting his face on fire with the brightest, sharpest pain.

'Can you stand up?'

'What?'

'Can you stand up?'

'Of course, I can stand up! What the hell is—?'

It was at this point that Gareth realised two things: one, that he couldn't see, courtesy of what felt like a hessian sack over his head. It smelled of grain or hay, and took him back to his childhood, making a den in a hay barn on Chris' parents' farm. And two, that he was pretty sure he recognised the voice he had just heard, but the ringing in his ears, from the booze and the bash to his head, plus the sack, was making it next to impossible to work out just who it was or what they wanted.

Gareth choked on his own fear, his brain so confused with what was now going on that it burst with an ache so full of barbs and spikes that he was sure his head would explode.

'Stand up.'

Gareth couldn't respond, couldn't breathe! What was going on? Where was he? What was happening? And why, if his eyes were open, couldn't he see?

'I said, stand up!'

Gareth was still choking, his voice trapped deep inside him. He was leaning against a wall. He tried to push against it, only to find that both of his hands were tied behind his back at the wrist.

'STAND UP!'

Gareth found strength in his legs, at last, forced them to work, to push and push and at last he could breathe, the fear and panic inside him loosening just enough now to allow him to suck in air.

'There, isn't that better?'

Gareth tried to focus on the voice as he continued to enjoy breathing again. He recognised it, was sure that he did, but there was something weird about it, muffled, and it was just off enough to ensure that his addled brain couldn't quite work out who it belonged to.

'Who are you?'

Nothing.

'Where am I? What's going on?'

Still nothing.

'What is this? What are you doing? Please, talk to me!'

No reply at all.

'I can smell paint,' he said. 'Why can I smell paint? Are we in my house? We are, aren't we?' Then another thought hit Gareth hard, winding him. 'Nick, is that you?'

Of course, it was, Gareth realised! Who else could it be? The mad bastard had come to his house, things hadn't gone according to plan, and he'd come back to have another go. Dear God, the man was completely insane!

'You've come back to have another go and you need to stop, Nick, do you hear?'

'WHATEVER THIS IS, whatever you're doing, Nick, stop. Right now, stop! Before you go too far.'

'Walk.'

Gareth walked and soon cold air and the crunch of snow swept at him and chilled him to his core. But was it Nick's voice? he thought. He just couldn't tell. It sounded like all the voices he'd ever heard in his whole life, all rolled into one. God, how much had he drunk to not even recognise a voice?

A hand was on Gareth's head, pushing him down into something, but he couldn't see it, and panic took hold again and he tried to resist but it was no good and then he was falling, falling, until something came up to meet him, something soft, and he felt his legs get shoved and a car door slam.

Gareth heard the sound of a car engine splutter into life, then he was moving.

'Where are we going? Where are you taking me?'

Silence. Just the journey. The car thrumming beneath him, the air warm from the heater. Gareth was terrified, confused, tired. His eyelids grew heavy. He wanted to stay awake, to understand what was going on, but the booze was still in control and the warmth of the car was so comforting, and perhaps this was all a dream? Yes, that was it, this was a dream! So, closing his eyes was fine because soon he would wake up with the mother of all hangovers and that would be that.

Gareth slept.

'Out.'

Gareth, even more groggy now, and queasy from the journey, felt himself guided from the car, and he moved without question, unsure of what was happening, why this dream was still insisting on continuing.

'Walk.'

Gareth walked, noticed the sound of snow crunching beneath his feet, felt a hand prod him and guide him onwards to whatever awaited. Probably some kind of mad joke, Gareth thought. It had to be. It was either Nick being a prick, and just really trying to put the wind up him, or it was all those old mates of his. But that didn't make sense, did it? None of it did.

The air changed, became still and calm and smelled of dust and stone and candles. It reminded Gareth of somewhere he recognised. But why the hell would they be here?

'Are we in a church?'

'Keep walking.'

'We are, aren't we? Is this Askrigg? Why've you brought me here? Who are you?'

Gareth heard a door open and a hand on his head made sure he lowered it as he was forced to step through.

Beyond the door, the air changed. This was a smaller room, Gareth thought. He could sense it, as though the place was closing in on him.

'Lift your left foot, please, and step forwards.'

'What?'

Pain and bright lights exploded in Gareth's head as something was brought down hard on his skull. He had no idea what he'd been hit with, but he could taste blood.

Gareth stepped forward to find his foot guided upwards onto a narrow step.

'We're going upstairs now, are we, Nick?' Gareth said, still convinced that was who was with him in the dark, even though he still wasn't sure about the voice. Because now, it was starting to sound clearer, as though its owner had been trying to disguise it. 'You're sick, you know that, don't you? Sick in the head! Just you wait till I get out of this!'

'Step up with your right foot now.'

Gareth thought about refusing but another flash of pain and light, this time to the other side of his face, had him moving.

'Continue to walk up the steps, please, until I tell you to stop.'

The voice was definitely changing, Gareth noticed. It was cracking and breaking and becoming something else, *someone* else. Or was it? The booze, the pain in his head, the queasiness, it was all too much.

Gareth hesitated then a new pain hit him, this time from his hands, and he screamed as he heard something go *snip* then a rush of warm fluid across his fingers and the sharp, metallic tang in the air of blood.

'Walk ...'

Gareth walked, the steps he was on wobbling. Hot tears flowed down his face, the pain from his hand cutting through him with the lightning heat of a welding torch.

'You cut off a finger! You cut off one of my bloody fingers!'

'Stop!'

Gareth stopped. The wobble now was quite pronounced. The pain in his hand was a deep, thick throb, which pulsed up his arm.

'Joke's over,' Gareth said, trying to gather some composure. 'I get the message, you're annoyed, you're angry, blah blah blah. So, stop now. Please?'

Something dropped over Gareth's head and cinched around his neck.

Gareth tried to speak but the thing around his neck was pulled in tight and his voice stalled.

Silence. The cold. His legs barely able to hold him as whatever he was standing on seemed to grow more and more unstable.

'Please, this has to stop!' Gareth begged, panic now taking over, because all sense, all reason, had abandoned him, washed away not only by his tears, but the blood still pouring from the raw stump on his hand where a finger had been.

Gareth went to beg again, except as he did so whatever it was he was standing on was kicked away. His body dropped and his feet tap-danced, searching for something to stand on, anything, it didn't matter what, just something to gain some purchase, to ease the pressure, to allow him to breathe.

But there was nothing but air and whatever it was that was tied around his neck only tightened and tightened and tightened, squeezing in as his weight dragged him down.

No breath was coming, Gareth knew that. He also knew that he was going to die. But the panic raking his skin, setting fire to his veins, was so violent, so all-consuming, that he couldn't stop trying to wriggle out of the bonds around his wrists, twisting and turning and whipping around his body to try and somehow snap whatever it was that was holding him up. Then he felt arms wrap around his legs and a jolt so violent that if he could have screamed then he was sure that the sound would've been loud enough to shatter glass.

The last thing Gareth saw was the sack over his head being ripped off, and below him, as his lungs finally gave up and his heart stopped, crying eyes staring up at him as, at last, the everlasting night welcomed him into its embrace.

CHAPTER THIRTEEN

Harry was nursing a large mug of strong coffee poured from the French press he had bought a couple of months ago. The flat may have been furnished when he'd moved in, but a couple of essentials had been missing. One was a simple way to make a decent coffee. The other was an egg poacher.

He had a feeling that this particular cooking utensil, and one which he was now standing over, was rather an old-fashioned thing to have at all, but it was how he remembered his own mum doing his and Ben's poached eggs at the weekend when they had been kids, and when his dad wasn't around—which was often, but never often enough—and it was still his preferred way of doing an egg or two on toast.

This one he'd picked up at random in a little antiques shop in Middleham one weekend. He'd been out for a drive to just have a look around the dales, explore little lanes and villages, get a feel for the land. It wasn't exactly the kind of recce he had been more used to back in his soldiering days, but it served the same purpose, allowing him the chance to understand the land more, the people.

The pan was a bit battered, and the four cups that held the eggs above the water were not exactly the more modern non-stick sort, so knobs of butter were dropped into each one to melt before Harry cracked in a couple of nice fresh eggs he'd picked up from a local farm, then ground on a bit of black pepper. Still, for four quid, it had struck him as quite the bargain. A few minutes later, when he slid the eggs out with a knife onto a slice of toast and sat down to enjoy them, bursting the deep gold of the yolks, it did the job more than adequately.

As he ate, the radio playing quietly in the background, he wasn't sure if Ben was home or not. His bedroom door was shut and he hadn't heard him come home that night, so it could have been a late one, or something else entirely. Whatever, it didn't matter, because what mattered the most to Harry was that Ben wasn't just there with him, but that he seemed to have so quickly become the brother, the man, that he was always meant to be.

Yes, it was early days yet, and Harry was still cautious, worried that at some point there would be a slipping back to his old ways, but so far so good, it seemed. Ben was enjoying life, meeting people, meeting girls. He had a job, seemed relaxed and happy in Yorkshire, and the worried, almost frightened look that he had worn for so long, like an animal constantly on guard against a predator, was gone. The dales, it appeared, were healing him, and that was all that Harry could have ever wanted.

Eggs finished, Harry topped up his mug of coffee, stood up, then went through to the lounge area, slumping down into an armchair. He had no plans for the day at all. It was to be a quiet one, made all the more so by the thick snow which lay beyond his front door, and which had folded itself, not just on Hawes, but on the hills and fields and lanes beyond. He would at some point take a walk into town to grab some supplies, perhaps enough to throw together a little roast dinner for him and Ben, a newspaper maybe, but that was about it.

Harry closed his eyes and almost as though it had heard his eyelids snap shut, his phone rang. And the damned thing was in his hand and up at his ear before he even had a chance to stop himself.

'Grimm,' Harry said.

'Harry, it's Jen. Sorry about calling you like this, but...'

Of course it was, Harry thought, rubbing his eyes, already weary, because he knew that any call from one of his team on a day off was never a good thing. Though, in those few words, Police Constable Jenny Blades had also shown just how different life was here in the dales, compared with down in Bristol. Back there, in his old stomping ground, everyone called everyone else by their surname or rank. Behind their backs or out of earshot, it was another matter entirely, and Harry had got wind of some of the nicknames he'd been blessed with. His favourite had been Balrog, on account of him apparently being a force of such grumpy darkness that no one ever wanted to go up against him if they had the chance to avoid it. Not even Gandalf.

Up here though, in a land of green fell and deep dale, where the weather changed on a pin from sunshine to storm, and where, if the rains really did come in, the water from the tap even turned brown, first names were fine. It had taken a bit of getting used to, but Harry had quickly realised that it was just the way things were. The people here were friendly, open, helpful. Well, not all of them, because he'd met some right awkward sods among the grey-slated villages and towns, but when it came to his team, they absolutely were. And, quite to Harry's surprise, they had somehow managed to bridge the gap between colleague and friend.

'You finished that with a *but*,' Harry said, 'and I'm assuming it's not because you've called to see if I want to go sledging,' Harry said. 'Which is a shame, because I'd probably be quite up for that in a few hours. Once I've woken up.'

'I wish,' Jen replied. 'Later in the week, maybe? I've a couple tractor inner-tubes which are a proper laugh. Go like the clappers and you're twisting round and round like you're on the Waltzers, though without the shady-looking fellas leering over you or the smell of candy floss and hotdogs.'

'Moving on,' Harry prompted, reaching for his coffee. He'd accepted that the only hot drink his team seemed to drink was tea, but he still needed a proper kick of the black stuff, particularly at the weekend.

'Yes, sorry, boss,' Jen said. 'Right, we've got an incident, over in Askrigg, at the church. Vicar's just called it in.'

'Called what in?'

'To be honest, I'm not exactly sure,' Jen said. 'All I've got is that there's a body in the tower. The vicar found it this morning while getting sorted for the morning communion service. That's all I know.'

Harry checked his watch. 'And what time was that, then?'

'Well, there's a communion service at eight-thirty,' Jen said. 'Then another service at ten-thirty, I think. The vicar was down there at seven to check that the heating was on. Apparently, it's been playing up a bit, what with this cold snap we're having, and the church is a bugger to get warmed up.'

'Cold snap? Is that what this is?' Harry asked. 'You call a foot or two of snow a cold snap?'

'This is nowt compared to what we used to get,' Jen said. 'You should see the photos my mum and dad have of their childhood in the 70s! Snow halfway up the house!'

'So, Askrigg then,' Harry said, tracing in his mind the road from Hawes that led to the village. 'And there's nothing else to tell? No other details of what it is the vicar found, just that it's a body in the tower?'

'That's all, yes,' Jen said. 'I'm on my way over in a couple of minutes. I'll give the others a call, then head off. Just thought it best to give you the nod first.'

'Who's off today?' Harry asked.

'Jadyn and Liz,' Jen replied. 'Liz was out last night and is off today with a couple of mates on their bikes, so she's about and can be called in I'm sure. Jadyn is away to a record fair or something.'

'A what?'

'That's exactly what I said!' Jen laughed. 'At least I think that's what he said. Not sure that can be a thing though, can it? I mean, a record fair? Don't people just stream music now?'

'Each to their own,' Harry said, not really listening to Jen's rambling. 'Best let them both know anyway and pre-warn them that we might need them.'

'No problem. See you there.'

And with that, the phone call was over.

Harry let his head slump back against the back of the armchair and closed his eyes. A body in the tower, he thought. Now there was a first. As a police officer, he'd attended crime scenes with bodies in all kinds of places. Usually back alleyways, cars, bedrooms. He'd been sent out to a particularly nasty one at a warehouse once, and he was never going to be able to forget it, of that he was quite sure. The victim's name was long ago lost to him, but the death wasn't and they had died badly. Not just over hours either, but days. But a body in a tower, and a church tower at that? It was a new one on him.

Five minutes later, Harry was dressed, wrapped up as warm as he could, and pushing his way through deep snow to his old Toyota Rav4. Knocking his boots free of snow and wondering why he still hadn't gotten around to buying some decent warm socks to wear with them, he climbed into the vehicle, started the engine, turned the heater up to full, then jumped out again to clear the windscreen. The air had a metallic tang to it, he noticed, the cold of it coming at him with a bite of the north. It was as invigorating as it was uncomfortable.

Back inside and behind the steering wheel, Harry stared over at the road leading through Hawes marketplace. Snow had fallen in the night, covering it in another thick layer that was all but untouched. Well, he thought, easing the gearstick into first and lifting the clutch to feel the tyres grip in the snow, time to try out that four-wheel-drive that Mike the mechanic had spoken so highly of...

CHAPTER FOURTEEN

As he drove through the snow, Harry was dealing with the usual grump that was always associated with having a day off snatched away by his job. It was all part and parcel of what he did as a career, and you either accepted it and got on with your life, or you moved on and did something else. Well, there was another option, but that usually involved finding solace at the bottom of a bottle, ruined relationships, and an early death. Dwelling on the negatives was a fast track to ruin because soon enough you'd become a bitter and twisted thing and no use to anyone. Not Harry's way at all, though he had been tempted now and again. He didn't know a police officer who hadn't.

On the one hand, the biggest crime that he'd never actually gotten around to investigating, was the number of weekends he'd had stolen from him over the years by his work, but the flip side of this was that no two days were ever the same. He enjoyed what he did, loved it actually and always had, and not only that, it was a job that he figured did some good, or at least tried to.

Harry was almost breathless with wonder at the land-scape he was now driving through, and he had a job keeping his eyes on the road ahead because they just kept wandering off to stare at the truly beautiful wonderland he was now driving through. Snow had been falling for a few days now, but today was the first time that Harry had not only ventured beyond Hawes itself, but actually driven on the roads in such conditions. The roads weren't impassable, but neither were they clear, demonstrated not only by the few inches covering them, but the drifts already growing across them, blown over walls and through gates by a north wind baring chilling teeth and an icy bite.

The old Rav4's four-wheel-drive seemed to Harry to be even more sure-footed on this terrain than it was on a normal road on a sunny day, but then he wasn't exactly gunning it, instead taking the journey good and steady.

Leaving Hawes, he followed the road out past Burtersett on his right and on towards Bainbridge and its stunning village green. On the way, Harry caught sight of a beck on his right, the snow having slumped into it to form a miniature crevasse. Along its edges, the snow had become ice, curtains of crystal hanging down, their edges lapped by the flowing water beneath.

Driving on, barns and walls poked out here and there in the snow, black eyes of stone dotting a landscape of white and Harry was reminded of the one book he remembered enjoying as a kid, and the land of perpetual winter it described: Narnia.

A couple of miles later, the road straightened out then swung up and right as it rose to wind its way into Bainbridge. Here, Harry could see the distant fells which had been hidden from him as he had driven along beneath lower slopes. They, too, were coated in white, and Harry was put in mind of being a kid and covering a great slab of Eve's Pudding—a cake his mum had made better than anyone on Earth—in fresh cream.

At the Rose and Crown Hotel, Harry took a left, and drove on past sleepy houses with fires lit, thin grey ribbons of smoke drifting out of chimneys to twist into knots as they rose skyward. He could smell it in the air, a comforting aroma of burning wood, pushing its way through the scent of more snow that the wind seemed to be intent on promising.

When Askrigg eventually welcomed him, Harry was almost sad to see his journey end, and promised himself that if the weather stayed calm, he would maybe venture off down some of the more lonely lanes later in the day. Though deep down he knew that this was all just wishful thinking, because experience told him that whatever today held, it most certainly wasn't an early afternoon and the chance to relax.

Crawling up the hill into Askrigg, Harry saw just ahead on his left two patrol cars already parked under large trees, beyond which he saw the church. He pulled in beside them, turned off the engine, then half jumped out of his skin at the sight of his driver's side window being filled with the presence of the largest and most orange jacket he had ever seen in his life. An arm raised to reveal a gloved hand, which waved at him, and from the deep darkness of the hood, Harry saw the smiling face of Detective Sergeant Matt Dinsdale.

Harry climbed out of the Rav4.

'Morning, boss,' Matt said. 'How was your drive over?'

'Rather enjoyable actually,' Harry said, clapping his hands together against the cold. 'How's Joan?'

Matt shrugged. 'Oh, she's fine,' he said. 'Comfortable, you know?'

Harry waited, expecting Matt to offer more, but he didn't. Well, he did, but that was just his usual cheery smile.

So, Harry thought, the detective sergeant wasn't going to say much. Fair enough. But that only made him more worried, not just as the man's boss, but his friend. Not only that, Matt wasn't exactly one for secrets, so whatever was going on, it was obviously serious enough to warrant him keeping quiet.

Matt spoke again: 'If you get a chance, you should head out up top,' he said, lifting an arm to point a finger up towards the hills behind the village. On the other side of them lay Swaledale, another place that had taken Harry's breath away. 'You'll need to be careful, like, but you've got four-wheel drive and decent tyres on that old thing of yours, so you should be fine.'

'Funnily enough, I was just thinking that on the way over actually,' Harry said.

'The old Roman road above Hawes is a bit of fun when it's like this,' Matt continued, a glimmer of excitement lighting up behind his eyes. 'But anywhere round here is worth a look. And take some cross-country skis with you, too. That way you can park up and go for a bit of an explore. I mean, you still can in boots and all, but skis are more fun, right?'

'I'm sure they are,' Harry said.

'And if you get stuck, you can just ski down through the fields to Hawes and get someone to come out and give you a tow!'

Harry couldn't help but smile at how happy Matt seemed to be with his suggestion.

'Except,' Harry said, 'there are two main problems with your idea.'

'Really?'

'Well, first of all, I don't have any cross-country skis,' Harry said. 'And secondly, I don't actually have any cross-country skis. I thought it was such a glaring problem that I'd mention it twice, just to make sure that was clear.'

'Oh, you don't need to worry about that,' Matt said. 'Soon as the weather hits, I throw mine in the back of any car I'm in, just in case!'

'Just in case of what?'

'Just in case of moments like this,' Matt said, 'or where I fancy nipping off for a quick explore myself. I can loan you a pair now if you want?'

'I should add a third thing to my list,' Harry said, 'that being that I've never actually used cross-country skis.'

'Seriously?'

Harry gave a nod. 'Snowshoes, yes. Setting up a tent in a blizzard and maintaining weapons in arctic conditions? Not a problem at all. Skiing? Never.'

'Well, that's something else I can sort out for you,' Matt said, 'because I'll teach you! It's dead easy, I promise you. I mean, if I can do it, anyone can, right?'

If there was one thing Matt Dinsdale wasn't lacking in, it was enthusiasm, Harry thought. And it never really seemed to matter about what. He was just the kind of person who approached life with open arms, someone who could find a spark of adventure in everything from a hole in the ground to trying a new cake or pie. In many ways, he was the human equivalent of a Labrador puppy.

Jen came over to join them.

'Jim's on his way,' she said. 'Gordy's on with something

else, but I've said I'll keep her posted on what's happening and she's going to head over when she can. Vicar's waiting for us in the church.'

A shiver snicked its way down Harry's spine and he shuddered.

'It's nippy, right enough,' Matt said.

Harry was again taken in by the detective sergeant's massive and eye-bleedingly bright coat.

'And you're feeling the cold are you,' Harry asked, 'in that massive satsuma you seem to be wearing?'

'What, this?' Matt said. 'I'm sweating like a glassblower's arse, if I'm honest! Russian arctic expedition jacket. It's good down to around minus seventy I reckon. Picked it up at a clearance sale. Proper bargain it was.'

Harry's own barrier against the cold was very dependent on layers and the hope that the weather didn't turn any nastier than it already had. Perhaps Gordy had a point about my jacket, he thought, as another shiver cut him in two.

'Should take the pathologist and her team a good while to get out here,' Matt said, as they left their vehicles to head to the church. 'Assuming of course that we're going to need to give them a call.'

'What about the divisional surgeon?' Harry asked.

'Oh, she won't be long,' Jenny said. 'She sings in the choir here and only lives a few miles away in Woodhall, just down the road.'

Harry remembered the first time he had met the force of nature that was Margaret Shaw, when, enrobed in her choral gown, which billowed in the wind with theatrical flair, she had marched over to him across a field down past Hawes to check on a victim of a supposed farm accident. She wasn't just the divisional surgeon either, but also the mother of his and everyone else's favourite pathologist, Rebecca Sowerby. Though Harry's relationship with Rebecca had thawed a little, which was good, it still wasn't exactly on the right side of chilly. Not yet, anyway.

'Right then,' Harry said, clapping his hands together, 'shall we get on, then, and see what's what, before we all freeze on the spot? Well, everyone except for Matt here, obviously.'

'Don't knock it till you've tried it.' Matt winked.

'It's that kind of attitude that could land you in serious trouble,' Harry said.

Walking along the path to the church, Harry breathed in the crisp morning air, again noticing just at the back of it the smell of home fires lit to ward off the chill of the day. Gravestones poked up through the snow like enormous mushrooms adorned with thick pats of snow, which sat precariously on top of them like huge hats.

At the church, he took point and went to lead Jen and Matt inside, through the large main door. It looked as old as the church itself, Harry noticed, made of thick, dark wood studded with ancient metal nails. The newer inner door, which led from the porch and into the church beyond, was still sturdy, but didn't have that same aura to it, of something that had silently observed the births, marriages, and deaths of generations. Then he noticed the lock.

'Someone's had a fair go at that,' Harry said, crouching down to get a closer look. Whereas the outer door was untouched, its own lock a huge cast-iron latch, this one had been got at with what Harry assumed, by the damage, to be a crowbar of some kind. Wood was splintered, the lock itself a twisted, ruined mess.

'The main door is always unlocked,' came a voice new to

Harry from inside the church, 'but this one is locked every evening without fail. Not that it did much good.'

Harry rose to his feet again to find himself staring at the owner of the voice, who was wearing, under a brace of fleece jackets, a black jacket and shirt, a square of white showing at the collar. On her head sat a bright yellow-and-white striped bobble hat so large that it was close to dwarfing her actual head.

'Detective Chief Inspector Grimm,' Harry said, introducing himself, and holding out his hand.

'Anna Fenwick,' the woman said, shaking Harry's hand firmly enough to have him take notice, and stifling a yawn. 'I'm the vicar.'

CHAPTER FIFTEEN

'So,' HARRY SAID, STEPPING FURTHER INTO THE CHURCH and out of the cold breeze thrusting its way into the old building from the open front door, 'how's about you run us through what actually happened and what you found, then?'

As he asked the question, Harry quickly took in what he could, not just about the church, but the woman who had welcomed them inside. She was, he guessed, mid-forties, five-six in height maybe. Her hair was a deep auburn, curly, and held back in a loose ponytail, which seemed utterly intent on breaking free. She wore an expression of open thoughtfulness, a face which said to Harry that she was the kind of person you could talk to in confidence for hours and probably lose track of the time. A good skill for a vicar to have.

'Of course,' Anna said, 'but I was just about to go and grab myself a coffee to wake myself up a bit. Didn't get much sleep last night. Don't suppose you'd like one yourselves?'

'Not tea?' Harry asked. 'It's just that usually everyone around here seems to only ever offer tea.'

Anna shook her head. 'Don't tell anyone, but I've never

really been a massive fan of tea. Tastes a bit like leafy drains if you ask me. Awful stuff. Not that I'm in the habit of drinking out of drains, but tea is just leaves in water, isn't it? I'm rambling. Sorry.'

Harry noticed that Anna's accent wasn't exactly local, ringing as it was with the musical notes of a born and bred Geordie. Last time he'd heard that accent was back in the Paras, courtesy of a soldier small of size and big in personality. He'd been born with the name Jason Dodd, but everyone called him Jack, on account of him going at life like a Jack Russell Terrier chasing a rabbit down a hole. The memory made Harry smile, but then other memories crowded in, reaching up from inside him to twist that smile into something else entirely, and he quickly hooked himself back into the now.

'We don't want to put you out,' he said.

'Oh, it's no bother at all,' Anna said. 'I always bring a huge flask of the stuff with me. Look!'

Anna then ducked behind one of the wooden pews to reveal a huge metal cylinder. To Harry, it looked like the kind of container more usually used to transport something slightly more volatile than coffee, such as radioactive waste or a tank shell.

'It's pretty strong and has quite a lot of sugar in it,' Anna said. 'And milk. And by milk, I mean cream. I'll just go and grab some mugs from the vestry!'

Harry made to stop her, but Anna had already headed off down the church at a brisk pace.

'A female vicar then,' he said. 'Bit unusual, isn't it?'

'Not really,' Matt said. 'I mean, it would've been a few years back, I suppose, but not anymore. Anna's been here for a few years now. Properly involved with the local community, too. Puts on a good quiz, does Anna!'

As Harry watched Anna make her way back towards them he noticed down at the front of the church that a small stage had been built. Microphone stands stood on top of it like thin saplings and he saw various leads trailing here and there as well as large, heavy-looking flight cases.

'Here we are!' Anna said with a disarmingly cheery smile and handing out mugs to Harry, Matt, and Jen. She then poured them a coffee each. The smell of it was rich and sweet and Harry took a sip immediately.

'Now that's good coffee.' Matt nodded.

'I'm a bit of a coffee snob if I'm honest,' Anna said, leaning in conspiratorially. 'I think it's because I like the ritual of it, you know? Measuring out the beans, grinding them, letting them brew. My dad was the same. Smoked a pipe. Said he spent more time messing around with the thing than actually smoking it! But then, last time I looked I was still a vicar, so I suppose ritual is probably a bit more of a thing to me than most people, isn't it?'

Considering what she had found earlier that morning, Harry didn't know if he was impressed by how calm she was, or worried. Usually, the shock of finding a body hit people hard, but Anna, so far, seemed okay. He had dealt with a good many people who were calm at a crime scene then crashed a good while afterwards when what had happened, or what they'd found, really hit home. But then Harry guessed that death came with the job.

'Is there an event on here, then?' Harry said, nodding towards the stage.

'There was last night, yes,' Anna said, and for the first time since they had met her, he saw a flicker of worry in the thin lines on her face. 'We had a concert. An album launch, actually. One of the church's homegrown stars, you might say. It was a wonderful event. The church was packed. Even had to bring in extra seating from the hall down the road.'

'Sounds exciting,' Jen said, but Harry noticed then that Anna wasn't smiling, as though the words she'd just said had brought with them a weight only she could feel.

'You mean Gareth Jones, right?' Matt said. 'Askrigg's other export.'

'You've heard of him, then?' Harry said. 'And what do you mean by other export?'

'Most folk round here who are my age and older have, yes,' Matt said. 'First, there was All Creatures Great and Small, which was filmed round here. The vets was set in the house just over the road from here.'

Harry remembered watching episodes of the series before he had driven up the motorway to Hawes from Bristol. He hadn't exactly taken to it and it certainly hadn't helped with how he'd felt about heading north.

'Then Gareth came along,' Matt said. 'He was a few years younger than me, but we all knew him. Everyone ribbed him a fair bit for it all. Then he wasn't around much. I think his parents had to get private tutoring for him, seeing as he was so busy with his music. He sung that song, remember? That Christmas one! You know which one I mean, don't you? That Christmas song! You must know!'

Harry didn't know. And he didn't want to know, either. He hadn't the faintest idea what the detective sergeant was getting at. Not that Matt was in anyway deterred.

'You must know it!' Matt said, humming what Harry assumed were notes, but which sounded more like angry wasps drowning in beer. 'Everyone does. It's everywhere at Christmas. It's that one that goes—'

'Please, don't sing it!' Anna said, holding up a hand to stop Matt before he went any further. Harry was thankful for her interruption, not exactly sure anyone should be party to Matt trying to sing. 'Or it'll be in our heads all day! Nope, too late, there it is!'

Again, Harry noticed that Anna was serious, despite the words she was saying being anything but.

'I get the impression you're not telling us everything,' Harry said.

Anna took a deep breath, sipped her coffee, then looked up to stare at Harry with the darkest of eyes.

'Gareth Jones grew up here,' she said. 'He was in the choir as a young boy. Then he won this choirboy competition back in the 80s, and the rest, as they say, is history. Singing all over the world, for the royal family, platinum albums, celebrity lifestyle, interviews in Hello magazine.'

'And he sung here last night?' Harry asked. 'Why would he do that? I mean, it's not exactly the Albert Hall, is it?'

Anna went to answer but her voice caught in her throat.

'I think you need to follow me,' she said, turning towards the end of the church where Harry saw a small door leading into the base of the tower.

'PPE, everyone,' he said, handing some to Anna as well, then pulled out a jar of vapour rub to hand around. 'And I think we're all going to need this.'

Together, they followed the vicar.

AS HARRY STEPPED through the small door and into the small room at the bottom of the tower, the vision of almost theatrical violence which greeted him and the others stopped him dead. As did the smell. He was thankful for the vapour rub, but the stink was still getting through. They'd all be needing to wash their clothes after this, that was for sure. A dead body in a warm room could start to stink in just a few hours. The ones found after a few days were the worst, though, Harry thought, as he tried to take it all in. The flies, the bloated stomach, skin stretched to the point of splitting.

This time, though, the reek wasn't so much one of decay, as the cold of the tower had perhaps in some small way worked a little like a fridge, slowing down decomposition. So that was something. But there were other smells, apart from decay, which could arrest the senses of anyone who was working something like this. And judging by the stained trousers and the puddle on the floor, whoever the corpse was, well, they were a few pounds lighter, that was for sure.

'Probably best you stay out there,' Harry called back to Anna, holding out a hand to emphasise the point and prevent her from coming in after them. 'Matt? Best you give Rebecca a call if you could.'

'Will do, boss,' Matt said, and popped back out of the tower.

'You're sure I'm not needed?' Anna asked, and Harry heard the relief in her voice.

'I'll ask you a few questions once we're done,' Harry said. 'If you could just let us know if and when anyone else arrives, that would be great.'

Harry turned back to what was in front of them, then a thought struck him, and he looked back at the vicar.

'You were down here to get ready for communion, am I right?'

'Yes,' Anna said, 'but don't worry as I've cancelled that

already. We have this sort of communication tree, you see, so you phone a couple of people who phone another couple of people and before you know it everyone has got the message.'

'That's good,' Harry said, 'but you didn't tell them—'

'Goodness, no!' Anna said, shaking her head. 'All anyone knows right now is that the heating is frozen. It isn't, but it may as well be for all the good it'll do when the weather's like this. Though with those police cars outside, I can't see that explanation lasting very long.'

Harry turned back into the tower, away from Anna.

For a few moments, no one said a word. And for that Harry was thankful. He was having enough trouble dealing with it himself and needed a bit of time to gather his thoughts and ensure that he kept his head. He had no doubt at all that Matt and Jen were doing the same.

Hanging from a bell-rope in front of them, and just a few feet off the floor, was the body of a man, smartly dressed, probably in the region of Harry's height. The rope was tied around his neck, not in a hangman's noose, but a decent slip knot by the look of it, and his face was not something to look at for very long if it could be helped, the eyes bulging and the tongue sticking out and horribly swollen. The walls of the tower had been painted in numerous signs and symbols, most of which were upside-down crosses, though scattered here and there was the odd pentagram or two. The roof of the room was in the process of being renovated, Harry assumed, which would explain the scaffolding, the huge pieces of wood stacked against the wall, and the various tools.

'You seen anything like this before, boss?' Matt asked.

'I'm not sure anyone's ever seen anything like this before,' Harry replied. 'I mean, you go anywhere in this world, you'll stumble on a few nutjobs running their own little Satan-worshipping cult, but this is, well, it's—'

'Properly messed up,' Jenny said.

Harry said, 'Am I right in thinking that this here is the late Gareth Jones?'

'It is,' said Matt. 'Joan and me, we actually had tickets for the show last night. Couldn't make it, obviously, so gave them to a mate and his wife.'

'Can't say I ever clocked you as a fan of choral music,' Harry said, wondering again about what exactly was up with Joan and why Matt was being so tight-lipped about it.

'I'm not,' said Matt. 'Just thought it would be something a bit different, like. Joan's a bit of a fan of old Gareth. He's on the radio a bit you see, well he was, and she likes listening to him. Anyway, it's not choral music. Well, some of it is, or was, or whatever. He sang other stuff, too.'

Harry tried his best to imagine Matt sitting through a concert of choral music. He wasn't really sure what choral music was exactly, but whatever it was, he was pretty sure that Matt wouldn't last very long if he was exposed to it.

'Doesn't make sense, does it?' Jen said, her voice quiet, solemn. 'I mean, Gareth here, he comes home to launch a new album, and then this?'

'He's had a bad time of it for sure,' Matt said. 'So Joan has told me anyway. But no, it doesn't.'

'Bad time of it?' Harry said. 'How do you mean?'

'Do you not read the papers?' Jen asked.

'Not if I can help it,' Harry said. 'All that bad news, politicians talking bollocks, celebrities, football. Not for me really.'

'He went through a pretty rough time of it,' Matt said. 'After an affair I think, wasn't it, Jen?'

'That was years ago,' Jen said, 'but it all came out in the press recently. Worst of it was that it wasn't that long after he'd lost his wife. I think this was supposed to be his way to have a fresh start.'

'Can't say he ever struck me as someone who'd be into all this kind of stuff though,' Matt said.

'What kind of stuff?' Harry asked.

'All those upside-down crosses,' Matt said. 'Satanism or whatever it is. And what's that snake about when it's at home? I'm assuming it's a snake. It's a snake, isn't it? It must be, surely. Though even if it is, why's it actually there at all?'

Harry looked at the snake when a voice called out from behind and he turned to see a stern face staring back.

'Good morning, Detective,' said the divisional surgeon, Margaret Shaw. 'Never clocked you as a churchgoer, though the good Lord welcomes all to his table, even surly old buggers like you. So, what have we got?'

CHAPTER SIXTEEN

'Wasn't really needed for this one, was I?' Margaret said, standing now with Harry in the main area of the church.

Jim had arrived while she examined the body as best she could—not easy with it dangling in the air like the world's most horrifying piñata—and had joined Matt and Jen outside with the thick rolls of cordon tape, to seal off the area. Jim had also popped into the office on the way over to pick up a decent-sized notepad and had already set himself up as scene guard. He'd left Fly at home, still spooked by what had happened a couple of days ago.

'Not really, no,' Harry agreed. 'But always best to be on the safe side, just in case.'

'Just in case of what, exactly, Detective?' Margaret asked. 'That's what I want to know.'

'To be honest, I haven't the faintest idea,' Harry said. 'The smell was enough without even seeing the poor bastard.'

'Any thoughts on what actually happened here?'

Margaret asked. 'This is going to hit the community hard, you know. He was a popular boy when he was in the choir. That was a long time ago, I know, but everyone was so proud of him when he went off and did so well.'

'I can well imagine,' Harry said.

'It was like his fame was theirs as well I think,' Margaret said. 'It's that kind of community up here, in the dales. Someone does well and everyone feels it.'

'No doubt,' Harry nodded. 'I tell you though, I've seen some sights in my time, but that in there? It's like I've nowhere in my head that I can store it. It just doesn't make any sense, does it, any of it, I mean?'

'I can't say that it does, no.' Margaret sighed, shaking her head.

'Any idea of time of death?'

Margaret rolled her eyes at Harry.

'Look, I have to ask,' Harry said. 'It comes on a list of questions you're given when you pass your detective exams.'

'Would that list be titled, *Annoying Questions To Ask At A Crime Scene?*'

Harry smiled. He had liked Margaret from the moment he'd met her. She had a warm abruptness that he appreciated.

'Indeed it is,' Harry said. 'Other questions include—'

'I'm stopping you right there!' Margaret said, holding up a hand, and Harry smiled. 'Anyway, in answer to your question, and bearing in mind that I couldn't actually examine the body properly seeing as it was dangling a few feet up in the air, I'd say between now and when the concert finished last night.'

'Helpful,' said Harry.

'Very,' Margaret replied. 'Rebecca will give you a better idea I'm sure, once she's had a good poke around inside.'

'So, did you know him, then?' Harry asked, if only to avoid thinking about what it was, exactly, that made anyone want to become a pathologist in the first place. Because giving a corpse *a good poke around inside* was surely one of the oddest things on Earth to actually enjoy, or at the very least gain some sense of fulfilment from.

'No,' Margaret said, 'I didn't. We moved here after he'd grown up and gone to the big city and made a name for himself. But folk certainly talked about him a lot. Not so much now, but in his early days, he was big news.'

'And this is how it's ended for him,' Harry said, rubbing his eyes in the hope that he might poke hard enough to jog some kind of thought as to what exactly had gone on. 'Did you know if he was involved in anything, you know, a bit, er ...'

'Weird?' Margaret said. 'Because that in there is very weird indeed, if you ask me. And my answer is no, I didn't or don't or whatever tense it is we're supposed to use in this situation. He was a clean-cut man, nice image. That was his whole thing, really, the boy next door, the lad from a small village in the dales who'd struck it big.'

'Jen mentioned that he'd lost his wife,' Harry said.

'There's losing your wife in a tragic accident, or perhaps to illness, that kind of thing, and then there's hanging from a bell-rope, surrounded by occultic symbols, your pants reeking of urine and excrement,' Margaret said. 'Can't say I'm seeing that the two are in any way connected, but that's for you to establish and me to go home and to try and forget about what I've seen here.'

'Yeah, that's what I thought,' said Harry. 'It's hard to see why he'd come all this way to launch an album then hang himself.'

'You think he did this to himself, then?'

'Has to be a consideration,' Harry said. 'Doesn't explain the symbols on the wall, but he could've easily climbed up that scaffolding, tied the rope around his neck, then go for one last swing.'

The conversation died and Harry found his eyes wandering around the church. It was a beautiful building and one that, were he so inclined, he was fairly sure he would enjoy attending, if only to sit in the peace and quiet for a moment and to just soak in the history. The stained-glass windows seemed to glow, casting the interior in the remnants of a shattered rainbow, which moved and swam across the floor. On the wall just a few steps away, he spotted a display of photos on the wall, which seemed a little out of place with everything else in the church.

'That's him, actually,' Margaret said, noticing what Harry was looking at. 'When he was just a boy, back in the choir.'

Harry followed the district surgeon over to have a closer look.

'He looks happy,' Harry said, leaning in to get a closer look. Gareth was easy to spot, a bright smile gleaming out of the past into a future Harry was glad that the boy hadn't ever been able to see. There were six children in the photographs, the youngest, a girl, a few years younger than the others, two other girls, and three boys, one of whom was clearly Gareth, looking maybe eleven or twelve, Harry guessed.

'How could you not be, growing up around here?' Margaret replied.

Harry had to agree. Though he was sure that being a kid

in such a place presented plenty of reasons to complain and grumble, the ups surely outweighed the downs.

'Right, I'd best be off,' Margaret said. 'Rebecca is on her way, I'm sure.'

'That she is,' Harry said.

'No, I mean I know she is,' Margaret said, and held up her phone. 'Just sent me a text. She's really looking forward to seeing you apparently.'

'You're a terrible liar, Margaret.'

'Yes, yes I am,' Margaret replied.

'This one should certainly keep her busy,' Harry said.

'And if there's one thing that my daughter the pathologist loves,' Margaret said, 'it's being kept busy. Means she doesn't have to think about other things. You know, like having a life outside of work, for example. But then, I wasn't exactly the best role model, you know. And neither was her father, God rest his soul.'

The district surgeon had never before mentioned her husband and neither, for that matter, had Rebecca. Harry wondered why but decided now probably wasn't the best time to enquire.

Margaret made to leave but stopped and turned back to Harry, reaching out to rest a gentle hand on his arm. Harry flinched at the touch, but then her fingers gripped and held him fast, her strength taking him by surprise.

'Whatever happened to Gareth, whether he did to himself or someone did this to him, it was no way for him to end up. No way for anyone. So, be careful, okay, Detective? Because this, well, it just seems a little more off than the usual, doesn't it, if you know what I mean?'

'It does that, and I do,' Harry said and watched as

Margaret Shaw gave a nod, let go of his arm, then swept off and into the day waiting quietly for her outside the church.

Inside, Harry took a stroll down the aisle towards the stage. He stepped up onto it and turned to face back down towards the tower. This was what Gareth would have seen, he thought, the pews filled with faces, fans, people who had come to hear him sing. And all the time, staring at him from the other end of the church, was the place that would see his end only a few hours later.

'So, what happens now, then?'

Harry turned around towards the altar-end of the church to see Anna the vicar looking up at him.

'We're waiting on the crime scene photographer and the pathologist and her team,' Harry explained. 'So, unless you've got anything to be getting on with, do you think you're up for talking it through and answering a few questions?'

'Of course,' Anna answered. 'Here or in the vestry? I say vestry, but it's more like a little cave where time has stood still for the last few hundred years.'

'Where's warmer?' Harry asked.

'Depends on what you mean by that,' Anna said. 'I've learned over my years in this job that it's not so much about degrees of warmth, as it is how much cold you can actually bear before your teeth start to chatter in the middle of the Lord's Prayer.'

Harry didn't quite know how to reply.

'The vestry it is!' Anna said, clapping her hands together and giving them a rub. 'Which is just through that tiny door over there at the side of the organ.'

Harry followed Anna through the door, which was set in stone like a passageway in a castle. Beyond it, and down a couple of steps, he found himself to be in a small room bereft of any real sense of what it really was. There was a filing cabinet against the far wall and on top of it sat some kind of machine with a roller and a handle. He saw an oak chest, which was clearly ancient. In the centre of the room was a table and around it a scattering of metal chairs. The white walls were decorated with a couple of fading cross-stitch Bible quotes, a number of black and white photographs of male vicars looking serious, and a schematic of the church itself. There was also a portable gas heater which Anna headed over to immediately, flipped open the top to turn on the gas, then pressed the ignition buttons in a small recess in the side.

'It's a bugger to light,' she said, pressing the buttons repeatedly, 'but when it gets going it's like a furnace in here.'

Harry was about to say that he could smell gas when the heater burst into life with a rather frightening explosion of orange flame, which lit up the small room.

'There!' Anna said. 'I'm afraid the only drink I have down here is water, though I can nip back and fetch the coffee if you prefer?'

'No, water's fine, I'm sure,' Harry said.

'I've got a couple of cases of communion wine as well, actually,' Anna said. 'But I wouldn't advise drinking it for the taste.'

The face Anna then pulled was enough to ensure Harry believed her.

Anna fetched a jug of water and a couple of chipped, blue cups, the handles of which were so small that Harry would've had trouble getting even his little finger through.

'No glasses,' Anna said. 'Sorry.'

Harry reached for the cup and took a sip. The water was so cold it was almost painful to swallow.

Placing the cup back down, Harry turned to face Anna.

'Firstly, I have to ask, can you account for your where-abouts last night? Obviously, we don't have a time of death as yet, but if you were able to give us some indication of where you were yourself, that would be useful.'

'I'm a suspect, then?'

'We just need to ask the question,' Harry said, somewhat noncommittally.

'Well, after locking up,' Anna said, looking up and into the corner of the room as though it was from there that she was collecting her thoughts, 'I just went home and straight to bed.'

'You live close by, then?'

Anna gave a nod.

'I only live a short walk away, along a path out the back of the churchyard,' she said, 'I look after the church here, as well as the ones over in Hawes, Hadraw, and Stalling Busk. I'm kept pretty busy, though rather too much of my time is spent trying to either work out how to stop the congregations dying off completely, or the buildings crumbling into the ground. I mean, where's all the sexy vicar stuff, that's what I want to know!'

'Sexy vicar stuff?' Harry asked, somewhat baffled. 'And what's that, then, when it's at home?'

'I mean, I do get to eat a tremendous amount of cake,' Anna said, 'which isn't a good thing, true, and then there's all the tea.'

'Can anyone confirm that you were at home?' Harry asked.

Anna shrugged. 'Sadly no,' she said. 'It's just me on my tod in that massive old vicarage. Does get lonely though, I must say.'

And you were at home the whole time until you came back this morning?'

'I was.'

Harry sat back in his chair. Was the vicar a suspect? Well, yes, but then the idea of it just seemed patently ridiculous. Yes, it was early to be coming to any conclusions about what had gone on and why, but the local vicar? Really? No, he wasn't buying that. Best just to get on with the interview.

'Right then,' Harry said, pulling out his notebook, his teeth still hurting from the icy water. 'Why don't you just take it from the moment you arrived at church.'

CHAPTER SEVENTEEN

'I USUALLY LEAVE AT AROUND SEVEN,' ANNA SAID, 'so that I've time to get the church sorted, check things over, make sure the heating has come on, get myself into vicar-mode as it were. The heating is supposed to be automatic, but it kind of has a life of its own. But with the weather like it is, I was here earlier, around six.'

'That is early,' Harry said.

'Well, the heating has been playing up, you see, so I needed to give myself enough time to have a decent breakfast —you can't do this job on a bowl of cereal and a glass of orange juice, that's for sure!—before I came over to check everything was okay and give it a quick dose of the old prayer stuff to help it on the way, just in case.'

'And that works?' Harry asked. 'Praying about the heating?'

'Always!' Anna grinned, the wink she sent on behind it fuelled by a mischief Harry hadn't really expected.

'Did you notice anything strange when you arrived this morning?' Harry asked.

'What do you mean by strange? I'm a vicar, remember, so I'm pretty used to strange.'

'The way I always think about it,' Harry explained, 'is to look for two things: either things that shouldn't be there, but are, or things that should be, but aren't. If that makes sense.'

'Ooh, I like that!' said Anna. 'Does that mean I can be a detective now, seeing as you've given me your trade secret?'

'You mean be a vicar detective?'

'Why not?' Anna asked. 'There's a television show in the idea, isn't there? Actually, I'm sure one already exists. Shame.'

Harry couldn't help but warm to Anna. She seemed to be not only very down to earth but also lit with a flame of humour that burned openly and warmly, an open fire in a comfy lounge. She was a person without malice, he thought, someone who really did genuinely care for the community in which she worked. His police brain told him to maintain an open mind, that this person in front of him wasn't just a witness, someone who found a body, but also a potential suspect. And such a ruse had been done more than a few times, Harry knew that for a fact.

'So, did you notice anything?' Harry asked.

Anna shook her head.

'Just a lot of snow,' she said. 'It's not been this bad in the dales for a long time, certainly not in all the time that I've been here, that's for sure. We still get it, yes, but not like this.'

'So, you walked up to the church and then what?'

'I opened up as usual,' Anna said. 'Except, I found that someone had already been in, hadn't they? The lock was all smashed up. And then when I came inside, I saw the marks on the wall. I was shocked.'

'I'm sure you were,' Harry said. 'Did you notice anything else?'

'The smell,' Anna said. 'But only when I walked over for a closer look. I saw those symbols, and after what happened last night, I figured they'd come back, you see? But the smell, well, that didn't make sense at all. So I had to find out what it was, didn't I? I had no idea what they had done!'

'What do you mean, *after what happened last night?*' Harry asked. 'Who did you think had come back? Did something happen during the concert, then?'

Harry wasn't one for getting his hopes up this early in a case. But if there was a link between something that had happened at Gareth's concert the night before, and what they were looking at now, namely the performer everyone had come to see swinging from his neck like a pendulum, then it was hard to not think that this could be an early break.

'Oh, these two idiots turned up,' explained Anna, rolling her eyes. 'No idea who they were or why they were here. They were clearly very drunk. And very stupid.'

Harry leaned back in his chair and it creaked just a little disconcertingly, so he leaned forward again, just in case, and leant his elbows on his knees, hands clasped.

'What happened, exactly?' he asked.

'They just barged in, that's what happened!' Anna said, and Harry heard anger in her voice. 'Right in the middle of the concert, interrupting Gareth during a song! Unbelievable! Never seen anything like it in my life! I've had all sorts turn up during services for sure, everything from homeless ex-soldiers to teenage mothers, but this? I didn't know what to think.'

'And then what?'

'They started saying some rubbish about claiming the

place in the name of Satan! Waving their arms around, being all weird and creepy. It was like they'd planned it. At least, that's what I thought, because no one just turns up and does that, do they? Why would you?'

'You'd be surprised at what people do on the spur of the moment,' Harry said. 'Did they leave?'

Anna nodded firmly.

'Yes, they absolutely did,' she said. 'Though only with a little persuasion.'

'How do you mean?'

'Thankfully some of the audience stepped in and removed them from the premises, shall we say?'

'Did it get violent?'

Anna shook her head. 'No, well, not really. There was no fisticuffs if that's what you mean.'

Harry thought for a moment. It sounded too good to be true, didn't it, these two from the night before, the Satanic link? And too good to be true generally was. Just a fact of life.

'Do you think you would be able to describe them?' he asked. 'And I would like to speak to those who helped remove them from the church, if that's possible?'

'Oh, I don't think I'll forget what they looked like for a long time,' Anna said. 'And neither will anyone else who was there, that's for sure! All dressed in black, lots of rips, chains, and tattoos. One had no hair at all, the other had long black hair stretching down his back.' She paused, then said, 'You know what they reminded me of? Heavy metal musicians! Yes, that's what they looked like.'

Harry jotted a few things down in his notebook.

'Do you think they did it, then?' Anna asked.

Harry said, 'It's too early to know anything, to be honest, but it does seem strange that we have two people turning up last night at Gareth's concert talking about Satan, and then we find lots of occult symbols on the wall at the crime scene the next day. That can't be ignored.'

'No, it can't,' Anna said.

'So, back to this morning,' Harry said. 'Anything else?'

Anna sat thoughtfully for a moment.

'Just the smashed lock, the symbols, the smell,' she said. 'I looked into the tower, but as soon as I saw what, I mean who, was in there, I stopped dead. I didn't go any further.'

'And you called us.'

'I did,' Anna confirmed.

Harry looked over his notes.

'The lock,' he said. 'Seeing that, well, I can't help but wonder why the alarm didn't go off. You must have one, right, for a place like this?'

At this, Anna laughed, but it wasn't a happy sound by any means.

'Security isn't something to laugh about,' Harry said. 'It's very serious, and I wish more people took it seriously.'

Anna shook her head.

'Detective, we currently need tens of thousands to carry out the repairs in the tower. The roof leaks. The heating is on its last legs. Our hearing-loop system is barely holding it together. The organ breaks down so often that we've taken to using backing tracks on CDs, though I think our organist, Mrs Howgill, is somewhat relieved, seeing as she's pushing eighty-five now. Our hymn books need replacing, the resources we have for any children who come along comprise a few Fisher-Price toys from the 70s, a number of illustrated Bible stories, and for some reason, a lot of Plasticene. Putting money towards a security system is impossible. For some things, I've no choice but to trust in God. And believe you me, it's not always easy.'

'No, I'm sure it isn't,' Harry said.

With little else Harry could think to go over, he thanked Anna for her time and left the vestry, the vicar coming up alongside as they walked down the aisle.

'This is really going to hit the community,' Anna said. 'It's awful.'

'It is that,' Harry agreed. 'But the team and I, we'll be doing everything we can to not only find out what happened, but to help as well.'

'That's very much appreciated,' Anna said.

Back at the front of the church, Harry was met by Matt.

'Everything's cordoned off,' Matt stated. 'Scene of Crime team are about an hour away. I reckon the roads are causing them a bit of bother.'

'You spoke with the pathologist?'

'Jen did,' Matt said. 'Apparently, she was even more abrupt than usual, which is saying something. Like I said, it'll be the weather. She won't be happy having to come out here in all that snow.'

'Do you have contact details of everyone who was at the concert?' Harry asked, turning back to Anna.

'Of course,' Anna replied. 'We have to be pretty hot on health and safety and safeguarding and all the rest of it. It's not like the 70s where you could just put on an event and leave the rest to chance.'

'And Gareth's team, the musicians and everyone else?'

'They're all staying down at The King's Arms. Worth a visit as well. Do a fantastic steak and kidney pudding!'

'All of them?'

'Everyone except for Gareth,' Anna said. 'He's got a

place of his own close by. Had a taxi booked to take him home I think. Sensible really as he was bound to get a bit tipsy after the concert, I'm sure. He was so happy when he headed off down to the pub, you know. I still can't believe that's he's gone.'

Harry heard Anna's words breaking as she spoke them.

'So, you saw him leave, then? The church?'

'I locked up,' Anna said. 'All part of the responsibility of this.' She pointed at the dog collar around her neck. 'The ring of keys I have to carry with me weigh about the same as a six-year-old, I'm sure. There was a little after-concert party here, with drinks and nibbles, but everyone was gone by eleven-thirty, and Gareth and the band had left before then, heading to the bar.'

'And do you know where he lives, then?' Harry asked.

'Actually, I do, yes,' said Anna, then tapped her nose conspiratorially. 'It's a bit of secret, because he was keen to just be left alone, but he gave me the address, just in case I needed to get in touch about anything.'

Harry asked Matt to fetch the others and soon the rest of the team were standing with him and the vicar.

'Gordy's just pulled up,' Matt said. 'Best we just give her a minute.'

'You're all very familiar with each other and friendly,' Anna said. 'I always thought the police would be more, you know, formal?'

'So did I, actually,' Harry smiled. 'But this lot soon put me to rights on that.'

'We don't really do formal,' Matt said. 'Not unless we really have to. And even if we do, we don't wear ties or anything.'

Harry heard footsteps and looked up to see Gordy at the

door stomping her feet clear of the snow. When she looked over, a yawn escaping from her, Harry saw her eyes widen at seeing the vicar.

'Oh, hi, Anna,' Gordy said, her voice displaying more than a little surprise.

'You know each other, then?' Harry asked.

Anna laughed. 'Oh, yes, we've met,' she said. 'And how are you, Detective Inspector?'

Harry was fairly sure that Gordy blushed at the question.

'I'm good, thanks, and yourself?'

'Well, a body in the tower certainly puts a dent in your weekend, that's for sure.'

'No, I can see that,' said Gordy, then turned her attention to Harry. 'So, what have we got, then?'

Harry gestured over towards the tower door.

'I'll give you the guided tour.'

CHAPTER EIGHTEEN

GORDY WAS OUTSIDE IN THE COLD, BRIGHT MORNING, sucking in great gobfuls of fresh air in the vain hope that it would somehow cleanse her from within of what was behind her in the church tower.

'You okay, there, Detective Inspector?'

'What? Yes, oh, I'm fine,' Gordy replied, turning to see the crime scene photographer standing close by. She didn't know his name and right now wasn't about to ask.

'Well, I can't say that I am, that's for sure,' the photographer said. 'That in there? Never seen anything like it. And I've seen a lot, believe me.'

'Oh, I do,' Gordy said, remembering then why she didn't know his name: it was because she didn't want to know it, because the man seemed to relish just a little too enthusiastically in the gory drama he froze in time with the click of a button.

'You know, there was this one time,' the photographer began, 'where I was called out to a crime scene where someone had been put through a muck spreader and—'

Gordy held up a hand to stop him dead.

'Whatever you're about to say, don't,' she said. 'I'm not sure another horror story is going to help cancel out the one we've all just experienced.'

'It was something else,' the photographer said, as though Gordy's instruction had just bounced off him. 'I mean, the victim, no it was *victims*, wasn't it? Yes, it was! Well, they were everywhere!'

'Please,' Gordy said, as the photographer just kept on talking.

'...like soup, you know that really chunky meat and veg kind—'

'Enough!'

The photographer's mouth snapped shut.

'There, that's a lot better!' Gordy said. 'Now you'll be on your way, yes?'

The photographer sort of just hovered for a moment, clearly not sure what to do next. So Gordy gave him the hint.

'On you go, then! Have a good day, now!'

And with that, the photographer walked up the path and away from the church, Jim signing him out as he left.

'He's an odd bugger, that one,' Matt said, walking out of the church to join Gordy in the fresh air. 'I mean, who chooses photography as a career and then, instead of deciding to do weddings and birthdays and those fancy, expensive family photos people get done, where they're all holding balloons and puppies and giving each other piggy-backs, ignores all of that and goes for crime scene photographer?'

'How's it going in there?' Gordy asked.

'Lots of white paper suits scurrying around like mice,'

Matt said. 'And in the middle of it is Grimm, doing what he does best.'

'Growling?'

Matt gave a nod. 'There's a man whose stare even sounds angry.'

Gordy laughed.

'And now he's our full-time DCI.'

'Well, we could've done a lot worse.'

'You sure about that?'

Now it was Matt's turn to laugh.

'He's all growl and grumble, but there's rarely a bite,' he said. 'He's like a massive Doberman, isn't he? Looks and acts all angry and then when you get to know him he's just a big softy.'

'Not that I'd like to be on the wrong side of him if he did get cross,' said Gordy. 'Though, I've a feeling cross is probably not the most appropriate or accurate word to describe how he'd be.'

'Who's that then?'

Harry's voice rolled into the conversation.

'You, boss,' Matt said, and Gordy laughed at the man's honesty.

'So, you all think I'm just a big, soft Doberman, is that it? All bark, no bite?'

'It is,' Matt nodded. 'Just need to keep you well-fed and know to leave you alone when you're lying on the floor in a patch of sunlight.'

'Though, we're neither of us volunteering for that tummy rub you like,' Gordy laughed.

Harry laughed, too, and the sound reminded Gordy of coal being tumbled into a fire.

'Joining us for some fresh air, then?' she asked.

'Well, you know how Sowerby gets,' Harry said. 'She likes to be left to get on with what she's doing, which is fair enough. Don't think they'll be much longer though.'

Gordy checked her watch and saw that the morning was already closing in on midday.

'Time flies when you're having fun,' Matt said.

'So that's what this is,' Harry said. 'I was beginning to wonder.'

A shout from the church caught everyone's attention.

'Sounds like you're wanted,' Gordy said, eyes on Grimm.

'And you can join me,' Harry replied. 'Come on.'

Inside the church, Gordy saw that the body from the tower was now in a black body bag, on a stretcher to be carried out and then driven back to the lab to be examined in detail. Rather you than me, Gordy thought, seeing the pathologist, Rebecca Sowerby, come over to meet them. At the far end of the church, she spotted Anna, who sent her the smallest of waves and the brightest of smiles.

'Well then, what have we got?' Harry asked.

'A mess,' Sowerby said. 'But then, when am I ever over this way looking at anything else?'

So, she's as barbed as usual, Gordy noted.

'I'm assuming your report will have a bit more detail in it than that,' Harry said.

'I'll walk you through it,' Sowerby said. 'Come on.'

Like Harry and Matt, Gordy had her PPE on, gloves and shoe covers and face mask, and she followed the ghostly form of the pathologist back over towards the tower and through the small door. Inside, the smell was still rich and putrid, tainting the air, and she wondered just how long it would take Anna to get rid of it.

Sowerby pointed at a wooden folding ladder leaning up against the wall.

'We think that the deceased was stood upon that, underneath the rope. It was then kicked away, causing him to drop.'

'And break his neck?' Matt asked.

The pathologist shook her head and Gordy closed her eyes at the thought of the horror of the victim's last moments.

'The neck wasn't broken. He strangled to death.'

'He did it to himself, then?' Gordy asked. 'Came here and killed himself? But why?'

'I didn't say that,' Sowerby said. 'His hands were tied behind his back, which is something he obviously didn't do himself.'

'Ah,' Gordy said, remembering then that rather stark detail from when she'd seen the body hanging from the rope.

'Someone bought him here, then,' Harry said. 'And strung him up.'

'They also cut off a finger,' Sowerby said. 'With what, I'm not sure as there's nothing here that was used to do it, no shears or a knife, so whoever it was took it with them. But they used the end of it like a pen and wrote on his forehead.'

'Saying what, exactly?' Gordy asked, remembering the bloody marks on the victim's forehead.

'I think you can probably guess.'

Gordy thought for a moment, and then it hit her.

'You're kidding me.'

'I never kid.'

'Now that I can believe,' Harry said.

'So?' Matt asked. 'What was on Gareth's head, then?'

'Six, six, six,' Gordy said.

'Exactly,' nodded Sowerby.

'Then this is a ritualist killing,' Harry said. 'Or it was

made to look like one. I was hoping it was all just a load of horseshit nonsense, but I'm guessing not.'

'I can't tell you what it is or isn't,' Sowerby said. 'All I can tell you is what we've found. And I've no doubt I'll find more when I get the body back to the lab for a proper examination.'

'What about the symbols?' Gordy asked, gesturing to the walls.

'The photographer will send you his files through,' Sowerby said. 'All occult, even the snake.'

'And you're absolutely sure it's a snake?' Matt asked.

'What else could it be?' Gordy asked.

'I'm just saying it doesn't look like any snake I've ever seen.' Matt shrugged. 'That's all.'

'Not sure how much DNA we'll get from any of this,' the pathologist continued. 'Despite the place looking like a proper mess, there's not that much here. And what is here, the blood, the fluids, it's all the victim's. And there's other stuff we'll be looking through, fibres we've found, and there was a stone in that corner over there which had been moved out of the wall with a little cavity behind it. Empty, but we check everything just in case.'

Gordy looked at Matt and then to Harry and both men were wearing looks of deep concern. And who could blame them? she thought. This wasn't a murder done in anger, this was planned, and to such a degree that Gordy couldn't ignore the sinking feeling in her gut that where there was one, others would follow. And the whole satanic, occultic side to it, added to the fact that it was all carried out in a church? God, the press was going to love it. But what it was going to do to the local community, she didn't dare think.

'One thing,' Gordy asked, 'with him hanging from a bell-rope, why no ringing bell?'

'That's a fair point,' Matt said, and everyone looked up then towards where the bells were hanging somewhere in the dark, high above them.

'Already checked that with the vicar actually,' Harry said. 'After we'd had our chat, I was wondering the same. All the work in the tower? It's not just a bit of fixing up. The place is a mess. The bells are currently in storage, for safety.'

'There is something else though,' the pathologist said. 'Not in here, but back out in the church.'

Gordy stepped in line behind Harry and Matt as they followed the pathologist out of the tower.

The pathologist came to a stop at the inner door.

'You'll all have noticed that the lock has been smashed,' she said.

'Hard not to,' Matt said. 'Must've really gone at it with something heavy and hard to damage it like that.'

'We dusted it for fingerprints, obviously,' Sowerby said, 'and as we did, we noticed something. You see here?'

Gordy leaned in.

'What are we looking at exactly?' she asked.

'The assumption is that the lock was smashed to break into the church, correct?' Sowerby said.

'Clearly,' said Harry. 'Why else would it be smashed?'

'If the door was locked, then the bolt would still be out. It would be damaged as well, from being ripped and torn out of the recess in the door frame, just here, see?' Sowerby pointed.

Gordy looked over to the door frame. There was damage, yes, but it certainly didn't look like anything had been ripped out of it.

'As you can see,' continued the pathologist, 'the bolt is still in the main mechanism. There is no damage to it because it was protected by being in there while the lock was smashed.'

'But the church was locked,' Harry said. 'They smashed the lock to get in! Anna found the lock like that when she came over this morning.'

'All I'm telling you is what we found,' Sowerby said. 'The bolt for the lock was not out when the mechanism was smashed. And neither was it in the recess in the door frame. It should be twisted and scratched, but it isn't.'

It was Gordy then who said what everyone else was thinking.

'Whoever did this, they smashed the lock after they'd got into the church.'

'Which means, it was either open when they arrived,' began Matt, but Gordy finished his sentence for him.

'Or they had a key.'

CHAPTER NINETEEN

HARRY WAS NOW STANDING IN THE SNOW-COVERED parking area just over the wall from the churchyard. The branches of the trees above him were laden with thick snow. Wary that the snow would soon slump off the branches to land on his head, he moved away.

'Boss?'

Harry turned to see Jim standing at the gate of the churchyard. His face was serious, a look that didn't really suit him, Harry thought, wondering when the cheery Jim of a few months ago would be back.

'Something wrong?' Harry asked.

'I'm feeling proper rough if I'm honest,' Jim said, rubbing his head.

'Headache? I'm sure we can find some paracetamol or something.'

'No, it's not just that, I'm feeling really ropey, like,' Jim said, his voice breaking a little. 'My guts are in bits.'

'You eaten something dodgy?'

Jim shook his head.

'Mum's food is never dodgy. Big, yes, and tasty, but never dodgy.'

Harry stared for a moment at his PCSO.

'You needing to head home, then?'

Jim nodded, though for a moment looked pained.

'And you're sure it's not because of what we've all just seen? Because your head will clear and we're done in there now.'

'I've been feeling like this since I woke up,' Jim said. 'Just tried to ignore it because I knew you needed me.'

'That's very good of you, very conscientious,' Harry said. 'But you throwing up all over a crime scene is never sensible. Get yourself home. Quickly.'

'You sure it's okay?'

'I am,' Harry said. 'Anyway, Liz is on her way over. Jen called her and whatever she was on with today was cancelled at the last minute, so she's free. She'll be here any moment now I shouldn't wonder.'

Jim hesitated.

'Go on, hop it!' Harry growled.

As Jim drove off, Harry heard the sound of an engine approaching. Then, around the corner at the bottom of the hill, and cutting a line through the snow, he saw a motorbike speed towards him, the back wheel sliding out on the snow, but the rider handling it with ease.

The rider pulled up in front of Harry, flipping up the visor on the helmet.

'Hello, Liz,' Harry said. 'Nice to see you're driving according to the conditions.'

Liz removed her helmet.

'I love it when it's like this!' She grinned. 'Don't get much chance to play in the snow nowadays.'

'Nearly came a cropper when you came round that bend down there, though, didn't you?' Harry said.

Liz glanced down the hill.

'The skid? That felt awesome!'

'Anyway,' Harry said, shaking his head, fully aware that riding a bike like that wasn't exactly the kind of thing that the police smiled at, 'I'm glad you're here because we've lost Jim to a bit of gut-rot.'

'Is he okay?'

'Just needs to sleep it off I think,' Harry said, then caught sight of Jen, Gordy, Matt, and the vicar heading their way from the church.

When they arrived, Gordy was nattering away to Anna. And Matt was obviously concluding a story that he found hilarious, but judging by the look on her face, Jen was simply baffled by.

'Right then,' Harry said, clapping his hands together as a sign that it was time for everyone to listen. 'The scene of crime team are done here so we'll be hearing from Sowerby early in the week if she's got anything else to add to what we already know.'

'What about the church?' Anna asked, and Harry heard the concern in her voice. 'It's horrible in there. I mean, not just the smell in the tower, but the mess, the symbols on the walls. And there's the lock and ...'

Her voice cracked and Harry saw Gordy rest a hand on the vicar's arm to comfort her.

'A team of forensic cleaners will be here as soon as they can be,' Harry said. 'They'll sanitise and decontaminate the whole area.'

'How soon?' Anna asked.

'Sowerby said they would be here tomorrow,' Matt said.

'They'll do a good job. It'll probably be cleaner than it was before, to be honest.'

Anna gave a small smile, comforted by that.

'Next task is to follow up on whatever we can,' Harry said. 'By which I mean, we need to get in touch with everyone who was at the concert last night. Gareth's team, close contacts, friends, and we need to see if we can find out who those two were who gatecrashed the thing.'

'You think there's a connection, then?' Matt asked.

'What we know, is that two blokes caused a disturbance last night at Gareth's concert. What they said, some nonsense about claiming the place in the name of Satan or whatever, well, we can't ignore that there's a link between that and everything that took place in the tower, can we? So, the sooner we identify them, find them, and talk to them, the better.'

'What about the lock?' Jen asked.

'All I know is that it was definitely locked,' Anna said. 'I locked that door. I always do.'

'Which means,' Harry said, remembering their earlier discussion with the pathologist, 'that they either picked the lock or had a key.'

'I can give you a list of key holders,' Anna said. 'It's the list I was given when I arrived here and I've been here ten years now and nothing's changed.'

'That would be very helpful I'm sure,' Harry said. 'But what about before you were here?'

Anna went quiet and thoughtful for a moment then said, 'I'm sorry, but I don't really know. I suppose there could've been other keys? That door looks new, I know, but that's only because the church is so old. I think it was put in back in the early 80s.'

'Well, a list will be a good place to start,' Harry said, then looked at his DI. 'Gordy, if you, Matt, and Jen here, can crack on with following up on finding and speaking with as many as you can from last night, Liz and I will head off to Gareth's house. He took a taxi there after the pub last night, so something happened between then and when he was in the tower. Might be a few answers at his house.'

'You've got the address, yes?' Anna asked.

'All written in my trusty little notebook,' Harry said patting his pocket. 'Right, let's get to it then. And stay in touch, everyone, okay? And, while you're at it, Matt?'

'Yes, boss?'

'I fancy you might need to give Mr Enthusiasm a call.'

'Jadyn?' Matt said, raising an eyebrow. 'You sure about that?'

'There's a lot of people to be tracking down,' Harry said. 'And I'm sure you can imagine just how excited he'll be to be thrown into a task like that, right?'

'That's what worries me,' Matt said.

As the team dispersed, Harry climbed into his vehicle, Liz sliding into the passenger seat.

'Ready?' Harry asked, clipping himself in.

'Always,' Liz replied, doing the same.

Harry turned the key in the ignition. He turned it again.

'Come on, then,' Liz said.

'I'm trying to!' Harry said, and turned the key once more.

'Something up?'

'No, I'm just pretending the engine won't start,' Harry said, trying again.

'Nothing?'

Harry shook his head.

'It's dead. I don't get it. Drove like a dream on the way over.'

'Cars are like sheep,' Liz said. 'One minute they're fine and healthy and everything's grand. Next, they're dead. No reason, no warning, either.'

Harry tried again, then yanked the key back out of the ignition. He turned to get out of the car to try and sort out some transport with the rest of the team, but they were already gone.

'Great!' Harry said. 'Just brilliant! Now what?'

Liz, Harry noticed, was grinning.

'What?'

'I've got an idea.'

'What idea?'

'You won't like it,' Liz said. 'But I don't think we've much choice.'

'Out with it, then!' Harry said. 'Come on!'

At that, Liz's grin grew even larger.

'Just one question,' she said. 'Have you ever ridden pillion?'

CHAPTER TWENTY

HARRY WAS TERRIFIED. HE'D EXPERIENCED FEAR IN ITS purest form many times in his life. From firefights where the rounds zipped past him like wasps, the crack of weapons fire almost deafening, and the horror of being caught and interrogated, to seeing friends blown to pieces and himself being the victim of an IED, but being on the back of Liz's police-issue off-road capable motorbike? Well, if he had been close to death ever before in his life, this was really pushing it.

With his arms wrapped around Liz's waist, his massive hands clamped together so tightly that he half wondered if he'd ever prise them apart again, Harry held on as tight as he could. He wasn't even worried about the cold, which with them being on the bike, was coming at them like sabres of ice, cutting and slicing as they rode through the snow towards Bainbridge.

The visor on the helmet he was wearing, the spare which Liz always had with her strapped to the bike, was slowly crusting over with ice crystals from the wind chill. He couldn't even shout to Liz because there was just no way that she would hear. Though what he would shout about, Harry wasn't entirely sure, other than an endless raft of expletives and the occasional roar of terror.

It wasn't that Liz was going fast, either, or that she was riding the bike like an idiot and taking risks. The opposite was actually true, because it became very clear very quickly to Harry that Liz really knew what she was doing, riding as though the bike was a part of who and what she was. In many ways, it was quite something to experience, except that all Harry could focus on was just how exposed he felt, gripping on for dear life to a woman who probably weighed about as much as one of his legs, on the back of a bike which, now that he was sitting on it, felt far too small for him on his own, never mind the two of them together. Harry was sure his arse was just too big, that at any point he was just going to topple off the back of the bike and go for a tumble, which would, he was pretty sure, end up with him in a river.

Having navigated their way through Bainbridge, the quaint village green hidden beneath a blanket of snow held down by the resolute army of snowmen that crowded it, Liz directed the bike to take a right, opposite the old Roman fort. The road ahead was narrow but surprisingly clear, Harry noticed, leaning to have a quick look-see over Liz's shoulder. Then, just ahead, where the road forked, and Liz took the left, Harry saw a problem; a tractor jackknifed on the road.

Liz pulled the bike to a stop.

'Reckon it's been here a while,' she said. 'Whoever was driving it probably just buggered off home for a cuppa and to wait for the snow to melt before they bothered moving it.'

Harry could see that the snow had drifted around the tractor, blocking the road utterly. There wasn't even space to squeeze past between it and the walls, because there were no walls, just huge drifts, their crests frozen in sculpted arcs.

'We'll have to take the Roman road,' Liz said, looking over her shoulder at Harry. 'That's the other lane just down there at the fork.'

Harry said, 'Isn't that just a dirt track, though?'

'It is,' Liz replied. 'But the snow will make it a soft ride and if the drifts aren't too bad we should be fine.'

'I don't really like the sound of the word "should,"' Harry said.

'Hold on!' Liz barked and Harry was only just quick enough to do exactly that as she spun the bike around, the rear end spraying snow out in a great fan, then headed them on down the Roman road.

Harry was pretty sure that describing this next part of the journey as "*a soft ride*" was really pushing it in the accuracy and truth department, as Liz thrust them along at what seemed to be a thousand miles an hour. She was definitely riding harder and faster, probably because they were no longer on an actual road, Harry thought, but it didn't make him feel any better about it. Some part of his brain was doing its utmost to tell him that he should be enjoying himself, that it was exciting and fun, but he was very aware that he was no longer in his twenties. He was older, creakier, and considerably more aware of his own mortality. Unlike Liz, it seemed.

When the Roman road met again with the road, Liz took a left, and soon Harry saw the valley open in front of them, the black depths of Semerwater sitting far below. Today was definitely not a day that he would be taking a dip in it.

At long last, Liz slowed down and pulled the bike to a stop in the tiny dwelling of Countersett.

'We need to be round the back here,' Liz said, pointing at

a lane on their left, which disappeared down a shallow slope to duck and hide behind snow-covered trees. 'Lovely place to live, isn't it?'

'It is that,' Harry said, off the bike now and rubbing his backside.

'Sore?'

'A little.'

'You're good on the pillion though,' Liz said. 'Some folk you put on there and they're all over the place, like. Leaning the wrong way, jumping about, but you just went with it. Made it a lot easier for me.'

'Can't say that it was intentional,' Harry said. 'Now, where do we go, then?'

Liz led the way and a minute or so later they were at the address that Anna had given them.

'Well, that doesn't look good, does it?' Liz said.

'No, it doesn't,' Harry agreed, as he stepped past Liz and led them both along a short snow-covered path towards an open front door.

STANDING IN THE HALLWAY, Harry took in the mess. Snow had blown in, covering some of the carpet with a small, sculpted snowdrift.

'Looks like we're going to have to give the SOC team another call,' Liz said.

'Today just gets better and better,' Harry sighed. 'Let's have a nosy around first though.'

It was clear to Harry that whatever had happened here, it had been violent. He saw a scrape of blood on the wall, yes, but the general state of the place was enough to tell him that something bad had happened here, before the final awful events at the church.

Gareth, Harry saw, had been in the middle of decorating, with dustsheets covering the floor and furniture in the lounge. Pots of paint had been kicked over, and one so violently that the top was lying a good distance away from it, red paint dashed across the place like a blood spatter special effect in a movie. He also saw other DIY tools lying about, having been spewed out by a toolbox lying open on the floor.

Harry dropped down to examine it.

'I get the impression this was all a bit new to Gareth,' Harry said.

'How so?'

'Look at this toolbox,' Harry said, pointing at the open shell of it. 'The tools don't look like they've been used. There's even this!'

Liz took a little booklet which Harry handed to her.

'That's the list of everything inside. Doesn't look like it's been thumbed much, does it? I reckon he'd only just bought it.'

'Doesn't tell us much though, does it?' Liz said.

Harry shook his head. 'Probably not, no.'

Stepping carefully through the damage, Harry made his way through to the small kitchen at the back of the house. Here he saw that the television was still on, though nothing was playing, the screen showing only the home screen of a streaming service. A bottle of port was open on the table.

Back out in the hall, Harry met Liz returning from a quick trip upstairs.

'Everything's fine up there,' Liz said. 'Bed's a bit ruffled, like it's been slept in.'

'Maybe he was in bed and he heard intruders,' Harry

said. 'Came downstairs to find them and then it all kicked off.'

'That doesn't seem to ring right with what happened at the church though, does it?' Liz said. 'And I'm glad I didn't get to see any of that. Sounds awful.'

'Looked and smelled it, too,' Harry said.

Moving through to the lounge again, Harry had another look around, wondering if anything would jump out at him, but doubting it very much.

'Over here's where the paint must've been stood,' Harry said, staring at various coloured rings on the dust sheet.'

Liz leaned in, then looked around at the other tins scattered across the room.

'I don't think they're all here though,' she said.

'How's that then?'

Liz dropped to her heels and pointed at the paint rings.

'These colours? None of the pots here match them. So where are they?'

Harry stooped down for a closer look.

'You're right,' he said. 'Well spotted.' Then something struck him. 'They're the colours from the church.'

'What?'

'The symbols painted in the church,' Harry said. 'They're the same colours as those were.'

'So, whoever did this was definitely at the church, then,' Liz said.

'Which means they either knew where he lived or followed him,' Harry said. 'And from what the vicar told us, this place and Gareth being here, well, that was a bit of a secret. Wanted to keep it private.'

'This is the dales though,' Liz said. 'Secrets don't stay secret very long. I mean, folk will go along with it, like something is still a secret, but deep down, everyone knows that it isn't.'

'That's not very helpful,' Harry said, pulling his phone from his pocket.

'No, I suppose it isn't.'

Harry made the call to Rebecca Sowerby, who was none too pleased to be hearing from him again so soon but confirmed that a team would be sent out to the house as soon as possible. Then, as he was about to stuff the phone back into his pocket, it buzzed in his hand.

'Grimm,' Harry answered.

'It's Haig,' Gordy said. 'How's things at the house?'

'Bit of a mess, to be honest,' Harry said. 'Just had to call forensics again.'

'Ouch.'

'Exactly,' Harry said. 'So, are you calling with good news or bad?'

'Well, we've been on it with tracking folk down from last night,' Gordy said. 'Jadyn has been working from the Leyburn station, ringing round. Didn't see much point having him drive all the way over here.'

'Sensible,' Harry said.

'Well, we've got some details on the two who broke into the concert. Sending you something now.'

Harry's phone vibrated and he glanced at the screen to see a photo of the rear of a beaten-up van, painted black, and its number plate.

'Who took that, then?' Harry asked.

'One of the blokes who saw them off the premises,' replied Gordy. 'He followed them to make sure they were gone and took a photo just in case it was needed.'

'Any details?'

'I'll send those through in a second,' Gordy said. 'But there's more good news.'

Harry couldn't believe what he was hearing.

'Go on,' he said.

'The van was caught on a camera. Jadyn's liaising with Traffic to see if they can find out exactly where it is now.'

'I'm impressed,' Harry said, then asked, 'How's Anna, by the way? She'll have had better Sundays I'm sure.'

'Oh, she's fine I think,' Gordy said. 'Clean-up team will be over tomorrow. So that's made her feel a wee bit better. Though it's going to be tough, I think, for the church to deal with what's happened.'

'It will have helped to have a friendly face,' Harry said. 'By which I mean yours not mine.'

'I suppose so, yes,' Gordy said. 'Anyway, best get on. I'll send those details now.'

And with that, the call was over, and rather abruptly, too, Harry thought. He stuffed the phone back in his pocket.

'So, what now?' Liz asked.

Harry thought about the journey over to Gareth's house on the pillion of the PCSO's bike. It was an experience he was fairly sure his rear end wasn't quite ready to repeat.

He also knew that he didn't have much choice.

'Hawes,' Harry said. 'That way I have access to transport with four wheels and a roof.'

CHAPTER TWENTY-ONE

Harry's afternoon wasn't the one he'd wanted, but it was the one the job had given him, and he made it bearable by drinking a lot of tea. What surprised him the most was that halfway through the afternoon he found himself munching on some fruit cake and Wensleydale cheese. He was pleased that no one was there to witness it, particularly Matt, because he would never hear the end of it.

Having been given a lift back by Liz, Harry had stayed around the Community Centre to make sure he was around if anything came in on what had happened over in Askrigg. He also took the opportunity to have another look through what they had on the sheep rustling and the murder of Jim's old school friend, Nick. Well, he would've done, if the file hadn't been rather lighter than it was supposed to be.

'Hello, Eric, is Jim there, please?'

Harry had made the call after the cheese and cake. Food in his stomach always had a calming effect on him and he needed that now. With what was going on over in Askrigg, what he didn't need was one of his PCSOs still playing silly buggers about another case. He understood Jim's need to do something about it, but he was losing focus on other things by being so obsessed with it. And that needed to be sorted.

'Harry?' Eric replied.

'It is,' Harry said. 'Sorry to bother you on a Sunday afternoon.'

'Ah, it's no bother,' Eric said. 'You're after Jim, then?'

'I am. I know he's not feeling too good, but—'

'Is he not?'

'I had to send him home this morning,' Harry said. 'Didn't look great. Something up with his stomach.'

'News to me,' Eric said. 'Though I've been out most of the day so he's probably upstairs. Fly's around and usually that lad isn't far away. Just a mo'...'

Harry heard Eric put the phone down at the other end of the call, then heard him shouting for Jim. Next he heard footsteps which grew quieter, then louder again.

'He's not here, Harry,' Eric said.

'What?'

'I shouted for him, went up to his room, but he's not there. Wait a minute, will you?'

Again the phone was put down and this time Harry heard a door being yanked open.

'Harry?'

'What is it, Eric?'

'His Landy isn't here either. You sure he came home, then?'

'It's where I sent him and where he told me he was going,' Harry said. 'Could he have popped out anywhere?'

'Nowt to pop out to,' Eric replied. 'We've already checked on the sheep, like, what with this weather we're having, and he'd have taken Fly with him if that's what he was on with, I'm sure. They can be a bugger to dig out if they get stuck in a snowdrift. But we bought them all down from up top early last week, so they're fine really. Been out to help a few friends with theirs, but not today, no one's called for help.'

'So, where is he, then?' Harry asked.

'Buggered if I know,' Eric replied. 'I'll just go and ask Mary.'

Harry again heard the phone thunk down on whatever surface it was kept on, followed by muffled voices, as Eric talked to Jim's mum.

'Nope,' Eric said, back on the phone again. 'Mary's not seen him either. Not since he went out this morning actually, to catch up with you lot.'

Harry fell silent.

'Something up?' Eric asked.

'Just give me a call if and when you see him, will you?' Harry said.

'I will.'

Harry said his goodbyes and hung up.

'Bollocks!'

The roar of his voice echoed around the office and Harry threw his phone across the table, frustration at Jim's behaviour bubbling over. The phone skittered across the table and bounced off into the wall with a clatter. At that moment, Harry didn't care if it was broken. What he cared about was that he had a PCSO who'd clearly gone AWOL.

Had the lad no idea what this could look like on his records? thought Harry. It wasn't that he needed to know where his team were at all times, but it was clear now that Jim had probably been lying earlier when he'd said he wasn't feeling well. And seeing as the file was missing, it didn't take much to put the two things together and come up with a situation that needed sorting quickly before it got out of hand. But just where the hell was he? No one knew, not his parents, not the team. And with the weather as it was, who was to say something really bad hadn't happened and the idiot wasn't upside down in a ditch somewhere?

Harry was furious. He could feel the anger burning through him, tension building in his muscles. He understood how Jim felt, but what he couldn't condone was what he was doing now. Okay, so he himself hadn't always done things properly, and wasn't that the main reason he'd been sent to Hawes in the first place? But Jim was young, Harry thought, and as angry as he was, he was more concerned than anything. If Jim was out there following up on a lead, no matter how tenuous, then what if that went wrong? The people who killed his friend, they were serious, not to be messed with. Then another thought struck Harry and he was back into the files, rifling through them, only to find a space where the one he was looking for should have been.

Harry found his phone and punched a call to Jim, knowing there would be no answer. And there wasn't. It didn't stop him trying a couple of times more, though.

Giving up on that, and with a message left on Jim's phone which made it very clear that he had better give him a call back if he still wanted a job in the morning, he sent a round-robin message to the team to tell him if any of them heard from Jim or knew where he was. Then he marched outside just to get some fresh air to clear his head.

The afternoon had drawn dark into early evening and Hawes was quiet. The road was clear now, or as clear as it could be. A plough had been through, but the going was still pretty treacherous and Harry watched a couple of cars ease their way up and through the marketplace, wheels spinning in the slush underneath.

Harry's phone buzzed in his pocket and he answered it without even checking the screen.

'You'd better have a good explanation for whatever it is you're playing at, Jim,' Harry began.

'It's Jadyn, boss,' said the voice on the other end. 'You alright?'

'No, I'm not alright!' Harry snapped back. 'You've heard from Jim, then? That's why you're calling?'

'No,' Jadyn replied.

'Did you not see my message?'

'Yes, but like I said, I've not heard anything from him at all. Should I have done?'

'How the hell should I know?'

Harry rubbed his eyes, forcing deep breaths down into his lungs to try and calm himself.

'Right, sorry about that,' Harry said.

'No bother,' Jadyn said. 'Just thought you'd like to know that I've managed to get more details on that van.'

'And they are?'

'It's in Catterick,' Jadyn said.

'And what's it doing there, then?'

'Parked up outside a pub, apparently,' Jadyn said, then gave Harry the establishment's name.

'You're having a laugh, aren't you?'

'Am I?' Jadyn said. 'I don't think I am, no.'

'You sure it's that pub?'

'It's the name I was given,' Jadyn said. 'Is there a problem?'

Harry shook his head and rolled his eyes. Of all the pubs in all the world, he thought... How many years had it been?

He didn't dare think. But surely it must have changed since then, when that particular pub was one of the main haunts of all the squaddies up at Catterick Garrison.

'Do you know it, then?' Jadyn asked.

'I do,' Harry replied. 'Anyone joining an infantry regiment in the British Army trains at the ITC.'

'ITC?'

'Infantry Training Centre,' Harry said. 'Including the Paras.'

'Oh, so this is like a trip down memory lane,' Jadyn said. 'Well, that should be fun then!'

'Fun?' Harry said. 'Fun? Do you have any idea what training for the Paras is actually like?'

'No, not really,' Jadyn said. 'Lots of running around and getting shouted at?'

'Yes, a lot of that actually,' Harry said. 'And that pub you mentioned? Well, if it's the same one, and I've a horrible feeling that it is, then it has a certain reputation.'

'It does? And what's that then?'

Harry's mind did a lightning-quick rewind to those younger days, when he was fitter, faster, and after a few beers, usually looking for a bit of a rumble.

'Let's just say that it was the kind of place you went to for a pint and a fight,' Harry said, flexing a fist as he spoke, his knuckles cracking as though they too remembered the pub.

'Do you want the address?' Jadyn asked.

Harry was pretty sure he didn't need it but asked Jadyn to send it anyway.

'Good work on this,' Harry said as he read the address, which confirmed that yes, it was indeed the same pub. 'You got anything else planned?'

'Well, I managed to get a couple of decent records this

morning,' Jadyn replied, 'before I came in on this. Mainly because the weather meant it was pretty quiet. So I'll be listening to them.'

'No, you won't,' Harry said. 'Because you're coming with me this evening on a little trip.'

'Am I?' Jadyn asked. 'Where to?'

'Down memory lane.'

CHAPTER TWENTY-TWO

HARRY PULLED THE LAND ROVER UP OUTSIDE THE PUB, bringing it to rest under the only security light attached to the wall that actually worked. In the front of the vehicle with him was Jen, with Police Constable Jadyn Okri squeezed in the back. It wasn't exactly the best way to travel for Jadyn, but one of them had to draw the short straw and it had been him.

Harry had been impressed with the enthusiasm with which the police constable had leapt into the back, as though the simple act of doing so, and swinging the door shut with a dull clang behind him, was some kind of signal that what they were about to do was some serious daring-do. And then, for the rest of the journey, Jadyn had plonked himself directly behind Harry, who had then had to drive all the way to Catterick with the world's most enthusiastic police constable jabbering on in his ear.

'Can I suggest,' Harry said, switching off the engine, the sound of it cooling down a faint tick-tock and pop under the bonnet, 'that on the return journey, you two swap places? Seems only fair, don't you think?'

'I don't travel too well in the back,' Jen said, doing a rather expressive impression of throwing up.

'Right now, I'm happy to risk it,' said Harry. 'PC Okri here, well, it's like trying to change gear sitting in front of an overly talkative octopus!'

'How's that then?' Jadyn asked.

'You kept jabbing your finger at things!' Harry said. 'Have you never seen snow before?'

'Not like this, no,' Jadyn said. 'And you saw the snow on that post box—it looked like a massive hat!'

'To you, maybe,' Harry said.

'And that car that someone had drawn a funny face on, with massive horns on top?'

'I'll admit that was a little funny,' Harry said.

'What about the snowman?' Jen asked.

'Which one? The one hitching a ride or the one with a pair of false legs sticking out of its mouth?'

'I liked the one with glowing eyes,' Jadyn said. 'That was well funny, that, like, wasn't it? Creepy, too! It was like it was just staring at us, wasn't it? Like it was alive!'

'No, it wasn't!' Harry said. 'Not at all! It was just a snowman! And if it's still there on the way back, can I ask that you don't bellow in my ear the words, *'Bloody hell, that one looks proper evil'*? Because driving in these conditions isn't easy at the best of times, never mind when you've a seven-year-old in the body of twenty-something sitting behind you constantly jabbering on about how he wishes he was out sledging and how tomorrow we should all have a snowball fight!'

Rant over, Harry heaved the driver's door open and dropped down into the snow. The night was quiet, the snow working to muffle the usual sounds of a world going about its business, but behind the quiet, he could hear the dull chatter and thump-thump-thump of a pub doing a roaring trade.

'Sounds pretty lively,' Jen said.

'From what I can remember, it was never anything else,' Harry said. 'A proper garrison pub. And if you've never been to one before, I warn you now, they're usually a bit on the wild side.'

'How do you mean *wild*?' Jadyn asked.

'No one goes to a pub like this for a quiet drink with their mates or to stuff themselves in a corner with a pint and a newspaper,' Harry said. 'It'll be full of exhausted soldiers grabbing a few hours of downtime, and that usually means too much to drink, lots of shouting, and a punch up.'

'Fighting then,' Jadyn said. 'Why?'

'You go through infantry training and you need to let off steam,' Harry said. 'You're wound up tight, fit as anything, and you're learning to kill, because that's really what it's about in the end, isn't it? So, you just need to have a blowout now and again.'

'Sounds like this is going to be fun, then,' Jen said. 'So, about the two we're here for?'

'Well, that's their van over there,' Harry said. 'So let's have a look at that first before we go in.'

The van was black, the paint job more paintbrush than professionally sprayed, and a good number of rust patches were blooming like flowers in dark earth. The rear doors were covered in numerous stickers of various instrument makers, from Gibson guitars to Drum Workshop and Zild-jian cymbals. And down the side of the van, in letters designed to look like they had been splashed on with fresh blood, was the word, 'Geryon'. Book-ending the word were two roughly daubed upside-down crosses.

'So, we're dealing with a band, then,' Harry said. 'And those crosses there look like some of what we found in the tower back at the church.'

Jadyn pulled out his phone and took some photos.

'We can compare them with the photos of the crime scene when we get them,' he said. 'Which should be tomorrow, right?'

Jen leaned in to cadge a look through the driver's window.

'And I'm going to take a wild guess, looking in here, that they're not exactly your normal, everyday chart-topping Pop act.'

Harry glanced over her shoulder. Inside he saw a silver skull gear knob, a collection of small, highly detailed models of what he assumed to be characters from horror movies, seeing as one had a head covered in pins, and most of the others were wearing masks and carrying massive machetes, and a footwell full of empty energy drink cans and crumpled crisp packets. There was also an open packet of Rizla and a pouch of hand-rolling tobacco.

'There's only one way to find out,' Harry said and nodded at the pub.

'After you, then, boss,' Jadyn said.

Harry led the way, scuffling across the grey snow of the car park and to a door that looked like it spent its holidays as a police riot shield.

Pushing through, Harry's senses were assaulted by such a wall of sound and smell that he took a brief step back before a shove from Jadyn coming along behind had him inside.

The pub was full, that was the first thing Harry noticed.

Rammed, was probably a better description. He saw a pool table to his left, coins lined up along one side, and the game in play down to the eight ball. The shot was taken, the ball sunk, and the crowd around the table erupted, spilling pints as much as sinking them. To his right were various scattered tables, all occupied, a jukebox against the wall, either side of which were various games machines, all being enthusiastically fed hard-earned money and devouring it greedily. The bar was front and centre and busy, the bar staff dancing around each other with well-practised ease.

'You getting the drinks in, then, boss?' Jadyn asked.

Harry whipped round to tell him exactly what he thought of that idea, only to catch the grin.

Jen said, 'Judging by the descriptions we've got of the owners of the van, I'm not seeing them here, are you?'

'No,' Harry said. 'But then, I didn't expect them to be.'

'Then why are we here?' Jadyn asked.

Harry pointed at the floor.

'There's a basement bar,' he said. 'Music venue. I say venue, it's more of a damp cellar with dodgy lighting and no ventilation.'

'Sounds a delight,' Jen said.

Harry walked across to the bar.

Catching the eye of one of the staff, a lad whose neck was nearly as wide as his head, his arms and chest straining beneath his black T-shirt, Harry said, 'Can I have a word?'

'Hang on, mate, I was here first,' said a young man at Harry's side, cash in his hand.

'Not biologically you weren't,' Harry said.

The young man's face cracked with confusion as the lad with the thick neck stared at Harry.

'Looking for a couple of blokes who might be here,'

Harry said. 'Own the van outside? I'm guessing they're playing here tonight?'

'What do you want with them?' the lad asked and Harry saw him bristle. That neck, he suspected, had an awful lot to do with banned substances.

Harry pulled out his ID.

'A chat,' he said.

'Downstairs,' the barman said, pointing to a door over to his left. 'They're playing now, so you'll have to wait till the gig's over or folk won't be happy.'

'Not my concern,' Harry said, putting his ID away again. 'I need to talk to them. Urgently.'

'It will be if things kick off,' the barman said.

Harry ignored the warning and turned from the bar to make his way over to the door. On the way, he heard a wolf whistle followed by a good amount of jeering laughter. Then a yelp. He glanced back to see Jen with a man's wrist twisted just enough to have him bending backwards to the point that he was just about to buckle and drop backwards onto the floor.

'Everything okay?' Harry asked.

'No problems here, boss,' Jen said. 'Just arresting someone for assaulting a police officer.'

'I didn't do anything!' said the man whose wrist Jen was twisting. 'I'm sorry, alright? I didn't know you were police!'

'And that makes it alright, does it?' Jen asked. 'Means you can just whistle and cop a feel whenever you want?'

'That's not what I'm saying!'

'Then what are you saying?'

'I'm sorry!' the man said, and Harry heard pain in his voice. 'I am, I'm sorry!'

Jen let go.

'It's a warning this time,' she said, as the man rubbed his wrist. 'And there won't be a next time, will there?'

The man shook his head, still rubbing his wrist.

'Ready when you are, boss!' Jen then said, sending Harry a smile.

Harry returned the gesture, then headed through a door and down a narrow flight of stairs and towards an ever-growing sound of drums, guitar, and grunting.

CHAPTER TWENTY-THREE

THE LAST TIME JIM HAD BEEN IN DARLINGTON WAS, well, he really wasn't that sure, if he were honest. His memory was telling him that it was way back when he'd been at school and for some reason had travelled all that way with his parents for a rare day out together and to buy some decent shoes for school. He'd wanted a pair of Dr Martens boots, but no way had that ever been going to happen. As his dad had pointed out, 'How can a pair of working boots be as much as a sheep?' Probably not the most accurate of comparisons, but the point had been made.

He had no idea if it had changed much. The snow was hiding a lot of the town and he wasn't really that fussed anyway. His heart belonged in the hills and there was no way he was ever going to try and convince it otherwise.

Having managed to convince Harry that he was feeling none too well, the effectiveness of the lie supported by the fact that he'd gone into work in the first place, he had then nipped back home to gather up what he needed for the day, before jumping in his Land Rover and going for a very long drive in not the best of conditions. But to the wheels beneath him, none of it was an issue, and he would have enjoyed the journey had it not been for the reason he was taking it in the first place, that being the murder of his old school friend a couple of months ago.

In the time since Neil's death, Jim had been tearing himself apart from the inside, blaming himself for what happened, angry at Neil for being involved in sheep theft in the first place, and never really being able to rip himself out of the endless cycle of blame and anger he was now in. Sense told him it was not his fault, that Neil had known what he was getting into, but another part of him insisted he should have been able to do something, protect his family's liveli-hood, help Nick. And now here he was, on a bitterly cold day, having driven for nearly two hours through thick snow, and for what? Well, he would just have to wait and see, wouldn't he?

It was the cigarettes that were to blame, the ones smoked by that bloke who'd tried to take Fly on Friday. They were the same brand that Neil had smoked. It was a long shot, yes, but it was one he'd had to take. Forensics wouldn't come back with anything, he was sure of that, and even if they did, he'd have to wait a few more days, and that was no use, was it? And then for that fancy solicitor to turn up? No, there was no way Jim was going to just let this slide. He was going to act. Which was why he was now parked up in a vehicle that smelled faintly of hay and lanolin and damp mud, on a street he'd never been on, staring at the door belonging to the address Timothy Renton had given them on Friday.

Having been sat there for a few hours now, Jim was beginning to wonder if going all lone wolf on this was such a good idea after all. He had a few snacks with him to keep him going, namely some of his mum's homemade fruit cake and a flask of tea, and it was cold, so he'd wrapped up warm in so many layers that he was now sweating like he'd just run a marathon in the sun. But evening was here and nothing had happened at the house, he'd seen no activity, no one going in or coming out, and doubt was settling in.

I'm an idiot, he thought, *and Harry's going to kill me.*

A yawn forced its way up and out of Jim's lungs and when it was done his eyes suddenly felt so heavy that all he wanted to do was close them and rest. But he couldn't because that would be foolish. He was here to do a job, to track down who had killed Neil, and even if this was a long shot leading to a dead end, he was going to see it through.

Another yawn, worse than the first, his eyes closing.

Jim sat up like he'd been stung on the backside, shook his head, saw the time on the dashboard: *twenty minutes? I was out for twenty minutes? How is that even possible?*

Jim stretched, rubbed his eyes, poured himself some tea, ate some cake, anything to keep himself awake. Even gave himself a gentle slap on the face.

Come on, Jim! Stick with it, now. For Neil, right?

Another yawn, only when Jim looked at the dashboard he saw that he'd lost another half-hour. How was that even possible? He hadn't even closed his eyes, he was sure of it!

He was knackered, needed to go home, but he couldn't give up now. *Just another couple of hours,* he thought, *give it that, then head back, and hope that Harry sees the funny side.* Not that there was one, he realised, seeing as he'd lied to his boss to go on what was looking to be nothing more than a wild goose chase.

Right, focus, Jim. Focus...

Jim forced himself to sit up straight, flexed his hands, his neck. He wasn't going to fall asleep again. And to make doubly sure of that, he slid open the window at his side and let in a flood of icy air that thrust inwards, bathing him in a chill that sent a shiver through him sharp as a dagger.

Shivering now, Jim got back to staring at the door. A light was on in the window to its side, so someone was home, or someone had left the light on and gone out. Hopefully, he'd find out which it was, sooner rather than later.

'Who are you, then?'

The voice was rasping and northern and caught Jim so by surprise that he jumped near high enough to hit his head on the Land Rover's roof.

Turning to see who owned the voice, Jim found himself staring at a man whose face was pockmarked like the surface of the moon, a gelled fringe hanging down onto his forehead like teeth from a comb. His eyes were sunken, dark things, cold and mean.

'What?'

'I said, who are you, then?' the man repeated. 'And don't be telling me porky pies, either, okay?'

'Porky pies? About what?'

'You're looking at those houses over there, aren't you?'

'I'm waiting for someone,' Jim said.

'Who?'

'An old friend.'

'Is that so, now?'

'Yes, it is.'

'Who?'

Jim wasn't liking where this was going and his eyes flitted from this man interrogating him to the house across the way.

'What's that got to do with you?'

The man leaned in, his face just through the window.

'I live here,' he said, 'so I think it's got a hell of a lot to do with me, wouldn't you say?'

Jim held the man's stare.

'So, who is it, then?' the man asked. 'Who are you here to see?'

'I've already told you,' Jim said. 'An old friend. He's supposed to be meeting me.'

'Is he now,' the man said. 'On a night like this? You sure about that?'

Jim nodded, fear starting to squeeze his stomach, his bowels.

'I'm not.'

'What?'

'I think you're lying.'

'Why would I lie to you? I don't even know who you are.'

The man grinned, and it wasn't a pleasant sight either, like staring into the face of a hungry predator.

'Now, that's a funny thing,' he said.

'What is?' Jim asked. 'Why is it funny?'

'Because,' the man said, 'I know who you are.'

'No, you don't,' Jim said, then reached down for the key that was still in the ignition, but as his fingers curled around it, the man ripped open the door and grabbed his hand.

'I wouldn't be doing that, now,' he said. 'Not while we're having our friendly little chat, here.'

Jim's eyes darted from the man's face to his hand, which was now gripped tightly around his own.

'Get off,' Jim said. 'Now. Or I'll call the police.'

'Will you now?' the man said.

'Yes,' replied Jim, tugging at his hand, finding it stuck fast in the man's grip. 'So, let go!'

The man leaned his face in further, close enough for Jim to smell the stink of tobacco and coffee and rot on his breath.

'You're police yourself,' he said. 'Aren't you?'

'Let go of my hand...'

'Thought so,' the man said. 'And I know who you're here to see as well. And he's not really an old friend, now, is he? No, he's not, not at all. And he's not best pleased that you've been out here spying on him. Because that's what you're doing, aren't you? Spying?'

Jim tried to snap his hand back, but the man's other hand grabbed him around the scruff of the neck, pinning him in his seat.

'It was a bad idea you coming out here, PCSO Metcalf,' he said, then he yanked Jim out of the Land Rover and threw him to the ground face first into the snow.

CHAPTER TWENTY-FOUR

Pushing through a door at the bottom of the stairs, Jadyn was hit by a wall of sound so thick that he could have probably chewed it. The assault on his ears was violent, but the rest of his body felt it, too, the terrifying conflagration of sound coming at them enough to send shockwaves through him, almost like he was being pushed back up the narrow stairs to the pub above.

At first, all he could see was darkness being twisted by swirling lights. Then, when his eyes adjusted, he could see the basement that he, Harry, and Jen were now in was small and rammed. People were jostling into each other, hands gripping bottles, and all of them facing the far wall of the space. The ceiling was low, lower than Jadyn had expected, and he guessed that was because it had been seriously sound-proofed so as to not disturb anyone upstairs or, indeed, anyone living close by.

Walking into the crowd, the sound from the band making it impossible to speak, Jadyn noticed how his feet seemed to not just stick to the floor, but crunch with every footstep. A quick look told him enough, that falling here would be bad, because the dance floor was slick with booze and fragments of broken glass. This was not a high-end establishment, that was for sure.

A tap on Jadyn's shoulder caused him to turn and find Harry leaning in close.

'Probably best we don't split up in here,' Harry said.

'Why?' Jadyn asked.

'Because I want this to go nice and smooth,' Harry said. 'We'll just head to the stage and when this song—I'm assuming it's a song, but I'll be honest, it sounds to me like they're killing someone up there—when it finishes and tell them we need to have a chat. Urgent, like.'

Jen leaned in. 'You think that'll work?'

'Haven't the faintest idea,' Harry said. 'Probably not, but I'm not going to stand around here all night while my ears bleed. We need this chat sharpish, agreed?'

Jadyn nodded, along with Jen. The music, if at all possible, grew even louder.

Pushing on, with Harry and Jen by his side, Jadyn started to make his way through the crowds. He thought back to his morning at the record fair, remembering what he'd managed to purchase—none of it actually expensive, because vinyl was silly money now, and it wasn't like he was earning loads as a police constable, but he'd still bagged some decent Funk and a couple of Soul LPs with covers to die for—and figured he wouldn't get a chance to listen to them for a few days.

A shove from his left knocked Jadyn from his thoughts and he turned to find himself staring into eyes that were more bloodshot than white.

'Sorry, mate,' the owner of the eyes said, a lad with buzz-cut hair, his shirt drenched in sweat.

Jadyn shook it off with a smile and a shrug and moved on, and the closer he drew to the stage the more the crowd was moving. At the back it was fairly stationary, people just listening, swaying, tapping their feet, drinking. A bit further in and the movements were more pronounced, arms joining in, beer being spilled. But ahead? Well, he'd been to gigs like this before. Plenty, actually. But he was wondering about Harry and what he was making of it. Stealing a look to his right, all he saw was Harry's scarred face and narrowed eyes; whatever the man was thinking it was, as always, impossible to tell.

A few steps further and Jadyn was in the thick of it now. He could see the band ahead of him, just two men, one with long hair, behind a microphone and armed with a guitar. Behind him, a man with no hair at all, kicking the living hell out of a drum kit. And between them and the band, the crowd was a jumping, spinning, unbalanced monster, swaying and leaping and pulsing, the air thick with the rich tang of beer and sweat and right in the background, vomit.

Pushing on, Jadyn was at the front now, except it was not a safe place to be. Arms were flailing, bodies crashing, and he felt as though he had walked into the middle of a perpetual earthquake, as the floor shook with it all.

'There! That way! Now!'

Harry's voice was enough to have Jadyn turn, see the man pointing to his left, to the edge of the stage and a door, then move.

Weaving as best he could through the masses, Jadyn heaved himself over to where Harry had directed, except when he got there he found that only Jen was with him.

'What's he doing?' Jen shouted, despite being close enough to Jadyn's ear to kiss it.

Jadyn looked over to see Harry standing in front of the singer and swiping his flattened hand across his own neck. With his other hand, he was displaying his warrant card.

'He's mad,' Jadyn said. 'He's actually asking them to cut the music!'

'Music?' Jen said. 'Is that what this is?'

'I've heard worse,' Jadyn said.

'How?'

Jadyn glanced back at Harry. He was now pointing over to where he and Jen were standing, the singer glaring at him, his sweaty hair clinging to his face in thick strands like he was staring through iron railings.

'I never thought two people could make that much noise,' Jen said.

'He's using loads of pedals and effects,' said Jadyn, pointing over towards the singer's feet. 'And the drummer's got some pads as well as a normal kit.'

'Sounds like you know what you're talking about.'

'I didn't always want to be in the police!' Jadyn said.

The sound from the band went up another notch, which was an achievement in itself, Jadyn thought, then he saw a disturbance in the crowd over by Harry. He was getting shoved now, people around him clearly getting frustrated with him trying to get the singer to shut it down and have a chat. The singer wasn't helping things either, leaning into Harry's face, tongue out, like he was trying to lick him.

'I don't think Harry's used to these kinds of places,' Jadyn said, as he saw the DCI finally give up and try to make his way over to them.

'Wait here,' Harry said, when he eventually arrived, and before Jadyn or Jen could do anything, he was through the door.

'Where's he going?' Jen asked.

Jadyn had a horrible feeling he knew the answer and when, a few seconds later, the sound of the band died like a plug had been pulled, Jadyn guessed that was exactly what had happened.

Harry came through the door again.

'That should get him to see sense,' Harry said.

Jadyn looked at his boss then over at the band. The drummer looked confused. The singer on the other hand looked furious. Then the crowd started to jeer and Jadyn had a horrible, sinking feeling.

'Maybe you should let them finish the gig first?' he suggested.

'No chance,' Harry said. 'This is a murder investigation. And I'm not going to stand around listening to whatever the hell that is, damaging my hearing for the rest of life, waiting.'

'He's coming over,' Jen said. 'They both are.'

Jadyn looked up to witness the singer, his long hair like wet string dancing in the air, leap off the small stage and throw himself at Harry.

'What the—' was about all Harry managed to say before he went crashing to the ground, the singer on top of him, and a wildness in his eyes clearly chemical in origin.

Instinct took over. Jadyn reached down to grab the singer, Jen at his side doing the same, when hands grabbed at him and heaved him back, turning him on his heels. Spinning round, he was eye-to-eye with a red-faced man full of rage.

'Ruin our night, would you, eh?' the man said, and catapulted his head forwards to crash into Jadyn's face. Jadyn moved quick enough to suffer only a glance on his chin, stepping sideways to allow the attack to fall past him and into the crowd.

More hands grabbed him and Jadyn shook them off.

'Police!' Jen shouted. 'We're police! Back off! Now!'

Someone didn't listen, went for Jen, who with cat-like agility, stepped out of the way of the assault. Then a roar barged its way into the moment as Harry rose from the ground, the singer on his back, arms wrapped around his neck.

'I think I've got his attention,' Harry said, then he prised the man's hands apart and a moment later had him with an arm trapped behind his back and walking towards the door. He then turned to face Jadyn and Jen as the sound of his phone chirruped in the air. Pulling it from his pocket, he raised an eyebrow as he looked at the screen, then said, 'You two mind grabbing the drummer?'

Leaving Harry to deal with the unexpected phone call and the singer, Jadyn turned back to the crowd. Around them, a circle had formed, the shout of the word *police*, and the way they had all dealt with their attackers, keeping any further trouble at bay, for now.

'Where's he gone?' Jen asked.

Jadyn looked over at the empty stage, caught movement at the other side of the room, and saw light glancing off a bald head.

'There!'

Jadyn pushed through the crowd.

'Police!' he shouted. 'We're police! Please stand to one side and let us through!'

The crowd, quite to Jadyn's surprise, mostly did as he asked. Which was a good thing really, because the door to the stairs leading back to the bar upstairs was swinging open and he saw the drummer making his escape.

With a final push, Jadyn was through and at the door.

Racing up the steps, the sound of Jen following behind, he was through the bar and out of the main doors barely a pace behind the drummer.

'Stop!' Jadyn yelled. 'Stop now! Stop!'

The drummer was doing anything but, though, sprinting through the snow.

Something white whizzed past Jadyn's face to explode on the back of the drummer's head. The shock of it making him stumble, slide, then crash to the ground in the snow.

Jadyn was on him in a beat.

'Nice shot,' he said, as Jen came up next to him to help drag the drummer to his feet.

'You hit me with a snowball!' the drummer complained, melting snow sloughing off his scalp and down his face. 'That's assault!'

'I don't think we did,' Jadyn said.

Jen stepped in. 'I saw some kids playing on the other side of the road. Maybe it was them?'

'Definitely,' Jadyn agreed. 'Because we're police officers, and the very last thing either of us would do is throw a snowball at someone trying to run away from us, now, is it?'

The drummer, on his feet now, looked at Jadyn, then at Jen, then finally back at Jadyn.

'What do you want, anyway?' he asked. 'What's this about? Why'd you ruin our gig?'

'Sounded to me like you were doing a good job of that yourself,' laughed Jen. 'But anyway, moving on, perhaps you can answer a question for me?'

'What's that, then?'

'When was the last time you went to church?'

CHAPTER TWENTY-FIVE

SNOW WAS IN JIM'S MOUTH AND IT TASTED OF SALT AND grit and muck and pain. He gagged, but something was pressing down on him and behind his closed eyes all he could see was fireworks bursting like it was November fifth.

'Think you can just roll on over here, do you, and spy on us, is that it, lad?'

The pressing increased and Jim's chest was struggling to heave in a breath, his throat sore from the effort already, panic gripping him vice tight and squeezing, just squeezing so hard.

'And for what? A dog? Really? God, some people really are proper thick, aren't they?'

The weight lifted but a sharp pain burst from a violent kick to his side and Jim tasted bile in his mouth. Was no one around to help? How was this even happening? But it was dark, wasn't it? he thought, as the pain radiated through him, and the weather wasn't exactly inviting. Which meant only one thing: he was alone. More alone than he'd ever been in his entire life.

Nausea twisting itself through his body, Jim made to get up onto all fours, but another kick swept in. This time, though, he was ready, and he rolled away from it, the wind from the booted foot fluttering his jacket.

'Come here, you little shit!'

But Jim wasn't about to do that. God, no! And neither was he about to stay and fight. He was up, on his feet, and legging it, muscles alive, legs pumping like steam pistons.

The snow and ice beneath his feet made the going tough, but he had a head start and that was enough. He'd no idea where he was going, just away, as far away as he could get, and quickly, so it was head down and on. Away.

Behind him, Jim heard footsteps making chase. But there weren't just two now, were there? Others had joined in. But who?

Risking a glance back, Jim saw three men chasing him now, and another two legging it towards him from the other side of the road, from an open door, the same door he'd been watching. So that made five in total, all after him, on a cold winter's night far from home. Which was enough to start him worrying that he might not see it again. Because that's how things like this ended, didn't they? Never well, someone dead at the end of it, tossed in a ditch to rot.

This was not good.

Jim turned back to look ahead, to focus on just keeping in front and hopefully finding somewhere to dodge out of the way, to hide, and give himself chance to catch a breath, and call for—

A stone dropped to the bottom of Jim's stomach. Who the hell could he call exactly? No one knew where he was! No one at all! And if he called Harry there'd be hell to pay, wouldn't there? What on earth had he been thinking? He was just a PCSO! He didn't have the training to cope with a situation like this! He was out of his depth and in very serious danger indeed. Whoever these people were, and whatever else it was that Timothy Renton was involved with, it clearly wasn't very good. They meant him harm. The worst kind. And to think he could have just stayed with the farm, taken it over from his dad. But no, he had to do something else, didn't he? Try something new, make a difference. Join the police! What an idiot.

The chasers weren't giving up, and that was a worry, because Jim wasn't sure how much longer he could keep running. He was fit, for sure, but sprinting was something different to just being able to keep going. And he was gasping for breath now, his legs on fire, and he could feel them slowing, feel his whole body starting to work like it was stuck in treacle.

Jim patted himself down, searching for his phone, found it, and called the only person he knew who could help, who was also the last person on earth that he wanted to call. But he had no choice.

'You'd better have a bloody good explanation for this!' the voice at the other end of the line growled low and deep. 'Lying to me? What the bloody hell were you thinking? Do you have any idea of how much tr—'

'Harry, I'm in trouble!'

'Too bloody right, you are!' Harry snapped back.

Jim could hear the sounds of other voices at Harry's end of the call, and the DCI's own voice echoing, like it was in a cave.

'No, I mean now!' Jim said, barely able to speak as he tried to keep ahead of the chasers. 'I need help, Harry!'

'What? What's up? What's wrong?'

Harry's voice had changed in a beat. Before it was angry and disappointed and confused. Now? Now it was hard, focused, and dangerous.

'What are you talking about, Jim? What have you done? What's wrong?'

'Timothy's house,' Jim said, slowing down even as he tried to speed up, to just keep his legs moving, then quickly blurting out the street and the house number. 'I was just watching it, that was all,' he explained. 'But then this bloke attacked me and now they're all chasing me!'

'Timothy's house? You mean Timothy Renton, the dog thief? What the hell are you there for? And who's they?'

'The cigarettes!' Jim gasped. 'The solicitor. I had to check. No one was taking it seriously and I couldn't wait. I had to see. Make sure.'

Slower still, they were gaining on him...

'You're not making any sense!' Harry said. 'Slow down!'

'I can't slow down!' Jim snapped back, his voice a rasp. 'I'm running, Harry! Right now I'm running, and they're after me and they're going to catch me and then I don't know what will happen! I was at Timothy Renton's house! I'm in the shit, Harry! Properly in the shit!'

'Right, Jim, I'm on my way!'

Jim went to answer but something came out in front of him, swinging around at neck height, and the next thing he knew, he was flying, his voice stuck in his throat. Then the ground came up bullet-quick and snatched away what little wind he had left, deflating his lungs like popped balloons.

Jim could hear Harry's voice far off, still calling his name, shouting for him to answer. Then nothing.

'This yours, is it?'

Jim looked up through blurry eyes to see his phone in the hands of a stranger, the screen smashed beyond repair.

'Oops.'

Then hands grabbed him, dragged him to his feet, and Jim knew that whatever was coming his way, none of it would be good.

CHAPTER TWENTY-SIX

HARRY WAS FIVE MILES INTO THE JOURNEY FROM Catterick to Darlington and didn't have a plan. Not yet. All he had was the memory of Jim's voice in his head and the panic ripping it apart. Right now, that was enough.

The sensible police part of his brain was telling him to call for backup, because he had no idea what he was about to face, no idea at all, and going at this on his own just wasn't sensible. The warrior soldier part of his brain was inclined to agree. Walking into a situation alone that he had no idea about was tantamount to suicide. A recce needed to be done first, get eyes on the target, work out what was going on, how many X-Rays he was dealing with, what state Jim was in, and only then would an extraction be actioned.

Then there was the Harry part of his brain. And that was the dangerous part, the dark and brooding animal which he kept chained up, and for good reason. Because when it got loose—and it hadn't done so in years, not since that time in Afghanistan—bad things happened. Very bad things indeed.

Harry was gripping the steering wheel so tight that his

knuckles had turned his skin almost translucent. He was going as fast as he dared, which considering what he was driving, wasn't exactly fast, and judging by the black smoke billowing out of the back, the engine really wasn't happy about it at all.

Following what had happened at the cellar venue under the pub, the very clear case of assaulting a police officer, namely Harry himself, by the singer, and the attempt at legging it by the drummer, Harry had been given no choice but to arrest them both. All he'd wanted to do was talk to them, bring them in for a chat, but their behaviour had warranted a stronger approach. Then, with Jim's phone call, he'd been put in a very difficult position, and he was still running through it all, as he tried to focus on the road ahead, which was clear of snow, but still treacherous.

Firstly, he had to go to Jim's aid. That was a given. The lad was in trouble, arguably of his own making, but still, Harry's duty was to help him, as his boss, as a serving police officer, as a friend.

Secondly, he had a murder investigation to be getting on with, the day was already night, and two possible suspects now needed to be questioned. He couldn't do both. Which was why, at the same time as Harry was heading off to help Jim, his two police constables, Jen and Jadyn, were now on their way to Harrogate in the police Land Rover, with the two less than happy members of Geryon in the back. It had been a long day, for sure, so Harry had put in a call to Gordy to head over and meet them there. She was rested a little from her evening and could take over. All sorted, they would then all have a chance at a rest before heading back to Harrogate at some point the following day to question them. And Harry figured a bit of time in a cell might give them both pause for thought.

Thirdly, and with the Land Rover needed by Jen and Jadyn, Harry had commandeered Geryon's van. The reek of the inside was an experience in itself and despite the biting wind, Harry was driving along with the window open. The air was rich and tangy, a mix of cigarettes, air freshener, sweat, dust, and right at the back of it, driving it all forward, the unmistakable aroma of cannabis. The interior décor was a demonstration of what can be done with leopard print faux fur and far too many plastic skulls. Also, and possibly most annoyingly, the keyring was a huge jangling thing comprising a metal chain and a fake shrunken head, and it kept smacking against Harry's knee like it was knocking at a door and trying to get in. And finally, Harry had to work out how he was going to play out what he was heading into, which was little more than the unknown.

Slowing down for a roundabout ahead, Harry pondered his options. The sensible thing to do was to call it in, go through the proper channels, but there were problems with that. He had no idea what danger Jim was in, or what the situation was on the ground. And the sudden arrival of the police, sirens and lights splitting the night, could be a problem. Plus, questions would be raised immediately.

He wasn't worried for himself at all, but for his PCSO. Jim had acted like an idiot, yes, gone off at half-cock, and ended up in a bad situation. Harry had no doubt how Detective Superintendent Swift would view it, and that the path he would take them down was career-destroying.

So, what could he do? What other options were there? All he had was a headful of weariness, a band van reeking of a bad night at Glastonbury loaded with musical instruments, and an address that was, at that very moment, just coming into view as Harry eased the van slowly into a narrow street lined on either side with Victorian terrace houses, spotting Jim's Land Rover parked up, just ahead, the driver's door ajar.

Lights off, Harry took stock. The house corresponding to the address he had been given by Gordy looked ordinary. But then at first glance, the street was exactly that and nothing else. It gave nothing away as to the people who lived on it.

Cars lined one side only, the same side as the target house, all covered in snow. Windows had curtains pulled against the night. It was the kind of street, Harry thought, where everyone kept themselves to themselves, where what the residents valued most above all was to be left alone, to not be disturbed. Which was just enough to start an idea forming.

Harry knew that the one thing he had to his advantage was the element of surprise. He wasn't in a police vehicle so no one would be sounding any alarm bells, not yet, anyway. And the vehicle he was in kind of looked like it fitted in rather well. What he needed was a closer look.

Climbing out of the van, Harry hunched his coat up against the cold, and went for a walk. He moved with just enough purpose to make sure he didn't look like he was doing anything other than trying to get somewhere else quickly. And when he came to the house in question, he slowed down just enough to cadge a look through the window, and to check if he could hear anything. Though the window had curtains drawn, he'd spotted a crack and through it, he saw a television and nothing else. As to sound, all he could make out was the wind gusting down the road.

Right, Harry thought, time to see who's home...

In situations like this, Harry knew that there were always two very different approaches. One was to be all quiet and sneaky about it. The other was to be brazen. Harry went for option two and after a quick search around the van for a few things, was outside, and standing opposite the house. He then furnished himself with a snowball made mainly of ice, crushed it till the thing was almost solid, and hurled it at the door of the house.

Nothing.

So, Harry did the same again. And again.

The door to the house was yanked open. Harry didn't move, just stared, as a man moved into the street, looked left, right, then directly at him.

'Did you just throw a snowball at this door?'

'Sorry, I can't hear you,' Harry said, holding a hand up to his ear then giving a shrug. 'Too windy.'

'I asked you a question! Did you just lob a snowball at this door?'

'I'm waiting for someone,' Harry called over.

'You're what?'

'Yes, it is rather cold, isn't it? Brrrr!'

The man stared for a moment at Harry, then went back to the door, slamming it shut behind him.

Harry lobbed another ball. This time the door was open in a heartbeat and two men were standing there.

'What's your problem, mate?'

'I'm not your mate.'

'Well, then, why don't you just fuck off, eh?'

Harry picked up another snowball, threw it, and it hammered into the face of one of the men, sending him sprawling.

The other man took a moment to realise what had

happened, then bolted after Harry, turning the air blue with his swearing.

Harry legged it, down to the end of the road and around a corner, only as soon as he was there he stopped and dropped to his knees in the snow.

The other man raced around the corner only to be rugby-tackled to the ground. Then, with Harry's bulk on top of him, he found his arms suddenly pulled behind his back.

Harry tied the wrists together with a guitar cable he had in his pocket from the van, checked that the other man wasn't coming after him, then tied his feet together as well.

'How many?' Harry asked.

'You're dead!'

'How many?' Harry asked again. 'In the house.'

'I'm not telling you anything!'

Harry held up a hand, three fingers showing.

'Three?'

The man smiled, cold and thin, the face of a snake.

Harry added a finger.

'Four?'

The same smile.

'What about five?'

The faintest of flickers of movement in the corner of the man's eye.

'And is there someone in there who shouldn't be?' Harry asked.

'You're mental.'

Harry leaned in.

'You have no idea,' he said, then stuffed the man's mouth with a pair of clearly very well worn and unwashed boxer shorts that he'd found in the van.

Standing, and leaving the man to his horrified silence,

Harry made his way back around the corner and towards the house. The door was shut so the man he'd hit with the snowball had clearly gone back inside rather than wait out in the cold for his mate to return.

Harry walked back to the van, opened the side door, then took hold of a very large cymbal, which was attached to the boom arm of a stand and a pair of drumsticks. Then he walked over to the house, knocked on the door, and waited.

Footsteps.

The door opened.

'Hello, there!' Harry said, then walked away from the door, smashing the living hell out of the cymbal with the drumsticks.

The sound smashed its way up and down the snow-covered street, loud and violent and out of control. Curtains were pulled, windows yanked open, then the shouts came.

'The hell are you doing, man?'

'Someone shut him up!'

'Call the police!'

A door opened from another house and out walked a somewhat overweight middle-aged man in tracksuit bottoms, a vest, and Wellington boots.

'You want to shut that up before I make you?'

Harry kept on at the cymbal like he was doing his all to embed the drumsticks in its metallic surface.

'Did you not hear me?'

Harry nodded at the house.

'They told me to do it,' he said.

'You what?'

'Told me to do this to wake you up. Thought it was funny. Ha ha, right?'

He smashed the cymbal again.

'Funny? How the hell is any of this funny?'

'Said you were funny actually,' Harry said. 'Stupid, too, I think. A proper idiot.'

'What?'

'The actual words he used were *"thick as pig shit and twice as ugly."'*

Another smash of the cymbal and Harry saw rage starting to burn in the man's eyes.

'Yeah, definitely all of that,' he said. 'Reckons everyone on this street is an idiot and that he's *the man*, if you know what I mean.'

'Did he, now?'

The man slapped the cymbal from Harry's grip, pointed at him as a warning, then turned towards the house, on the way, shouting over for some of his neighbours to join him from a number of other doors which had swung open to welcome in the cold.

Harry followed.

At the house, the argument was short-lived and went from verbal to violent before anyone really had a chance to put across their point of view. And coming to the rescue of the first, others piled out of the house to join in the brawl.

In the confusion, Harry slipped through the door. He checked upstairs first, found nothing, then downstairs, and found Jim in a back room, bruised and scared and tied to a chair.

'Harry...'

'To the rescue, it seems,' Harry said, and quickly had Jim out of his bindings. 'You good to walk?'

Jim nodded.

Harry said, 'Behind me, okay? Hold onto me and don't stop. Understand?'

Another nod.

'Just a mo', though,' Harry said, and removed a package of something wrapped in plastic from his jacket, and stuffed it deep inside a tired-looking sofa which was up against the wall.

'What was that?' Jim asked, grabbing hold of Harry's jacket as the DCI turned to the door.

'A gift to the local police force, I think,' Harry said, then moved off, and fast.

Out of the room and down the hall towards the front of the house, Harry pulled Jim. A shout came from behind and he recognised the voice from the previous Friday. Timothy Renton.

'Hey, what are you doing?'

Harry felt Jim tugged backwards, heaving them to a halt. Snapping round, Harry came face-to-face with Timothy once again.

'You!' the weaselly man spat.

'Surprise!' Harry said and with the drumsticks still in his hand, jabbed them hard into Timothy's solar plexus. Timothy coughed, went white, and dropped to the floor, gasping for breath and retching.

'Grab on!' Harry said.

Jim held on tight and Harry charged onwards again, into what had now turned into a full-on street brawl in the snow. Except that as they made their way around it Harry couldn't help but think how pathetic it all looked, as at least a dozen men of varying ages, sizes, and numbers of cigarettes a day rolled around in the snow, grunting and groaning and slapping each other.

Across the road, Harry lobbed Jim into the van, jumped into the driver's seat, and had the key in the ignition as

Timothy appeared in the doorway of the house, pointing at them and yelling obscenities, trying to get the attention of his friends, but to no avail.

With a wave, Harry eased out of where he had parked, and drove away, making sure to send a wave to the man around the corner, who was free of the cable around his ankles and looking distinctly upset about everything. Harry was pretty sure his smile didn't help things either. As the man saw him, surprise shook him, and he made to make chase, slipped, and landed on his arse.

A few miles on, Jim finally broke the silence.

'Harry,' he said. 'I'm... sorry.'

'And so you bloody well should be!' Harry said back, keeping his eyes on the road.

'And thank you,' Jim said then, his voice cracking. 'For coming to get me.'

Harry glanced across at the PCSO to see him leaning against the passenger door window, pain etched into his face, tears in his eyes as he stared off into the middle distance.

'There was never any question,' Harry said, and drove on, taking them both home.

CHAPTER TWENTY-SEVEN

Monday morning arrived in much the same way as a drunk and unpopular relative at a wedding: loud, smelly and unavoidable.

Having dropped Jim off back home at an hour no one was happy to see, and after a brief chat with his mum and dad, Harry had managed to get back to his flat and drag himself into bed. However, he was still awake and up at eight in the morning regardless, courtesy of his brain refusing to accept that what he really needed was a rest.

At the office, Harry had found Liz and Jadyn already off on separate jobs, while Jen was still doing a phone around of the contact list from the concert. Matt had filled him in on various bits and bobs about who they'd managed to get in touch with so far. The board had plenty of notes on it, and names, too, but it was a bit of a jumble. They'd be sorting that out soon enough, by Jadyn no doubt, but right now it was important that everyone just cracked on with what needed doing, and that meant for Matt and the team to follow up what they had been doing with tracing names, contacting people, and going to chat with anyone who they thought might be able to help with their enquiries.

Harry's gut was telling him that whoever had murdered Gareth had been at the concert, because what had happened, it hadn't been random. It had been elaborate and weird and violent, and he just couldn't see it being the act of some passing killer stopping off during their wintery holiday in the dales to do over a celebrated singer simply because they didn't like his music.

'And you're happy to continue with that today?' Harry asked. 'Interviews and whatnot?'

'No problem at all, boss,' Matt said. 'We've got a good number of names to go talk to, starting with the band, and then there are Gareth's old choir friends. The ones in the photos at the back of the church.'

'They were at the concert, then?'

'All of them, and at the pub,' Matt said. 'They're most of them local, so it shouldn't be too much hassle.'

Harry remembered Anna telling him the same about the friends and the pub.

'We've got the list of key holders to go through as well,' Matt continued. 'Though I've a feeling that over the years there's been more keys given out and lost than there are names on it.'

'Well, just do what you can,' Harry said. 'We'll be expecting photographs and the report from Sowerby at some point, so we'll look through that when they arrive. And if, I mean *once* you've a list of people to have a proper chat with, just let me know how they go.'

'Oh, I will boss, you can count on it.'

'Anything else going on?' Harry asked.

Matt looked thoughtful for a moment, rubbing his chin.

'It's still snowy out,' he said.

'Very observant.'

'Actually, it's worth being aware of,' said Matt. 'There's always the possibility of some hill walkers taking on a winter's walk and getting caught out. Then there'll be farmers out on the fells and in their fields, checking on stock. Plus we're bound to have a few prangs, aren't we? Most folk know how to drive in these conditions, but there's still going to be a few accidents, people drifting into a wall or each other.'

'So, a busy week, then,' Harry said.

'Nowt a bit of tea and cake won't sort.' Matt smiled.

'What about the cheese?' Harry asked.

'Bit too early, even for me,' Matt laughed. 'Oh, and I'm going to give the vicar over in Askrigg a call as well. Check she's all okay and that the clean-up is happening. And just so you know, news has already leaked out about what happened. Flowers are starting to be left at the church gate apparently.'

'Really?'

'Look...'

Matt showed Harry a photo on his phone showing a small collection of bunches of flowers in the snow.

'Anna sent that to me earlier, which is why I thought it wise to check on her later. This isn't going to be an easy one for her to deal with.'

'No, it isn't,' Harry said, then added, 'You know what this means, don't you?'

'The press?'

Harry gave a nod.

'Well, we'll just have to deal with that when it happens,' Matt said, then suggested, 'I reckon Swift is due a call about what's been going on anyway, wouldn't you think?'

Harry caught the hint of what Matt was suggesting and grinned.

'You know, that's not a bad idea at all! Anything from Jadyn and Jen?'

'Jen will be in later on. Jadyn's been called out to a snowball fight that got out of hand over in Leyburn.'

'What? How?'

'Well,' Matt said, 'there's a little bit of friendly rivalry between this end of the dale and down dale, like.'

'So?'

'So, the roads are clear now, and the school bus managed to make its slow way there, only to then be ambushed by a whole group of kids as it pulled into the car park at Wensleydale School.'

Harry tried not to smile.

'What happened?'

'Like I said, it got a bit out of hand,' Matt said. 'Everyone on the bus piled out and retaliated. Wasn't much the teachers could do as the whole school then erupted into an all-out war.'

'And Jadyn's been called in, why?' Harry asked, leaning in.

'Basically, to give everyone a damned good bollocking!' Matt said. 'One of the bus windows was smashed thanks to some snowballs being a little heavier on account of the grit and stones in them. Some kids had glasses smashed. I don't think anyone was injured though.'

'Jadyn will be loving that, I'm sure,' Harry said, imagining the young police constable standing in front of a few hundred teenagers.

'So, what are you on with, then?' Matt asked. 'No, wait, I remember now. You're off to Harrogate, right?'

Harry nodded.

'Meeting Gordy there,' he said. 'Have a chat with our two suspects. Apparently, they weren't much help last night. Hopefully, they'll be more communicative in the light of day.'

'You think they're involved?'

Harry thought for a moment.

'Seems a bit of a coincidence that there's all those occult symbols at the crime scene, and there's those two turning up a few hours before talking about Satan.'

'You don't sound convinced though,' Matt said.

Harry shrugged, pushed himself to his feet.

'Right, I'll be off,' he said.

'Don't forget to call Swift,' Matt said.

'Oh, I won't,' said Grimm, then made his way out of the office, phone already in his hand.

WITH HARRY GONE, Matt walked over to the wall where the board was already starting to look a little full. It was a disorganised and tangled mess currently, with names and details jotted down by each of them at different points that morning. With Jadyn busy over at the school, Gordy meeting up with Harry, that left Matt with Liz and Jen. Well, it would've done if one of them hadn't had to head off to a traffic incident on the road out towards Ribblehead Viaduct. Liz had volunteered first, clearly keen to get back out into the snow on her bike.

'Jen?'

The police constable looked up from the laptop, her phone at her ear.

'Oh, sorry, didn't realise you were still on the phone,' Matt said.

'No answer,' Jen said, putting the phone down. 'Not many to check now.'

'Anything interesting?'

Jen gave a shrug. 'Everyone's backing up the sequence of events from the concert.'

'Nothing else?'

'Not really. I've spoken with a few B-list celebrities, which was a little odd. Everyone seems to have just gone along to see Gareth, enjoyed the drinks and canapes at the end, then gone home. And fair enough with this weather. Nice to know folk are sensible.'

'The roads aren't that bad,' Matt said.

'So?'

'So what?' Matt said.

'So, you were about to ask me something,' Jen said. 'At least, I think you were. Unless you just like to say my name out loud at random now again, which I can understand.'

Matt had to take a moment to think, then he remembered.

'Oh, right, yes, I was going to ask if you were busy.'

'Well, I won't be in about five minutes,' Jen said. 'Why?'

'I think it's time we interviewed the band,' Matt said.

'Sounds dangerous,' Jen said.

'Oh, it is,' said Matt. Then he leaned in and said in hushed tones, 'They could be very, very pretentious...'

CHAPTER TWENTY-EIGHT

THE CONVERSATION WITH DETECTIVE SUPERINTENDENT Graham Swift was short, to the point, and finished off with Swift feeling important. Harry was pretty sure that the fact they were dealing with the death of a celebrity was what swung it, as Swift had almost tripped over himself to volunteer to be the point of contact for any and all communications with the press. To that end, he wanted a frank and detailed discussion about the case with Harry later that day, once he was done over in Harrogate. And if he had time, he might even pop over and meet him there.

Now, though, Harry was sitting in an interview room with the lead singer of Geryon, a Mr Andrew Robinson, who was insisting on being called by the pseudonym he went by as singer, guitarist, composer, and screamer of Geryon, that being Charon, having named himself after the ferryman of Hades in Greek mythology. Harry wasn't exactly playing ball.

'Right then, Andrew—'

'I don't answer to that name. I'm Charon, son of Erebus, and I ferry the souls of the dead over the River Styx!'

'You're a lot of things, Andrew,' Harry said. 'A lot of things...'

'And what's that supposed to mean?'

'Plenty, actually,' Harry said and looked at the notes in front of him. 'Turns out you've a reputation when it comes to being a bit of a naughty boy, haven't you, Andrew?'

'Charon...'

Harry ignored him.

'Driving without insurance, disturbing the peace, drunk and disorderly. And I think we can add to that assaulting a police officer, can't we?'

'I didn't assault you,' Andrew said. 'It was part of the art.'

'The art?'

'The show,' Andrew said.

'Oh, you mean whatever it was you were doing last night.'

'It's art,' Andrew said. 'You wouldn't understand. It's too dark, too beyond your vibration.'

Harry's eyes widened as Andrew made weird shapes in the air with his hands.

'Moving on,' Harry said, glancing at Gordy, who rolled her eyes. 'Like I said, we can add assaulting a police officer. Oh, and possession!'

'What?'

Harry brought out a large parcel wrapped in plastic.

'Recognise this, do you, Andrew?'

Now that it was out of his pocket, and even though it was wrapped in plastic, the smell from the cannabis was very evident.

'What's that, then?' Andrew asked.

'Well, it's not your average approach to snacks bought for a long journey, that's for sure,' Harry said. 'You see, we brought your van in and had a look around.'

'You can't do that! You don't have a warrant!'

'Someone's been watching too much television, haven't they, Detective Inspector Haig?'

Gordy nodded. 'Did DCI Grimm show you his warrant card when he asked you to speak to him at your concert?'

'Yes, but that doesn't count!' Andrew said. Then turned to the solicitor and said, 'I didn't know what he wanted! This isn't right, is it? I'll sue! That's what I'll do! I'll sue the police!'

Gordy spoke again, her soft Highlands accent making her every word sound reasonable. 'Once a police officer has shown you their warrant card, which is their ID, they can search you, anything you're carrying, and your vehicle.'

'No, that's not right,' Andrew said, shaking his head, his eyes on the solicitor. 'Tell them!'

'I'm afraid she's entirely correct,' the solicitor said.

Andrew's face did a good impression of not fitting very well on his skull, like it was trying to wrestle itself off and escape, as he turned back to face Harry, confusion and anger in his eyes.

'Someone must have put it there,' Andrew said.

'Anyway, moving on,' Harry said, 'because right now, that not-insubstantial bag of weed is going to haunt you for quite a while I'm sure, shall we go back to Saturday night?'

Andrew leaned forward on his elbows and stared at Harry through his long, black fringe.

'We were told to do it.'

'What?'

'We were told to do it,' repeated Andrew. 'That's why we

were there.'

Harry couldn't believe what he was hearing.

'You mean someone told you to go to the concert at the church?'

'Yes,' Andrew said, a smile creasing his mouth.

'Who?' Harry asked. 'Who told you?'

Andrew's smile was suddenly all teeth and no charm.

'Satan!' he said, thrusting his arms in the air, fingers outstretched. 'Satan commanded us! And we claimed that place in his name!'

'Like bollocks he did!' Harry roared, and Gordy stepped in.

'Who told you about the concert?'

'Satan!'

'Why were you there, Andrew? Why did you gatecrash it?'

'To glorify Satan!'

'I'm not listening to this horseshit nonsense,' Harry said and stared at the solicitor. 'And I suggest you have a word with your client before I start to lose my patience!'

'Is that a threat?'

'Too right it's a bloody threat!'

Gordy stepped in once again, showing Andrew a photograph of Gareth Jones she'd printed from the Internet.

'Do you know this man?'

Andrew stared at the photograph and gave a nod.

'He is Satan's enemy!' he said. 'You all are! Ha! Flies and lice, that's all any of you are!'

'Dear God, do we have to listen to this?' Harry grumbled.

'And where were you that night,' continued Gordy, 'between the hours of eleven pm and approximately three am?'

Andrew's smile was fixed to his face and Harry was forcing himself to not just reach out and slap it right off.

'I am the devil,' Andrew said, 'and I am here to do the Devil's work!'

'You're a pillock,' Harry muttered.

'Answer the question, please,' Gordy said.

'I just did.'

'So, you are unable to confirm where you were between those hours?'

Andrew shook his head slowly.

Gordy then showed some other printouts.

'These are screenshots from your YouTube channel,' she said. 'Can you explain what they are?'

Andrew leaned forward for a quick look.

'Gigs, churches burning,' he said. 'Fun, right? Look at the flames!'

'I watched some of the videos you've posted,' Gordy said. 'In one you spend the whole gig holding an upside-down cross, claiming that you are a demon sent by Hell.'

'Because I am.'

'The burning churches, they're videos from other pages,' Gordy said. 'Black Metal bands from Norway. That was a while ago now, but a lot of churches were burned.'

'Good!' Andrew said. 'Because that's all they are, fuel for the fires of Hell!'

'Is that why you were at the concert?' Gordy asked. 'To post a video to add to your collection? Something for the fans?'

Andrew said nothing, just stared.

'Your friend, the drummer?' Gordy said. 'He filmed the whole thing, didn't he? We have witness statements to that effect. And we have his phone, obviously.'

'So?'

'So,' Gordy said, 'and allow me a moment here to just explore an idea, but I think all of this, your name, the way you dress, turning up at the church, this whole Satan thing, it's all about image, isn't it? Notoriety? That's what you crave? I mean, you don't actually believe any of it, do you, all the occult stuff?'

Harry saw a flicker in Andrew's smile as it weakened.

'We are Satan's soldiers—' Andrew said, but Gordy was in before he could continue with whatever it was he wanted to say next.

'No, you're not, Andrew,' Gordy said, her voice firm now. 'What you actually are is a drama school dropout, low on cash and high on your own self-importance, with well-off parents, who for some reason keep funding your every whim, and all you really want, all you really truly crave, Andrew, is fame, and by any means necessary!'

Andrew's smile weakened further.

'You want notoriety,' Gordy said, the Highlands in her voice now blowing a wind cold enough to freeze his blood. 'You want to be known as this supposed dark, satanic band. So, what I need to know, is how and why you were there on Saturday night, Andrew. How you found out about it, why you went there in the first place, and where you were afterwards.'

'And why should I tell you anything?'

'Because,' Gordy said, and this time Harry saw a keenness in her eyes that a tiger on the hunt would've been proud of, 'sometime after the concert, Gareth Jones was murdered. And right here, right now, I can't help but think we're looking at suspect number one.'

CHAPTER TWENTY-NINE

'So, these photos, then,' Matt said, placing them on the table between himself and Jen, and the final members of the band to be interviewed, Mick Johnson and Lisa Shaw, who were sitting across from them in a small, cosy lounge with the largest fireplace Matt had ever seen. They were at Lisa's parents' house, having arranged to stay there for a few days after the concert.

'Yes, they're from years ago,' Lisa said. 'Seems like yesterday though, you know?'

'Time's a funny thing,' Matt said.

'It is, indeed,' agreed Mick, 'but I think we've answered all your questions, and Lisa is really quite upset about what's happened.'

'I'm sure,' Matt said. 'It's a very upsetting thing.'

'And like we said earlier, the whole thing was her idea in the first place, to do the concert here. So, there's no reason on earth why she would have anything to do with any of it.'

'Yes, and we've noted that,' Matt said. 'We just need to

ask a few more questions to help us get to the bottom of what actually happened. I'm sure you understand?'

'No, of course, I really do,' Mick said. But—'

'Also, we've actually only been here for a few minutes,' said Jen. 'And you've done most of the talking.'

'But there's not much else to say, surely,' Mick said. 'What else do you need?'

'First of all, can you tell us where you were between the hours of eleven pm and approximately three am?'

'In bed!' Mick said. 'Where else do you think we were?'

'And you have witnesses?'

'Yes, each other!' Mick said. 'We were in bed. Together.'

'Righto, fair enough,' said Matt, jotting something down in his notebook. He also noticed how Lisa seemed rather nervous, fiddling with something in her hands, like it was calming her, perhaps. Though what it was, Matt hadn't the faintest idea. And he was working very hard to not just reach over and take whatever it was from her hand just to get her to stop.

'We're engaged, you see,' Mick said, and Matt noticed a change in the man's tone, from anger and indignation, to one of pride, though it was a little more than that, he thought. The way he said it was almost as though he was telling them that he'd won. But then perhaps he had, Matt thought, so there was no point thinking less of him. Not yet, anyway.

'It was a bit of a spur of the moment thing, if I'm honest,' Mick said. 'Didn't even have a ring, so I used a drinking straw.'

Lisa showed her hand, and there on the ring finger was the red-and-white stripe of a plastic straw, tied in a knot.

'That from the pub?' Jen asked.

Lisa shook her head. 'Parents had some,' she said. 'We'd

planned to stay here a few days after the concert, anyway, so here we are, and engaged. I can hardly believe it! I know Gareth would've been so happy for us, too.'

Lisa's voice cracked then, and she began to sob.

'It's alright,' Matt said, 'just take your time.'

Lisa wiped her eyes.

'Just doesn't seem fair though, you know? I mean, yes, he had an amazing career, but he'd had it rough, too.'

'The loss of his wife, you mean?' Matt said.

Lisa nodded.

'I was on holiday at the time,' Lisa said. 'South of France with my parents. They'd taken me away to cheer me up after another relationship went south.'

'We weren't together then, you see,' Mick said. 'We met a couple of years ago, doing some work for the BBC.'

'I remember the day, everything about it,' Lisa said. 'We were in the garden, having this amazing barbeque, just myself, Mum, and Dad, when I get this text from Chris, telling me about it.'

'Chris?' Jen said. 'Oh, you mean Christopher Middleton.'

'Yes,' Lisa said. 'It was the shock of it, I think. They were both in hospital, you see, after what happened.'

'And what was it that happened exactly?' Matt asked.

'Stolen car,' Jen said. 'Drove into them. The driver was never found. Gareth survived. His wife didn't.'

'It was awful,' Lisa said. 'I don't think he ever really recovered.'

'No, I can't see how he would,' Matt said.

For a moment, everyone was quiet, then Matt coughed and attempted to get things back on track.

'So, you were with each other between the hours mentioned?' he asked.

'Yes,' Mick said, his voice hissing through his teeth.

'Can I ask about your relationship with the deceased?' Matt asked.

'He's a, I mean, he was an old friend,' Lisa said, and Matt could see how upset she was, as well as hear it in her voice. 'The photos show that. We've known each other since we were kids.'

'So, you knew him before all the fame and fortune, then,' Matt said.

'I did, yes.' Lisa smiled, then she added something extra, her voice almost wistful, Matt thought. 'In fact, if it hadn't been for all of that, what Gareth did, I wouldn't have ended up becoming a classical pianist.'

'How's that, then?' Jen asked.

'How's what?'

The question had clearly caught Lisa off guard.

'You were saying about why you took up piano, I think,' Jen prompted.

Lisa nodded.

'I played the piano anyway,' she explained. 'Then Gareth hit the big time and part of me just wanted to keep up, so that's what I did.'

'You became a professional pianist to follow him?'

Matt saw Lisa blush.

'Well, if you put it like that, it does sound a bit ridiculous, but yes, I suppose so.'

'Were you ever anything more than friends?' Matt asked.

'Well, of course they weren't!' Mick said, jumping in. 'It was only ever platonic. A schoolgirl crush, really.'

'It's a long time ago, now, Detective,' Lisa said. 'We're all a lot older.'

Matt jotted down a few notes.

'And what about yourself?' Jen asked, glancing now at Mick, and taking him rather by surprise.

'He was an amazing talent,' Mick replied. 'I was lucky to have been able to perform with him at the concert and on his new album.'

Matt noted how that wasn't exactly an answer to the question.

A laugh came from Lisa then and Matt saw that she was holding one of the photos, looking at the back.

'We signed it!' Lisa said. 'I'd totally forgotten! How amazing is that?'

Matt looked over to see lots of faded, child-like writing on the back of the photograph.

'May I see?'

'Of course,' Lisa said, then handed the photo over.

Matt had a cursory look, not really sure why, now that the photo was with him, so handed it to Jen sharpish. As he did so, a niggling thought then caught in his mind and he nearly asked for the photo back, except Jen spoke then and knocked whatever it was from his brain.

'Now, the two who gatecrashed,' Jen said. 'What can you tell us about them?'

'They nearly ruined the concert,' Lisa said, her words spitting like cobra venom. 'Pair of proper idiots, for sure. Who does that? Have they no respect?'

'Oh, I couldn't agree more.' Matt nodded, still trying hard not to say anything about Lisa's fidgeting hands. 'Had you seen them before?'

'You're having a laugh, surely!' Mick said. 'At what point would we ever in our lives have any interest in whatever it is people like that do to musical instruments to make them sound as though they're in actual pain!'

'They're a band, then?' Lisa asked.

'Very much so,' Jen explained. 'I've done a bit of looking around, you see.'

'How can two people be a band?' Mick asked. 'Ridiculous!'

'The White Stripes are a two-piece,' Matt pointed out. 'Royal Blood. The Black Keys. The Proclaimers.'

'Well, listen to you!' Jen said, raising her eyebrows at Matt.

'Blame Jadyn,' Matt said. 'Give him a few spare minutes and he'll talk you to death about music.'

'They're not signed, though,' Jen added. 'According to their website, they're looking for a deal. They've done a few indie things, pressed an EP, and they've got a pretty good following on social media, which considering their sound and image, is quite the surprise.'

'Not really,' Lisa said. 'It's a nightmare trying to get signed now.'

'Sounds like you know what you're talking about.'

Lisa shrugged, then she seemed to jump forward like she'd had an electric shock.

'You okay?' Mick asked.

'I've just remembered something,' Lisa said.

'What?' asked Matt.

'Saturday night, at the concert. It was the mention of getting a record deal that reminded me!'

'Of what?'

Lisa leaned forward.

'I saw someone there who really shouldn't have been.'

'Who?'

'Nicholas Straub,' Lisa said.

'And who's he, then?' Matt asked, at least he thought he

did, but really he was only seeing Lisa's fidgeting and he was going to have to say something soon for sure.

'Someone who really hated Gareth,' Lisa said. 'He's the record producer who blamed him for his marriage collapsing. That's what jogged my memory. Don't know why I didn't mention it before, you know, when you phoned me? Sorry.'

'Well, you've mentioned it now,' Matt said, before asking Jen, 'Do we have this Mr Nicholas Straub's details?'

'We do,' Jen said. 'But I don't think you're going to like it.'

'And why's that?'

'He's not exactly local.'

'How much not exactly?'

'Lives in London,' Jen explained.

'Ah.'

Lisa was fidgeting again.

'Do you mind if I ask you to stop that, please?' Matt asked. 'Just need to gather my thoughts, that's all.'

'Stop what?'

'Playing with whatever that is in your hands,' Matt said, sure his voice was coming across a little snappy now, which was unlike him, for sure, but sometimes, fidgeting really did wind him up.

Lisa raised a hand to show a couple of keys, the fob still in her palm, though Matt could see that whatever it was, it was furry. Probably one of those weird Japanese plushy toys, he thought.

'Just my key ring,' Lisa said. 'Sorry. Didn't realise it was so annoying.'

'Will there be anything else?' Mick asked.

'No, I think we're good,' Matt said, his train of thought lost now, thanks to Lisa's keys, and this was confirmed with a nod from Jen. 'We'll just leave you be now. Though, can I ask you how long you'll be staying up here?'

'Oh, a few days I should think,' Mick said.

Lisa nodded her agreement.

'And with the weather like it is, I'd rather not risk any long journeys anyway,' Mick added. 'I'll show you to the door, then.'

Outside, Matt was thoughtful.

'Something up?' Jen asked.

'A case like this, something's always up,' Matt said, thinking back over the interview, sure he'd seen something or heard something, but for the life of him couldn't remember what.

'So, what now?' Jen asked.

'Nicholas Straub,' Matt said. 'I think he's our next port of call.'

'London, then?'

'If you don't say it out loud, then it can't be true,' said Matt.

'Oh, sorry,' Jen said. 'Harry's not going to be happy.'

'No, he's not,' Matt said. 'But then again, when is he ever?'

CHAPTER THIRTY

'And you've charged him, then, this lead singer?'

Swift's question was to the point. He'd arrived midmorning on Tuesday and made sure that his presence was obvious by bustling around the small office like an overpowered vacuum cleaner on full.

'No,' Harry said. 'We haven't. But we applied to keep them both in for thirty-six hours, considering the seriousness of the crime.'

'Why?'

'Why what?'

'Why haven't you charged him?'

'We've nothing to charge him with,' Harry said. 'Or his mate, either, for that matter. Not really. I mean, there's the cannabis we found in the van, but it's not enough to make us think they're dealing.'

'It is illegal though,' Swift said, and Harry couldn't believe that the man thought the words were worth uttering. He was glad the rest of the team were out, following up on what they could, as well as dealing with the various effects of a heavy snowfall, which comprised mainly of broken-down vehicles and unavoidable shunts. Gordy was with him, though, and they'd been going through what they knew about the case so far, but Swift had put an end to that.

'Yes, of course it is, and that'll all be followed up, and is, but what's most important right now is what happened to a certain Mr Jones on Saturday night, not the fact that two musicians like to get stoned in their van.'

'So, what about the symbols on the tower wall,' Swift said, 'and all that stuff about Satan? It's no coincidence, is it?'

'No, it isn't,' said Harry, 'but neither is it a big arrow pointing at them both, saying *here be murderers*!'

Harry caught a glance from Gordy that said enough to have him curb his tongue.

'I think, sir,' he said, forcing himself to calm down and to ignore the tiredness crawling like woodlouse through his body, 'that they're just playing this for fame. Mad as that sounds, I know, to you and me. Yes, there's a link, and my gut tells me that someone put them up to what they did, but we've no reason to charge them, not for this, anyway.'

'So, what are you going to do?'

'Well, like I said, we've got them for a few hours more for further questioning,' Harry said. 'Andrew, the singer, he's really sticking to his story, because he's clearly the most hungry for this to be something he can use as part of his image as a man of darkness, or whatever it is he's trying to prove. But his mate, the drummer?'

'He has a name?' Swift asked.

'Keith, would you believe,' Gordy said. 'I mean, I've nothing against the name, it's just he doesn't look like a Keith, does he?'

'I would have no idea about what Keiths are supposed to look like or not,' Swift said. 'So, what about him?'

'He's not as into it as Andrew,' Harry said. 'We interviewed him first. I don't think he buys into it all in quite the same way.'

'For a start, he doesn't have a stage name.' Gordy laughed.

'Exactly,' Harry said. 'So, I think, with a bit of work, and the fact that they're apart, Keith will crack first, probably without even realising it. Right now, he's already looking like he just wants to go home.'

'And you're leading on this?' Swift said, looking to Harry.

'I'm heading over there to see if I can get any further with them before they're released,' Gordy said.

'And no one's posted bail?'

Harry shook his head.

'I think maybe their parents are leaving them there to stew a bit.'

'You really don't think they're guilty, do you?' Swift asked.

'I think they're caught up in something, somehow,' Harry said, 'and we're trying to work out what. But the murder? I'm not seeing it.'

'So, what next?'

'Well, you've got everything on the case so far,' Harry said. 'And I'll be keeping you up to date as things progress.'

'I know you will,' Swift said, 'but what exactly are you doing next, Grimm? By which I mean you personally?'

'Heading over to have a chat with my favourite pathologist, actually,' Harry said. 'There's a few things she wants to go over about what the forensics team found.'

'Well, I won't be keeping you then,' Swift said and went to stand up, but paused. 'Oh, and about the press...'

'What about them?' Harry replied.

'I'm going to do a press conference this afternoon, as you know.'

'Yes, we do,' Harry said.

'As Gareth was somewhat the celebrity, they'll be all over it, won't they, all over us?'

'You make them sound like a rash,' Harry said. 'Which if you ask me, they are.'

'Is there anything I can give them?'

'How do you mean?' Gordy asked.

'I don't want them to think we're not doing anything.'

'I don't care what they think,' said Harry. 'So, sir, and if you don't mind me being blunt, I'll tell you exactly what you can give them.'

'And what's that?'

'Bugger all!'

And with that, Harry was up, out of his seat, and leaving the room, heading off to meet with Rebecca Sowerby and already wondering if Tuesday was now just working really hard to see if it could keep him awake for longer than both Sunday and Monday had.

'SO, THERE HE IS, THEN,' Harry said, staring at the shroud-covered body of the late Gareth Jones.

'You look tired.'

Harry was rather taken aback by the statement. It was the first time ever, he was sure, that the pathologist had commented on him in any way other than disdain.

'Been a long weekend,' Harry said. 'I'm sure it should be Friday already.'

'I can well imagine.'

'So, what have we got?'

'Ready for this?'

Harry had already daubed enough vapour rub under his nose to make sure his sinuses stayed open for at least a month, and he was wearing the required PPE.

'Never readier,' he said.

Rebecca reached out and pulled back the cover to reveal the body of Gareth Jones, folding it down all the way till he was fully exposed.

Harry stared at the body. He remembered back to when he'd first started in the police. His first time seeing a body on the slab had, it turned out, been a typical police initiation, designed to freak out newbies. He'd been standing next to the body, the pathologist opposite, a body between them. The pathologist had then made some excuse and left, leaving Harry alone. Then, just when Harry had started to wonder if the pathologist was ever going to return, the body in front of him had sat bolt upright and screamed. The trouble was, Harry's response hadn't exactly been the one expected, that being to essentially soil himself and run out of the room in a wild, terrified panic.

Instead, Harry had reacted instinctively, and punched the shrouded, screaming head of whoever it was who'd volunteered for the role. And the only person who had then left the room screaming had been the very not-dead corpse. Harry had, after all, seen more than enough death in his life as a soldier. And he had his own way of dealing with surprises designed to scare.

'You can see the marks around the neck very clearly,'

Rebecca said. 'And we can confirm that he died of asphyxiation.'

'And the bruises to his face and forehead?' Harry asked, seeing the purple welts on the swollen, pallid face of the dead man in front of him.

'They were inflicted prior to the hanging,' Rebecca said. 'Violent enough to cause a concussion, possibly unconsciousness.'

'So, you think he was out when whoever it was strung him up?'

'Not sure,' Rebecca said. 'The bruising shows signs of a struggle, so he may well have regained consciousness at that point or been conscious anyway. It's impossible to say.'

Harry scanned down the body, down the lines of stitching from where Rebecca had been at work, wondering how Gareth had been moved from his cottage to the church. If unconscious, then either someone strong must have carried him, because he couldn't recall any signs to show that he had been dragged, or at least two people had been involved.

'There's more bruising,' Harry said, pointing at Gareth's chest.

'Here, here, and just here, too.' Rebecca pointed. 'Injuries like what are usually sustained in a fight.'

'And what about those marks on his legs?' Harry asked.

These were longer, larger bruises, around the lower thigh and knees.

'They suggest that something heavy was wrapped around them,' Rebecca said. 'Tightly, too, to cause those marks. Squeezed.'

'Why?'

'At a guess, someone pulled down on him to hasten his death,' Rebecca said. 'It was something that happened back when hangings were a public spectacle. Friends, relatives, they'd try and hurry things along to reduce the suffering.'

Harry paused for a moment, trying to take it all in. And there was a lot, not just from Gareth's body, but from Rebecca who, for reasons he couldn't fathom, was still being decidedly pleasant. It wasn't that she was ever unpleasant as such, just that they always seemed to be able to rub each other up the wrong way. And today, so far, that hadn't happened. Yet.

'We also found marks on his head which contained flecks of paint from his house, perhaps where he had fallen or been pushed. And the paint used in the tower matches that from his house, which he was decorating.'

'So, whoever did this, definitely took him from his house, then,' Harry said.

Rebecca said nothing. Harry knew that she didn't need to.

'Anything else? The fingers?'

'Nothing to tell other than that one was snipped off and the blood used to write the number six-six-six on his forehead.'

'Not getting much, are we?' Harry said.

'Well, I'm giving you as much as I can!' Rebecca said, and Harry heard that familiar edge there again, keen and deadly.

'No, it's not you,' Harry said, refusing to get riled up. 'It's just this, all of it. Sometimes, actually a lot of the time, you'd think there'd be something to go on, something really obvious, and then there just isn't.'

'Well, I've not quite finished,' Rebecca said. 'There are a couple of other things, actually. First, something from the tower.'

'What?'

'The team found one of the stones in the wall to be loose,' Rebecca explained. 'Looked like it had been recently disturbed.'

'And what did you find?'

'Something rather odd, actually,' Rebecca said. 'I mean, there wasn't much, but there was enough in the samples we took of the fur.'

'Fur?' Harry said. 'Why would there be fur in a hole in the wall of a church tower? Was it a dead rat? A stray cat?'

'No, a rabbit, actually,' Rebecca said. 'We found evidence that at some point, rabbit remains had been put in that hole. For how long exactly, we can't say. Definitely rabbit, though, and clearly placed there deliberately. By which I mean, it didn't crawl in there and die.'

'Well, that doesn't make any sense, does it?' Harry said.

'No, it doesn't,' Rebecca agreed. 'And neither does the fact that whatever had been in there was, by all that we could tell, only recently removed.'

'So, what's the second thing?' Harry said. 'If rabbit fur in a hole in the church wall was the first, I'll be honest, I'm rather dreading what this next thing could be.'

'A wallet. At the cottage,' Rebecca said. 'You can collect it on your way out.'

'A wallet?' Harry said. 'Whose wallet exactly?'

'A Nicholas Straub,' Rebecca said. 'Ever heard of him?'

'Never,' Harry said.

'Well, that's whose wallet we found. Oh, and there was something else, too.'

'Dear God, it's like the gift that just keeps giving.'

Harry noticed the hard stare he was being sent by Rebecca and shushed.

'There was a toolbox,' Rebecca said.

'I remember it,' Harry said. 'Knocked over, tools everywhere.'

'Quite literally, too, actually,' said Rebecca. 'We've two tools missing, namely some scissors, probably for wallpapering, and a hammer.'

'You sure?' Harry said. 'I saw the toolbox and it looked pretty organised to me, and new. Can't see that Gareth would lose any.'

'Well, we went through that place as carefully as we always do,' Rebecca said, 'and all I can tell you, is that if those two specific tools were there before whatever happened in that cottage, then they're not there now.'

Harry rubbed his temples in anticipation of a headache he was pretty sure was going to hit him sooner or later.

'So, what we've got, then, is death by hanging, which was sped up by someone hanging from the deceased's legs, rabbit fur, and some missing tools.'

'Yes,' Sowerby said. 'I'll be doing a bit more research though,' she said. 'The rabbit fur has baffled me. Might be that it's the killer's calling card.'

'Dear God,' Harry said, 'I hope not. Last thing we need is some mad, bunny-obsessed serial killer.'

'I'll let you know what I find,' Sowerby said. 'Even if it's nothing.'

A few minutes later, and with the as-ever joyous conversation with Rebecca Sowerby over, Harry was making his way back home to Hawes, when his phone rang.

'Grimm.'

'It's Matt.'

'What now?'

'We think we've got another person of interest,' Matt said. 'Nicholas Straub.'

'Really?' Harry said. 'Now, that is interesting.'

'Is it? Why?'

'Because I've just heard that name myself. Forensics found his wallet over at Gareth's cottage.'

'So, you'll be wanting a chat with him, then, I suppose?' Matt asked.

'Indeed I will,' said Harry.

'And therein lies the problem,' Matt said.

'And what's that, then?'

'He lives in London,' Matt said.

'Bollocks,' said Harry.

'Thought you'd say that.'

CHAPTER THIRTY-ONE

'So, how's Joan doing, then?'

Grimm's question drifted across to Matt on a cloud of billowing steam from the kettle, which was getting even more use than usual, thanks to the weather. And with Wednesday having already demonstrated, by dropping a couple of degrees, that it was not going to be having anything to do at all with a thaw, Harry was beginning to wonder if it might be sensible to buy another, just to keep up with the demand for steaming hot mugs of tea.

He had gathered the whole of the team together for two reasons. The first, was to go through what they had so far on the case. The second, was to take up the time between waking up and when he would have to get on a train in Darlington and head to London to have a little chat with a certain Mr Nicholas Straub. They'd already spoken, and the man had agreed to see Harry the following day at his office.

Harry wasn't looking forward to it. London was not his idea of fun. Bristol he could manage, because it felt more like a large town when compared to a village, but compared to

London? Well, London was incomprehensibly big. And it felt like there was no escape from the place once you were there. Also, Harry suspected that he'd already grown rather too fond of the green vales and dells of Wensleydale, and the thought of having to head away from them to spend a day surrounded by concrete just didn't fill him with glee.

'She's good, thanks,' Matt answered. 'Very good, actually. Which is quite the relief!'

'Out of hospital, then, is she?' Harry asked.

'Oh, she wasn't in for too long,' Matt said. 'Just a check-up, you know. Make sure everything's okay.'

'But you had to rush her in though, didn't you?'

'I did,' said Matt. 'But we're all good now, which is a big relief, let me tell you! Oh, and cheers for the tea, boss.'

Harry really wanted to ask what exactly was up with Joan, why she'd been rushed into hospital in the first place, but Matt had already turned away and moved to go and sit with the rest of the team. Whatever was up, he was really keeping it all very close to his chest.

Harry went to follow, only to be nearly tripped up by Fly, the dog automatically flipping over onto its back.

'Jim?' Harry said, keeping himself calm. 'Your dog?'

The PCSO was up out of his seat and over to Fly. His face, Harry saw, wasn't looking too bad, with most of the bumps and scrapes healing enough to not be too noticeable. If and when anyone had asked what had happened, the story was that he'd taken a fall in the barn with the sheep and got a hoof in the face. It was funny enough and likely enough to be believable and Harry was happy with that. What happened was their secret and that's the way it was going to stay.

As for the delightful Timothy, Harry had a little smile on

his face about that. Turned out that Geryon had not just one, but two bags of cannabis in their van, and one of those just so happened to end up stuffed in the sofa at Timothy's house. Then the police had turned up, courtesy of an anonymous tip-off, the place searched, and apparently more than that single bag had been found. Not just drugs either, but a shed out the back of the house in which a small number of very terrified dogs had been found and then quickly returned to their owners. Timothy's life, Harry suspected, had really taken a turn for the worse, and it couldn't have happened to anyone more deserving.

'He's a bit nervous still,' Jim said, 'after what happened last week.'

Harry ruffled the hair on the dog's head.

'I'm sure he is,' he said. 'But he'll be right soon enough, I'm sure.'

Fly's tail wagged vigorously as Jim picked him up and took him back to sit under his own chair.

'Looks like we've got ourselves a full house,' said Liz.

'Which just goes to show we're all a little too keen if you ask me,' said Gordy. 'Weather like this, any normal, sensible person would have stayed at home.'

'Well, we're none of us normal nor all that sensible,' Matt said. 'And who'd want to be, that's what I want to know?'

'I'm normal,' Jadyn said, lifting a hand.

'Are you, though?' Jen asked. 'I mean really normal? Like all of us?'

'Yes, I am,' Jadyn said. 'It's you lot who's weird.'

Harry moved to stand in front of his team, behind him, the board.

'Right then,' he said, but noticed a hand was already in the air.

Harry's eyes rolled around to see to whom the hand belonged and they dropped on the ever-keen face of Jadyn.

Harry liked Jadyn a lot. They all did. What he hoped, though, was that the keen, bright spark that burned inside Jadyn didn't get put out too soon, or ever. But there was always the chance it would happen, as it happened to so many in the force, and Harry included himself in that. Though moving to the dales had certainly brought that spark back, hadn't it? he thought.

'You want me to do the board, boss?'

'Of course, Officer Okri,' Harry said. 'Be my guest!'

Jadyn was up and at the board like he'd been stung, pens grabbed and at the ready.

'Right then, who wants to start?' Harry asked.

As one, not a soul raised a hand.

'Don't all overwhelm me with your amazing insights,' Harry said. 'Why don't we start at the beginning? The call from the vicar, I think?'

'She found the body when she went in on Sunday morning,' Jen said. 'Which was when I called you.'

'Indeed you did,' Harry agreed. 'So, let's roll it back a bit further then and start with the victim, shall we? What do we know about Mr Gareth Jones?'

'He's a singer, boss,' Jadyn said, writing, 'Gareth Jones' and then 'singer' on the board. 'Famous for that Christmas song, you know, that one that goes—'

'Don't!' Gordy said, her voice raised, and a hand in the air as though barring the way to traffic. 'Nope, you've done it now, just by mentioning it. Now it's in my head for the rest of the day!'

'Oh, sorry about that,' Jadyn said.

'Anything else?' Harry asked, working to keep the discussion moving rather than stalling early on.

Jen had her notebook out, and that was a good sign, Harry thought, suspecting that the lacklustre response from the team was due to tiredness rather than anything else, which was completely understandable.

'I've quite a lot here,' Jen said, 'and it's a bit jumbled. But I'll just go through it. Jadyn?'

'Hmm?'

'If this gets confusing, just tell me to slow down, okay?'

'I'll be fine, don't you worry,' Jadyn said, a smile of unbounded confidence on his face.

'Right then,' said Jen, 'I'll start with the grim details first.'

'Always for the best, I think,' Harry said. 'And I should know, right enough.'

'What? Oh, no, that's not what I meant!' Jen spluttered.

'Of course you didn't, now on you go.' Harry laughed.

'Yes, right,' Jen said. 'So, anyway, Gareth Jones, aged forty. His body was discovered by the vicar, Anna Fenwick, at approximately six-thirty on Sunday morning. Forensics have come back to confirm that he was strangled by being hanged by a bell rope around his neck. There were signs of a struggle as well, both on his body, but also back at his cottage in Countersett. He also had a finger snipped off.'

'It was a bad one, this,' Harry said. 'So, what else do we know about him?'

'We know that he lived in London, though he'd recently bought a place over at Countersett,' Jen said. 'He'd had a very successful career as a recording artist and is worth a few bob. Just three years ago he lost his wife, and most recently, was embroiled in a rather bitter divorce case between record producer Nicholas Straub and his then-wife Cassie.'

'How's that then?' Harry asked. 'What did he have to do with it, this divorce?'

'He had a fling with Mrs Straub,' Liz said. 'It was all over the press. Can't remember the exact details, but I think it was all nonsense, in the end, wasn't it?'

'Oh, that's right, yes,' Gordy said. 'Something about him not knowing she was even married at the time, wasn't it?'

'Anyway,' Jen said, 'the concert in Askrigg on Saturday was to launch his new album.'

'And I'm visiting Mr Straub later today, as a matter of fact,' Harry said.

Gordy laughed. 'Your excitement is palpable.'

'You have no idea.'

Matt said, 'He was spotted at the concert by Lisa Shaw. She's the pianist.'

'And forensics found his wallet over at Gareth's cottage,' added Harry.

'That makes him a suspect, for sure,' Gordy said.

'That it does,' Harry nodded, the sound of Jadyn's frantic scribbling behind him difficult to ignore.

'Let's keep this going,' Harry said. 'What next?'

'Well, there's the two members of the band, Geryon,' Gordy said.

'What kind of name is Geryon when it's home?' Jim said, shaking his head in bemusement.

'I looked it up,' Jadyn said. 'It's the name of a demon from an RPG.'

'RPG?' Gordy asked.

'Role-playing game,' said Jadyn.

'And did you get much from them yesterday?' Harry asked.

Gordy shook her head. 'Same nonsense as before,' she

said. 'But with nothing to charge them for, they were released yesterday afternoon.'

'But what about all the occult stuff?' Jim asked.

'There's nothing actually connecting them to what happened to Gareth,' Gordy said. 'Just one of those strange coincidences, that's all. Nothing more.'

'I'm not so sure,' Harry said. 'But like you said, there's nothing we can charge them with really. But we know where they are if we need them.'

'Exactly,' Gordy said.

Jadyn said, 'Everyone I spoke to when I was ringing around all those who were at the concert, they all seemed to think it was funny.'

'In what way?' Harry asked.

'I don't know.' Jadyn shrugged. 'Just that loads of people thought it was funny that in the middle of this really nice concert, these two men turn up and talk about Satan. Quite a few think it was a publicity stunt.'

'By Gareth?' Liz said. 'Why would he have ever done that?'

'No, by the group,' Jadyn said. 'It's the kind of thing that goes viral, isn't it? And they filmed the whole thing, too, you know? So, viral kind of makes sense.'

Harry thought back to the interview with the lead singer.

'It's still all a bit strange though, isn't it?' he said. 'All that occult stuff on the walls and them talking all that bollocks about the devil.'

'Some people will do anything for a bit of fame,' said Jim. 'Can't see why anyone would want it, though. Can you imagine?'

'What else, then?' Harry asked.

Jen spoke again, reading from her notebook. 'We know

that Gareth joined his old choir friends in the pub after the concert.'

'And what do we know about these friends?' Harry asked.

'Not much really,' Jen said. 'They've all got alibis for the night in question. Two of them are now married to each other, namely Penny, who was Edley, and Andrew Firth. They went home afterwards as they had a babysitter looking after their two kids. Claire Sykes was there with her husband, and they went home, too. Christopher Middleton— he's the one who confronted the gatecrashers—lives locally and walked home. Lisa was with her boyfriend, Mick, staying at the pub. And Gareth got a taxi home.'

'This Christopher fellow,' Harry said. 'What do we know about him, then?'

'Runs a local gym,' Liz said. 'He's got guns on him like you wouldn't believe.'

'What did he have to say for himself?'

'He was pretty shocked,' Matt said. 'I got the impression, from all of the friends actually, that Gareth had kind of lost touch with them all, but that they had all been close as kids. I reckon this was a bit of a reunion for them.'

'Alibi?'

'He was dropped home by Penny and Andrew, very, very drunk. He doesn't really drink, what with his chosen career of being all buff, so he's not exactly used to it. They say he could barely walk.'

'Difficult for him to get to Countersett, then, in that state,' Harry said. 'Which leaves us with Lisa and Mick, then.'

'They're engaged now, for one,' Matt said. 'They told Jen and me that on Monday.'

'And I think Lisa had a little bit of a crush on Gareth as a kid,' Jen added. 'Well, I say little, but it seems it was big enough for her to follow him into the music business.'

'Not so sure it was just as a kid either, actually,' Matt said. 'She remembers when Gareth's wife was killed, like properly remembers everything about it.'

'She was on holiday though,' Jen said. 'I mean, if you're away getting a tan in the sun and sloshing down the wine, finding out that your mate's been in a hit-and-run and lost his wife in the process is something you're probably going to remember.'

'I guess,' Matt said. 'Anyway, there's Mick as well. And he's a bit of an odd one.'

'How so?'

Matt shrugged.

'Can't say for sure,' he said. 'One of those types that clearly thinks the police are simply out to waste people's time. Can't say I warmed to him. Oh, and Lisa doesn't half fidget. She kept on playing with her key ring while we were talking to them. It was all I could do to not rip it out of her hand and throw it out of the window!'

Harry laughed. It sounded like just the kind of thing that would annoy him, too.

'We've been through the photos from the church as well,' Matt said. 'And we found that one of them had their signatures on the back, which Lisa seemed to think was particularly wonderful, though I can't really imagine why.'

'You have them here?' Harry asked. 'The photos?'

'I've got them,' Liz said, handing over a little folder to Harry. 'Here you go.'

Harry opened the folder, looked through the photos. Young kids, just having fun, that's all he saw in them. No sign that later in life one would end up dying horribly. But then, why would there be? He turned the photos over, looking for the writing, finally coming across it. The hands which had scribed their names were young, Harry thought, as he read them, full of dreams and ideas and hope and everything else that goes on in the head of a child. He slipped the photos away again and closed the file.

'On that,' Matt said, 'there's something about that writing that struck me as odd, but I can't remember or work out what.'

Harry removed the relevant photo again from the folder, turned it over, and looked at the signatures. He then handed it over to Matt.

'In what way?'

Matt stared at the writing then shook his head.

'You know, I've got no idea right now. I was hoping looking at it again might jog my memory. Obviously not.'

Harry took back the photo. 'I mean, it's just their names, isn't it?'

'Nicknames, I think,' Matt said. 'I remember that as a kid myself, everyone having nicknames.'

'So, what was yours, then?' Liz asked.

'Tiny,' Matt said. 'On account of me not really shooting up till I hit sixteen. Before then, I was a proper little short arse!'

'So, which one's Gareth, then?' Harry asked, then he stared at the writing closely to decipher it, as it was rather faded now. 'According to what we have here, we've got Doughnut, Bonny, Quidsy, Rambo, Psycho, and Toots.'

At which point the room erupted.

'Doughnut?' Jim said. 'That's brilliant! One for you there, Matt!'

'Don't be mean to old Tiny,' Liz said. 'Anyway, I reckon we should call him Cake, on account of how he never eats anything else!'

'Psycho, though?' said Gordy. 'Who calls a kid that?'

'I reckon that's Claire,' said Jen. 'Claire Skyes, Psych-oh, you see?'

'Clever.'

'Quidsy, then,' asked Harry. 'Someone rich, then?'

'Nope, I've got that one, too,' said Jen. 'Penny. As in a penny, money, you know? They've just gone for Quid, as in a pound.'

'Tenuous,' said Harry, 'but I see where you're coming from. But as I can't see this being at all useful to what we're investigating, fun though it is, shall we move on? What about the vicar, Anna?'

'What about her?' Gordy asked. 'You can't think she's guilty?'

'I didn't say that I did,' Harry replied. 'But right now, as you well know, and though we have to view everyone as inno-cent until proven otherwise, we have to consider the fact that everyone we talk to in connection with this could be a suspect.'

'Of course, yes,' Gordy said.

Harry stared at the DI for a moment, wondering what was up, remembering then how it was pretty clear when Gordy had turned up at the church on Sunday not only that she recognised Anna and knew her, but that she had been more than a little surprised to see her, and vice versa, too. So, what the hell was that about? Harry was pretty sure it had nothing to do with the investigation, but still, it did have him a little baffled.

'So, what do we actually know about Anna, then?' Harry asked again.

'She's been vicar of the parish for over ten years,' Gordy said. 'Spends her free time either cooking, walking out on the fells, or adding to her extensive and weird book collection. And she's a massive fan of The Golden Girls. Loves horror movies, too, apparently.'

Harry wasn't sure how relevant any of that actually was, or how Gordy had come by the information in the first place.

'You sure that's the same person?' he asked. 'Anna Fenwick, the vicar?'

'Very much so,' Gordy nodded. 'As Jen said earlier, Anna discovered the body early Sunday morning, when she'd headed into sort the church out for the day.'

'And from the church, we've a few things to be going on with,' Jim said, joining in, having been a little too quiet up until then for Harry's liking. He was obviously still a bit shaken up from what had happened over the weekend.

'You are getting all this down, aren't you, Officer Okri?' Harry asked, glancing over to Jadyn.

'No bother at all,' Jadyn replied confidently. 'I'm all over it, boss.'

'Jim?' Harry said. 'Go on...'

'We've got evidence of rabbit remains from a hole behind a stone in the wall of the tower,' Jim said. 'Though, I'm not really sure what use that is to us. More useful, is that we have the same paint on the walls of the tower as found at Gareth's cottage. Also, the lock to the church was smashed on the inside, suggesting whoever got in, did so with a key, or the church was already open.'

'And how've you got on with the list of key holders?' Harry asked.

'Been through them all,' Liz said. 'Again, they all have an alibi. Not only that, none of them have either a reason to harm the victim or the capability.'

'How do you mean?'

'They're all old,' Liz said. 'It's a church, right? So, the congregation, well, they're all pretty old, aren't they? It's not one of those hip and happening happy-clappy jobs, like that one over in Leyburn.'

'Old people can do terrible things, too,' Harry said.

'I know that,' Liz replied. 'But the alibis all checked out.'

Harry thought on all that he'd heard, staring for a moment at the mass of scrawl Jadyn had plastered all over the board. It was, in almost every possible way, a disgraceful mess, but done with such enthusiasm and verve he didn't want to say anything. Not yet, anyway.

'There's the missing hammer and scissors,' Jim said, interrupting Harry's thoughts. 'From the toolbox at the cottage.'

'Well remembered,' Harry said. 'And I'd put money on those being used by the killer, one to remove Gareth's finger, the other to smash the lock of the church door.'

'We need to find them, then,' Matt said.

'Trouble is, right now, we've no idea where to start a search,' Harry said.

'So, what next?' Jim asked.

Harry cast his eyes across his team. They were all keen to get to work, and that was good. He'd had too many meetings such as this where all anyone really wanted to do was as little as possible and then go home.

'Gordy, I want you to head over to have another word with our two gatecrashers. Take Jadyn with you. Matt, I think we need to have another chat with everyone on those photos, all of Gareth's old friends, so if you and Liz can get on with that? Jen, could you go and check up on Anna, make sure everything's okay, and see if there's anything else she might have seen or noticed? Jim, I want you to do a bit of background research for me, on Geryon and Nicholas Straub. And whatever you find, send it through to me as soon as you can.'

'No problem, boss,' Jim said. 'Where will you be when I contact you?'

'On my way to London,' Harry said. 'Which reminds me, I need a lift to the station.'

CHAPTER THIRTY-TWO

HAVING CALLED AHEAD TO MAKE SURE THAT ANNA WAS in, Jen was now at the door to the vicarage. The house was a huge thing, sitting just down from Askrigg church along a footpath, and set in its own walled garden. Snow had drifted up against the walls and large icicles hung down from the gutters, crystal spears glinting in the sun. She noticed that those directly above the front door had been deliberately broken.

The front door opened and there stood the vicar, though not in the expected garb of her profession. Instead, she was wearing faded jeans, Homer Simpson slippers, a fleece jacket, and a Lord of the Rings T-shirt.

'Officer Blades!' Anna smiled. 'Quick, get yourself in out of the cold, now.'

Jen did as she was bade and stepped into the house. It welcomed her with a comforting gloom, though not much of a difference in temperature.

'Let's get you through to the study,' Anna said. 'I don't bother heating the whole house, because there's no point. It's just me rattling around in the place, so I've a fire going in the one room I spend most of my time in. Come on.'

Jen followed Anna across the hall, past the large sweeping staircase, and through a deep brown, oak door.

'It is a little big for someone on their own,' she said, as they stepped into a room that smelled of burning wood, coffee, and books.

'I don't think a family has lived here in years,' Anna said. 'I'm currently trying to persuade the powers that be to sell this place, buy somewhere modern that's smaller and doesn't require the same amount of fuel as the Titanic to heat.'

'Makes sense,' Jen said, heading over to the large open fire, around which were sat several worn, comfy-looking armchairs.

'A walk to the bathroom in the middle of the night feels like an expedition through the Arctic,' Anna said. 'And when I come down that staircase, it's like I've walked onto the set of some costume drama. It's lovely, yes, and I'm very lucky, but really, it's a bit silly, isn't it?'

'Oh, I think I could get used to it,' Jen said, warming up her hands.

'Coffee?' Anna asked.

'That'd be lovely,' Jen replied, then sat down to take in the room. Beyond the collection of comfy chairs, which were huddled around the fire as though they were trying to stop it from escaping. A large desk, which looked pre-twentieth century, but not in a good way, was up at the window, facing out. The wall opposite the one containing the fire was floor-to-ceiling bookshelves, all of them full. And the final wall comprised a small table, on which were sat a kettle and a small fridge, and a couple filing cabinets which looked to Jen as though they had, quite literally, fallen off the back of a lorry. The room was scruffy, but in a nice, cosy lived-in way, and she liked it.

'Here you go,' Anna said, handing Jen a mug of coffee. 'And some biscuits. Now then, is this a nice polite police check-up, or do you have some other questions?'

With a chocolate digestive in one hand, coffee in the other, Jen smiled and said, 'A bit of both I suppose. How are things, now, after the weekend?'

'I'm not really sure,' Anna replied. 'It's not a situation that my training prepared me for. Births, deaths, funerals, listening to people, getting out into the local community, quoting bits of the Bible just to confuse people, all of that was covered. But murdered celebrities in church towers? Not on the syllabus.'

'How was the cleanup?'

'Effective,' Anna replied. 'Though I'm not a big fan of going back into the tower right now. And I don't think anyone will be for a good while. The smell's gone, so that's good, but there's a feeling to the place now, like what happened there is in the walls.'

'How's the congregation been?'

'Very concerned,' said Anna. 'And not just those who attend on a Sunday. The community has been really hit by this. Gareth, well, he was a bit of a local hero, wasn't he? No one can understand what happened.'

'No, I can see that,' offered Jen.

'I've not actually told anyone the full details,' Anna said. 'I don't think everyone needs to know about the nitty-gritty, do you? The hanging and the symbols and whatnot. It'll only turn this into goodness knows what.'

'Have the press been in touch?'

Anna gave a nod and a roll of her eyes.

'The phone calls were nonstop yesterday. Though I think the weather is a bit of a blessing. I don't think the journalists are too keen to travel all this way when it's like this. Hopefully, they'll have other things to think about when it finally thaws.'

'With what happened, is there anything else you've remembered?' Jen asked.

'Like what?'

Jen shrugged. 'Honestly, I don't know. Could be anything. Even if you don't think it's important, in the end, it might be.'

'Well, it's not something I remember, but it is relevant I think,' Anna said. 'I've been doing a bit of my own research.'

'Really? Into what?'

'Those marks on the walls,' Anna said. 'Bit of a hobby of mine.'

'What is?'

'The occult, witchcraft, pagan beliefs, all that kind of thing.'

Jen spluttered her coffee.

'But you're a vicar!'

'Some people do find it a bit odd, true, but what can you do? I deal in belief, life after death. It's my actual job. So, learning about the development of belief in the supernatural isn't actually that weird if you think about it. Look, I'll show you.'

Anna stood up and walked over to the bookcase. Jen followed and found herself confronted with a collection of books with titles she really would not have expected to find in that room.

'Wow...'

'Yes, isn't it?' Anna said, and Jen saw the smile on the

woman's face. 'I love books, you see. I've got stuff here on everything from Tarot, astrology and scrying, to modern day satanism, ancient Babylonian beliefs, witchcraft, folk beliefs, and goodness knows what else. It's a little bit of an obsession.'

'I can tell,' Jen said, not quite sure how to take in what she was now looking at. 'You said you'd been doing a bit of research?'

Anna pulled out a hefty book, the spine thick as a concrete breeze block, the cover a worn, red leather.

'This one is basically an A to Z of every possible known sign or rune or engraving or whatever from every known religion and/or belief across the world.'

Flicking through the pages, Anna said, 'The signs on the walls of the tower? They bothered me, you see. As soon as I saw them, I was pretty sure something was off.'

'Off? In what way?'

'Look here...'

Anna flicked through the pages of the book.

'See this one? That was on the wall.'

She flicked through to another section.

'And this one. Do you see?'

Jen shook her head.

'No, not really.'

'They're random,' Anna said. 'From different religions or beliefs.'

'Does that matter?'

'I don't know,' Anna said. 'It's just that this is the kind of thing you see in the movies, you know? You've got some weird, black magic stuff going on or whatever, a director needs whatever they're filming to look evil, so the props people just flick through whatever books they've got and choose stuff that looks right.'

'Don't tell me, you like horror movies, too,' Jen said.

Anna grinned. 'Love them! It's the only genre that takes the supernatural seriously.'

Jen walked back to the fire and didn't really know what to think. Should she be worried, was right at the top of the list, because surely there was something weird about a vicar into this kind of stuff, particularly considering what had taken place just a few days ago. But surely there was no way Anna was a part of it! Now that really was crazy! Why would she be a party to the events that had occurred?

'You okay, there?'

Jen turned at the sound of Anna's voice.

'Not freaked you out, I hope?'

Jen smiled but knew it wasn't convincing, her thoughts racing now. Because there wasn't just the symbols to consider here, was there, but the whole thing with the door lock, that whoever had murdered Gareth had a key. And the vicar definitely did. All of the keys, actually. But where was the motive? There wasn't one! This was madness, surely!

'No, I'm good,' Jen eventually answered. 'But it is strange.'

'My parents always said the same. Could never understand how I had this supposed Christian faith, but at the same time, an interest in any of this. More coffee?'

Jen shook her head.

'No, I'd best get going. Thanks, though, for your time. And for what you said, about the symbols.'

'Well, it might be useful,' Anna said. 'I hope so.'

Back outside, and having left the warmth of the vicarage behind, Jen tried to get her thoughts straight, which wasn't easy. And it was made even less so by the ringing of her phone.

'PC Blades,' Jen answered.

'Jen, it's Jim.'

'Something up?'

'You still in Askrigg?'

'I am.'

'Right, can you go have a chat with the landlord at the King's Arms? He's just been on the phone about something.'

'What?'

'The night of the murder,' Jim said. 'Seems that either Mick or Lisa, or both of them, weren't exactly telling the truth.'

CHAPTER THIRTY-THREE

HARRY STRODE FROM THE TRAIN AND WAS IMMEDIATELY swept along by the tsunami of people racing along, desperate to get into the city. It was clear to him that they were all very much late for something hugely important and needed to get there very quickly. So much so, that a good number of them were already on their phones and talking ten to the dozen. Harry tried to hang back and stay out of the crowds, but it was impossible, so he gave up and just went with it, half wondering if he could just lift his feet and be carried.

Through the barriers and out into the main area of King's Cross Station, Harry made his way to the London Underground. When he got there, he had no recollection of how he'd found the place, almost as though the station had read his mind and simply transported him.

The journey beneath London was a rich and unpleasant meal, with tastes and aromas ranging from crippling body odour akin to the stench of mince, and aftershave strong enough to cut through lead, to dust and dirt and fast food, sucked down from the world above by the air conditioning.

Relieved to be back outside, Harry eventually managed to make his way to the address he had been given at which Mr Nicholas Straub had agreed to meet him. London was cold and bleak and icy, but the snow was nowhere near what it was in the dales. What surprised Harry was that it wasn't an office, as he'd expected, but a club, and a rather exclusive one by the look of it.

Outside, the building was tall and white and maintained to a very high standard. The paintwork shone and was clearly either cleaned regularly or repainted annually. Or both. Pushing through the double doors, Harry was greeted with a pleasant reception area and a very well-dressed man so clean-shaven that his skin looked like plastic.

'I'm here to see Mr Straub,' Harry said. 'I'm Detective Chief Inspector Harry Grimm.'

The man behind the reception desk spent just a little too long staring at Harry, looking him up and down, before heading off to check whatever it was that he clearly felt he needed to check. It was certainly important, Harry thought, judging by the way he swept off and through a door.

Returning, the man told Harry that Mr Straub was running a little late, but that a room had been booked for their meeting.

'A room?' Harry said. 'Here?'

'Follow me,' the man said and without waiting scuttled off.

Harry raced off after him to then find himself, a few minutes later, in a room with a moderately sized snooker table in the centre and an extensive drinks cabinet against one of the walls. The furniture was bright and comfy and Harry suspected, hideously expensive.

'Help yourself,' the man said, gesturing at the drinks, before turning and leaving Harry on his own.

Harry hadn't the faintest idea what to do with himself. The room was plush and he really wasn't, having not bothered to dress up for the occasion, but also having just spent close to three hours on the train from Darlington, then dashing across town.

He walked over to the drinks cabinet, examined a few bottles, put them back. Then he turned around and stared at the snooker table. It was all set up and ready for a game.

Harry shuffled over to a stand against the wall holding several cues, chose one, and was then down at the white. He was just about to cue off when...

'Do you play?'

Harry stood and turned to face the new arrival, a man in leather shoes, jeans, shirt and jacket, and a scarf around his neck, though what purpose it served other than to look expensive, Harry couldn't tell.

'Mr Straub?'

'And you must be DCI Grimm,' Straub said.

'If I'd known we were meeting somewhere so, well, exclusive, I'd have dressed a little more appropriately,' Harry said.

Straub dismissed Harry's words with a wave of his hand.

'This place? Oh, it likes to look posh, but the clientele? They're creatives. You know the type: musicians, writers, artists. So, scruffy is their default setting, albeit expensive scruffy. It's only the television presenters who bother. God knows why. Probably to make up for their complete and total lack of personality.'

'So...' Harry said, not really sure what to say next, feeling even more out of place now that he knew the kind of people he might bump into.

'You wanted to have a chat,' Straub said, gesturing at a seat opposite one that he then sat down in himself.

Seated, Harry said, 'Yes, you see, it's about Saturday night.'

'What about it?'

'The concert, up in Askrigg? Gareth Jones?'

'I've seen the news,' Straub said. 'Awful what happened to Gareth.'

'Yes, that,' Harry said. 'But perhaps we're skipping ahead a bit too quickly. You were there, yes?'

At this, Harry saw Straub's expression flicker.

'Ah, yes, about that...'

'I understand,' Harry said, 'that you knew Mr Jones?'

'In a way, yes,' replied Straub.

'And in what way would that be?'

'A bad way,' Straub said, and there was an edge to the man's voice now which, up until that moment, had been all politeness. 'That man! He... well, I... Look, it's difficult.'

'Take your time,' Harry said.

Straub went to speak, but they were interrupted by a young woman, smartly dressed, carrying a menu.

'My name's Jackie and I'll leave this with you for the moment,' she said. 'I'll come back in a few minutes to see if you want anything.'

'We don't,' Straub said.

Harry, however, noticing Straub's edge, said, 'You know, I wouldn't mind me a nice iced coffee, if you would be so kind? Can't say I've had one for a very long time indeed. And with an extra shot.'

'Not a problem,' Jackie said, her face the kind of smile that would make the rising sun jealous. 'Anything to eat?'

Harry said, 'Do you have anything pastry and sugar-based that will bring on an early death?'

Jackie laughed. 'I'm sure I can find something!' She turned to Straub and Harry noticed that the man was clearly growing more and more impatient. 'And you, sir?'

'Just some iced water, please,' he said. 'And could you hurry it up, as I'm sure we won't be here very long.'

Once Jackie had left, Harry said, 'I think you were about to tell me all about how you know Gareth Jones.'

'Look, I don't wish to speak ill of the dead,' Straub said, 'but that man? That clean-cut, butter-wouldn't-melt man? He ruined my marriage!'

Harry said nothing, just allowed Straub to speak.

'He had an affair with my wife. A long time ago now, but when I found out, I confronted her and our marriage fell apart. Because of him! He tried to hide behind his own personal tragedy, yes, very clever, but I wasn't having it. He was to blame!'

'Your marriage fell apart, then,' Harry said.

'A very messy divorce, indeed,' Straub explained. 'Cost me a fortune! Take my advice, Detective, and never get married. All it leads to is pain and an empty bank account!'

Harry had a sneaking suspicion that not only did Mr Straub have no idea as to the meaning of pain, but also had never really experienced an empty bank account in his life. And as for his views on marriage? Well, he was wrong there, Harry was sure. He should probably have been a little more down on the whole institution, what with what had been and gone with his own parents, but they weren't the norm. And what about people like Matt and Joan? They had something very special indeed, Harry mused, realising then that Straub was still ranting, clearly built on stronger foundations than the ones on which Straub's own marriage had been constructed.

Straub stopped speaking when Jackie returned with their order.

Harry took a long, long drink of the coffee, then reached for the pastry, which broke apart as he took a bite, filling his mouth with the rich taste of butter and sugar and cream. What would Jen say? he thought, smiling to himself.

'Anyway, I don't see how any of this is relevant,' Straub said.

'But you were there, weren't you?' Harry stated. 'Saturday night, the concert? You were recognised, you see.'

Straub's expression twisted into one of irritation.

'Yes, I was there,' he said defiantly. 'So what? You don't think I killed him, do you?'

'Can I ask why you were there in the first place?' Harry said.

'What I do is my own business,' Straub answered.

'And, right now, it's also police business,' Harry said, wiping his mouth. 'So, please... ?'

Straub huffed.

'I was there because I wanted to be,' he said. 'Is there a law against that?'

'Not that I know of,' Harry said. 'But it does strike me as a little strange that you would drive all the way up from London to go to the concert of someone you blame for the failure of your marriage.'

'I was there to see if he was lying,' Straub said. 'Yes, that's why. Because he had played on the broken man thing, how his life was a mess, after what had happened with his wife, but I didn't believe him. And, after seeing that concert, I'm pretty sure he's absolutely fine, thank you very much!'

Harry was now finding it hard to resist the urge to reach over the table between them and ricochet Straub's head off its surface. He was, to Harry's mind, deeply unpleasant in almost every way.

'So, that's why you went, is it?' Harry asked. 'To spy on him? No other reason?'

'None,' Straub said.

'And you're sure about that?'

'Absolutely.'

It was now that Harry decided to reveal that, thanks to Jim's digging, he had a little more idea about Straub than the man realised.

'You're a record producer, are you not?'

'I am, yes,' Straub replied. 'So?'

'So,' Harry said, 'you get a lot of demos in, I'm assuming? Would that be correct?'

'We do,' Straub said.

Harry pulled his phone from his pocket, switching it on.

'And you're sure there's nothing else you want to tell me about Saturday evening? Nothing at all?'

'Not a thing,' Straub replied.

Harry flipped his phone around for Straub to see the screen.

'And what's this I'm looking at, then?'

'It's a blog post,' Harry said. 'At least, I think that's what it is. Something to do with social media, anyway, so obviously something I've got no interest in. Except with this here thing you're staring at now, that is.'

'But what is it?' Straub asked.

'If you read that little paragraph in front of you,' Harry

explained, 'you'll see that it mentions your name, your company, yes? Whoever wrote this, did so to tell their fans that they'd posted a demo off to you. Well, not just to you, but a fair number of record companies. But yours is there, in the list.'

'I'm not sure I'm following,' Straub said, shaking his head, pushing himself back in his chair.

'Then let me remind you,' Harry said, and quickly zoomed in on the screen. 'See that? Well, that's the band in the photograph. And that's their name, Geryon. And you, Mr Straub, received last month, their first demo. Which means I think you need to be a little more open in telling me exactly why you were at Gareth's concert, why you paid Geryon to gatecrash, and, one final thing, what exactly you were doing at Gareth's cottage that very same evening?'

Straub opened his mouth to protest, but Harry shut him down.

'You left your wallet,' Harry said. 'This one, to be exact,' and he threw onto the table between them the wallet Sowerby's team had found at Gareth's cottage, safely sealed inside a clear plastic evidence bag.

CHAPTER THIRTY-FOUR

THURSDAY MORNING AND THE TEAM WERE ONCE AGAIN gathered at the Community Centre. Harry was weary from his journey to and from London, but it had been worthwhile for sure.

'How was London, then?' Matt asked.

'Definitely somewhere I visited,' Harry said. 'And somewhere I won't be hurrying back to any time soon if I can help it.'

'Can't say that I blame you,' Matt said.

'How was your day?' asked Harry.

'Lots of questions, not many answers,' Matt said.

'You look pretty tired,' Harry then said, noticing the grey shadows under the detective sergeant's eyes.

'Yeah, I was up in the night with Joan,' Matt explained.

'Really?' Harry asked. 'She still not right, then?'

'Oh, she's right as rain, actually,' Matt said. 'Just a bit of sickness, that's all. Nowt to worry about.'

Before Harry had a chance to ask anymore, Matt was away to the kettle to make another brew.

A few minutes later, Harry had everyone gathered around the board once again. It had not gone unnoticed that Jadyn had been working at it while he'd been in London. Now, rather than just one board, it was two, with all the information laid out neatly. Harry was impressed.

'Not bad, is it?' Jadyn said, going to stand beside his handiwork. 'Took me a while to do, but I think it's a lot better.'

'You've done a cracking job,' Harry said. 'Well done.'

'Really?' Jadyn said, surprise in his voice. 'You mean that?'

'Of course I mean it,' Harry said. 'Why wouldn't I?'

'No, fair point,' Jadyn said.

Harry turned to the team and clapped his hands to bring them together.

'Right then,' he said, 'after my trip to London yesterday, I figured it would make sense to tell you what I uncovered. Then we'll see where we are with everything else.'

'Did you not bring us back any souvenirs?' asked Liz. 'I mean, to go all that way and to come back with nothing? Seems a bit rotten.'

Harry reached round to the table behind him and handed a bag to Jim.

'Take one and pass the bag on if you could,' Harry said.

Jim reached into the bag and pulled out a keyring.

'You're too generous!'

'I am that,' Harry said, as Jim stared at the tiny red London bus hanging from his fingers.

'What, nothing for Fly?' Jim asked.

'He's still got that bone lying around that I got him last week!' Harry said, noticing then that Fly was having a good old gnaw on what was left of it.

Jen was next, revealing another keyring, this one of a black cab. Liz reached in and found herself to be the lucky owner of a small red letterbox. Then it was Matt who revealed a London Underground sign. That left Gordy and Jadyn. Gordy pulled out a tiny teddy bear with no mention of London anywhere to be seen, but Jadyn got the worst of the lot, revealing a rabbit's foot.

'Yeah, I can't really explain those last two,' Harry sighed. 'I was rushing to catch the train, you see, and I just grabbed the first ones that came to hand.' He smiled, then added, 'It's the thought that counts though, right?'

'I guess,' Jadyn said, sniffing his new keyring before stuffing it into a pocket.

'So, anyway,' Harry said, keen to move on, 'my meeting with Mr Straub...'

'It went well, then?' Gordy asked.

'It was certainly interesting,' Harry said. 'And I can now reveal why the band Geryon were at Gareth's concert! Jim?'

Jim sat up with a start.

'What? I mean, yes, boss?'

'Perhaps you'd like to share with the others what you and I learned yesterday?'

Jim made to stand, but Harry waved him back down into his chair.

'I was doing research on the band, like you asked,' Jim said. 'And they have loads of social media stuff going on, with Twitter and TikTok and Instagram and Facebook. They've got a YouTube channel and a blog, too. Can't see how they've time to play if they spend all their time on everything, but there you go.'

'So, what did you find?' Matt asked.

'I was skimming through their blog,' Jim explained.

'There was a lot in there about how they were looking for a record deal, how difficult it was to get one, that kind of thing, and how they'd sent off a load of demos to record companies.'

'I'm not following you,' Matt said.

'I don't think any of us are,' Jen said.

'They listed all the record companies they'd sent demos to, on their blog,' Jim said. 'They called it their Kill List because, and I quote: *"We're gonna kill 'em with our darkness, make 'em bleed with it, and those that don't get what we're about, let them burn!"'*

'They wrote that?' Gordy asked.

'They did,' said Jim.

'How pleasant! But again, like Matt said, I'm still not with you.'

'Turns out, one of the record companies belongs to a certain Nicholas Straub,' Harry said.

'So what?' said Jadyn.

'So,' Harry said, 'he went trawling through all the demos, found a band desperate enough for fame to do literally anything, and sold them on this idea to gatecrash Gareth's concert as a promotional stunt, stringing them along that they'd have a better chance of a deal.'

'But why?' Liz asked.

'So that he could gloat,' Harry said. 'He drove all the way from London to watch Gareth's comeback concert fall apart. It didn't. Which was why he then went to see him at his cottage.'

'He was there, then?' Liz said.

Harry nodded.

'He's a bitter and vindictive man, is Mr Straub,' Harry said. 'And between all of us and these four walls, I think he's more than a little bit, you know...' Harry tapped the side of his head.

'So, he did it, then?' Jadyn said. 'Did you arrest him?'

Harry shook his head.

'Yes, he was there, had a big old barny with Gareth back at his cottage, lots of shouting and pushing and shoving, but afterwards, he went back to where he was staying, a rather exclusive bed and breakfast in Bainbridge.'

'But he still could've done Gareth in, couldn't he?' Jadyn said. 'Like you said, he's got motive, he was up at Gareth's place.'

'Solid alibi, I'm afraid,' Jim said. 'All checked out. He was back just after midnight. Couldn't find his key so had to call the owner, who was none too impressed, and very much remembered everything about Mr Straub, the state he was in with his cuts and bruises, and the fact that he was then in bed until way past midmorning before heading off back to London.'

'Even took his keys off him,' Harry added.

'That's that, then,' Gordy said. 'And I'm glad, because I got nothing from Geryon yesterday.'

'Why's that?' Harry asked.

'A wall of legal threats from both Andrew's and Keith's parents. Not that it amounts to much if we've reason to go on questioning, but I thought I'd wait on what I learned today. And I'm glad I did.'

'So, there we go,' Harry said. 'Jadyn, I think we can put a line through Geryon and Mr Straub.'

Jadyn did as requested.

'What about the rest of you?' Harry asked, then looked over to Jen. 'How was the vicar?'

'Turns out she collects books on witchcraft,' Jen said.

'Well, not just witchcraft, but beliefs in general. She's not what you'd call a normal, everyday vicar, that's for sure.'

'That's a bit odd though, isn't it?' Jim asked. 'We've got this murder and all this occult stuff and it just so happens that the vicar is well into it?'

Gordy laughed. 'I don't think that's what she said.'

'But what about her alibi?' Jadyn said. 'We've only got her word that she was on her own, haven't we?'

'She's telling the truth,' Gordy said.

'But how do we know that?' Jadyn asked. 'Vicars can be murderers too, you know.'

'Because—' began Gordy, but her voice stuck in her throat.

Harry looked over at his DI.

'Everything okay, there?'

Gordy nodded. 'Look, she was alone, okay? She's telling the truth. Trust me.'

'Is there something you know that we don't?' Harry said, puzzled now.

'She asked me not to say,' Gordy replied. 'She's a very private woman, and with her job, and how people are, she, well, she just needs to be careful. Not that she doesn't trust people, you know, but... oh, God, I'm rambling...'

'Yes, you are,' Harry said. 'This is not only a murder investigation though, this is also the very definition of confidential. Whatever it is the vicar doesn't want people to know, I can't see it getting beyond these four walls.'

Gordy, Harry noticed, looked a little awkward.

'Please, Gordy,' he said.

'I know she was alone because I was on the phone with her for most of the night,' Gordy said. 'Remember that date I said I went on last week?'

Harry did, and at the same time remembered how he'd noticed that Gordy and Anna had seemingly recognised each other Sunday morning.

'Well,' Gordy continued, 'it was with Anna. And I know the Church of England is pretty okay about things now, I mean it's not perfect, but it's working on getting there, but anyway, we met a good distance away from Askrigg, and then Saturday night I called her to see how the concert had gone. She'd mentioned it, you see, and was pretty excited about it. She then told me about what had happened, and we just talked and talked. Before either of us knew what we were doing, it was gone four in the morning. So, I'm her alibi, if she needs one at all.'

CHAPTER THIRTY-FIVE

'WELL, WE'RE CERTAINLY DOING VERY WELL AT FINDING out who didn't do it,' Harry huffed. 'Jadyn, strike the vicar off the suspect list, would you?'

'You didn't really suspect her though, did you?' Matt asked.

'To be honest, no,' Harry said. 'But still, an open mind, and all that. Now, what's left?'

'I went round all the friends again,' Matt said. 'Alibis stack up. Except, it seems, for Lisa Shaw and her now-fiancé, Mick Johnson.' He then turned to Jen. 'You want to tell, or shall I?'

'You start,' Jen said. 'I'll jump in as and when.'

'You see, boss,' Matt said, 'while I was talking to Lisa and Mick, neither of whom were best pleased to see me, Jen here turned up at the door. Turns out, she'd just had a little chat with the landlord of the King's Arms, where they all stayed Saturday night, remember?'

'He'd called in with a bit of information,' Jen said. 'So, I popped over there for a chat, then headed over to speak with Mick and Lisa.'

'As you know, they were each other's alibis,' Matt said. 'After the pub, they went to bed, and that was that.'

'Not so, it seems,' Jen said. 'Because the landlord remembered seeing one of them leave the pub in the early hours. I think he'd nipped to the toilet and heard a disturbance.'

'So, who was it?' Harry asked. 'Who left the pub?'

'It was Mick,' Matt said. 'The landlord also said that when he looked in the car park he saw that their car was gone. He didn't hear it, but that's no surprise, what with all the snow, and all.'

'They lied, then,' Harry said.

Matt nodded. 'That they did, boss.'

'Why?'

'As far as they're concerned there's nothing to tell,' Matt said. 'Mick couldn't sleep and went for a walk, that's it. And Lisa didn't notice because she'd had too much to drink and was out for the count.'

'But what about the car?' asked Jim.

'They both think that the landlord must have been mistaken, and I can see their point. I went and had a look at the car park for the pub and it would be pretty difficult to see what's what in the middle of the night, and even more so with tired eyes.'

'Mick also said he would never drink and drive,' Jen added. 'He was pretty adamant about that. Started on about how an old school friend of his had been killed driving over the limit. He really hammered that point home. Even stood up and started waving his hands about, telling us that we couldn't arrest him!'

'But they still lied,' Harry said. 'And I don't like that. Particularly when I can't see any real reason for it.'

'The vicar lied,' Jadyn said and Harry rounded on him with such wide eyes that the police constable backed down immediately.

'She didn't lie,' Harry said. 'She was alone all night, correct? She simply didn't tell us that she had been on the phone, which is a different thing entirely, and the detective inspector's explanation was clear. Understood?'

'Yes, boss,' Jadyn muttered. 'Sorry, boss.'

Harry turned back to Matt and Jen.

'What do you think, then? About Mick and Lisa?'

'I don't actually know what to think,' Matt said. 'None of this is working, is it? What evidence we do have is pointing nowhere and if we're honest that evidence in itself doesn't amount to much.'

'Perhaps we should take a break,' Harry said.

'Good plan,' Matt said. 'Because this absolutely calls for copious quantities of tea and a positively illegal amount of cake and cheese.'

Harry groaned.

'Don't give me that,' Matt said. 'We've all seen you eating it, and enjoying it, I might add.'

'Okay, then,' Harry said. 'Do your worst.'

WITH THE TEAM splitting off into their own little discussions and having munched his way through a far too large piece of cake and cheese, Harry was outside trying to see if fresh air would help, his large hands wrapped around the now half-empty but still positively enormous mug that Matt had given him the year before.

It didn't.

'You alright, boss?'

Jadyn's voice bounced out to greet Harry as though it was excited to see the snow and couldn't wait to go for a play in it.

'Not exactly, no,' Harry said.

'Maybe you should have a rub of this, then,' Jadyn said, holding out the rabbit's foot Harry had given him. 'Meant to be good luck, aren't they? Though, I can't see how that's fair on the rabbit.'

'Sorry about that,' Harry said. 'Bit of a rubbish gift really, isn't it? I'm not good at stuff like that. I think I was just mulling over what the pathologist had said, about finding that rabbit fur, and then I saw that, and before I knew what I was doing, I'd bought the thing. Feel free to throw it away.'

'What now, then?' Jadyn asked.

Harry shook his head.

'I think I'll head off for a chat of my own with Mick and Lisa. And while I'm on with that, would you mind giving the pathologist a call for me? Said she'd get back to me if she'd found anything else. I doubt she has, or she'd have rung, but you never know.'

'No bother,' Jadyn said.

Harry drained his mug and headed back inside.

'Where are those photos from the church?'

'Here,' Jen said, handing Harry a folder.

'Right, I'm going to go and have a chat with Mick and Lisa,' Harry said, having a quick flick through the photos, then slipping them back into a pocket. 'Probably nothing will come of it, but it might stir something else up. Can someone give them a call for me, let them know I'm on my way?'

'I will,' Jen said. 'And if they're not in?'

'Then tell them they had bloody well better be!' Harry said, and with that, was gone.

THE JOURNEY over to Lisa's parents' house, which had Harry driving over to Askrigg and past the church to head out towards Carperby, was nice and clear. Harry allowed his eyes to just relax and take in the scenery as he mulled things over, once again driving his old Rav4, thanks to a swift repair of something Mike the mechanic had explained in great detail to him, but which Harry had then forgotten almost immediately.

Nothing seemed to make sense.

He had a dead celebrity singer, a growing number of suspects clearly not guilty, and so much weirdness that he was pretty sure he was well over his quota for one lifetime just from this case alone. Add to this the ongoing struggle that Jim was still having over his friend's murder, and the shadow cast by that particular case, Harry was of a mind that what he really needed more than anything was a holiday. Though, what he'd do with one he had no idea. He couldn't remember the last time he'd had a proper holiday in his life. He'd had time off, for sure, but to actually go away somewhere, to relax? No idea.

A couple of miles out of Askrigg, Harry took a right down a narrow lane, stopping at a rather grand-looking house, set back from the road. A small commuter car was out front. A Fiat something or other, Harry guessed, judging by how the vehicle not only looked too small for anyone over five and a half feet in height to fit into, but also was so overly designed as to look as though it was little more than an oversized perfume bottle.

Harry knocked at the door, which was pulled open a moment later by a tall, slim man, probably in his mid-sixties, Harry thought.

The man smiled at Harry.

'Hello,' he said. 'Can I help?'

'I'm Detective Chief Inspector Harry Grimm,' Harry said. 'And I'm looking for a Lisa Shaw and Mick Johnson.'

'Oh, is this about what happened at church? Such an awful thing. Perhaps you should come in.'

Harry stepped through the door and into the house to follow the man down a hall and into a lounge.

'I've just lit the fire,' the man said. 'This cold snap really isn't budging, is it? I'm Stuart, by the way. Lisa's father.'

'Good to meet you,' Harry said, noticing that Stuart's Yorkshire accent was barely noticeable, as though it had been educated out of him at some point. 'And this is a very nice house you have here, I must say.'

Harry wasn't one for jealousy or envy, but sometimes it was impossible. Lisa had obviously grown up in very comfortable surroundings.

The room was decorated and furnished somewhat traditionally, as though for inspiration, Lisa's parents had visited various stately homes and decided to reproduce the look, only smaller. The sofas were deep burgundy and looked comfy enough to swallow you. An impressive wooden sideboard, probably oak, Harry guessed, sat against one wall, and by another was a drinks cabinet. The windows were large and through them cast the brightest of sunshine. And as for the fireplace? Well, Harry had never seen one so large, the fire in it comprising logs which were heading on the way towards trunks. The walls were decorated not only with various pictures in gilt frames, but numerous photographs, and in all of them Harry could see that Lisa was there, front and centre, be that on her own, with her parents, or with friends.

'Thank you,' Stuart said. 'That's very kind. Now, can I get you something to drink? Probably a little early for a nip of something stronger, but what about tea or coffee?'

'No, I'm fine, thanks,' Harry said.

'Are you sure? My wife gave me this rather wonderful coffee maker for Christmas and I can't get enough of the stuff! Probably why I'm not sleeping much at the moment, but then who does at my age, always getting up in the middle of the night, visiting the loo?'

'Quite,' Harry said, stuck for anything else to say.

'Well, if you're sure.'

'I am,' Harry said. 'Now, I'm assuming Lisa's here, yes? One of my team called ahead for me.'

'Oh, yes, I remember,' Stuart said. 'About half an hour ago, wasn't it? Yes, Lisa got the message, told me you were coming over.'

'So, she's here then?'

'No, she isn't.'

Harry took a very slow, very deep breath, then exhaled just as slowly.

'Well, is Mick here, then?'

'Michael? No, he's with Lisa.'

This was already going badly, Harry thought, and realised that he was pacing.

'Do you know when they'll be back?'

'I don't think they'll be long,' Stuart said.

Harry was now by one of the walls and looking at various photographs of Lisa. Some were from school, the Girl Guides, family holidays, but a good number were also of her,

Gareth, and the others. Harry recognised them as copies of the ones he'd seen back at the community office. And there were others, of Lisa older now, graduating, skiing, sitting in the sunshine with her parents.

'I'm rather a fan of photos,' Stuart said. 'My wife, Milly, well, she thinks I have too many, but I disagree. It's like surrounding myself with lovely little snapshots of my past. Almost as though each of those memories are with me whenever I walk into this room.'

'Looks like she had a very happy childhood,' Harry observed, and it was true. The smile on her face in all of the photos was broad and genuine and full of joy.

'I hope so,' Stuart said. 'One can only do one's best as a parent. And you know, you never stop being one. I mean, there she is, a child, and then there's these others, an adult. But she's still our little Lisa.'

'It's good to be close to family,' Harry said.

'We're very lucky,' Stuart said. 'She even still comes away on holiday with us sometimes, you know?' He pointed at the photos Harry had seen of Lisa in the sun. 'France, three years ago. Wonderful time. She needed cheering up, so we stepped in, as parents do.'

Harry had little he could add to what Lisa's dad had said, so he asked, 'The car out front, is that yours?'

'Good God, no!' Stuart laughed. 'Mine's in the garage. That little thing's Lisa's.'

'They went in Mick's car, then?'

Stuart nodded and Harry leaned in for a closer look at the photos.

'Here's a question,' Harry said, thinking back over everything and pretty much just looking for something to talk about to fill the silence, 'and it might sound a little odd, but it was something we were discussing as a team earlier.'

'Go ahead,' Stuart replied. 'Not sure I'll be able to help though. I'm no detective!'

Harry smiled. 'No, it's not important, I'm sure, but do you remember Lisa and her friends all having nicknames?'

At this, Stuart laughed.

'My God, I'd completely forgotten that, you know! How on earth did you stumble across that little fact?'

'A photo from the church, they'd all signed it,' Harry said, then gently tapped the glass on one of the photo frames. 'They'd all signed it and I was just wondering which nickname belonged to which of this lot here, that was all.'

Stuart came over to stand beside Harry and leaned in to have a closer look.

'Well, I remember that Gareth was Toots,' he said. 'It was Christopher who gave them all their names. Quite creative, that boy. Loved reading, writing stories.'

'Toots?' Harry said.

'On account of him being the best singer,' Stuart said. 'Well, he thought he was, anyway. Christopher was just as good, you know. He was Doughnut. Penny was Quidsy and Claire, that poor girl, she was Psycho!'

Harry laughed. 'Well, we guessed right then,' he said. 'Amazing! But why Doughnut for Christopher?'

'He was, shall we say, a little on the larger side as a child,' Stuart explained. 'Children can be incredibly cruel.'

'That leaves Rambo and Bonny,' Harry said.

'Rambo was Andrew,' said Stuart. 'He was obsessed with the film, had ideas of heading off to join the army when he was older. You know, I think he even tried out for it?

Anyway, he works over at the auction rooms in Leyburn now.'

'So Bonny was Lisa, then,' Harry said.

'Bonny?' said Stuart. 'No, she was never Bonny. Bunny, yes, but not Bonny.'

'Bunny?' Harry said, and was about to ask why, when a line of cold carved itself down his back.

'Something wrong, Detective?' Stuart asked.

Harry was staring at the photo. It couldn't be, could it? He thought. What was the reason, the motive, never mind the how...

'Do you know where they've gone, Lisa and Mick?' Harry asked.

'They're at Christopher's,' Stuart said. 'I've no idea why. He rang, while you were on your way, and off they went.'

'And you're sure her nickname was Bunny?' Harry asked.

'Very much so,' Stuart replied, then nipped out into the hall to return a few seconds later with a set of keys. 'See?'

'That's a rabbit's foot!' Harry said, remembering his conversation with Jadyn earlier, amazed to be staring at another of the macabre things on the same day.

'She's had it for years,' replied Stuart. 'Ever since she was a child.'

But Harry wasn't listening. He was already out of the door and on the phone to the office back in Hawes.

CHAPTER THIRTY-SIX

HARRY WAS SITTING JUST A LITTLE WAY OFF FROM Christopher's house when he saw two police incident response vehicles pull up behind him. He climbed out to be met by the rest of the team.

Gordy was over to him first, with Matt and the others gathering around.

'So, what have we got?' she asked

'Our suspect, I think,' Harry said.

'Who?' Matt asked.

Harry cast an eye around the team, then said, 'Lisa. Lisa Shaw.'

He saw a wave of disbelief sweep through them all, eyes widening at the name.

'I know,' Harry said, 'and what you're all thinking now is what I've been thinking while I've been waiting for you.'

'Lisa Shaw, though?' said Jen. 'It can't be, can it? How's that even possible?'

'And what's the motive?' asked Jim.

Harry scratched his chin as he tried to get his thoughts in

order, spotting Fly staring at him through the window of one of the police cars.

'Right, you remember what the pathologist told us about the tower, yes?'

'Too much and not enough, if you ask me,' Matt said. 'What with the paint from Gareth's house all over the tower walls, that door lock smashed from the inside, and something about rabbit fur.'

'Exactly,' Harry said, pointing a finger at Matt. 'Rabbit fur!'

'Nope, no idea,' Liz said.

'The nicknames,' Harry said. 'On the photo. Remember? Rambo and Psycho and the others?'

'Doughnut, Quidsy, Toots, and Bonny,' said Jadyn, reading them out from his little notebook.

'Well, we were right, or you were, anyway, Jen,' Harry said, giving a well-done nod to the police constable. 'Psycho was Claire Sykes, and Quidsy was Penny. As for the others, Gareth was Toots, Christopher was Doughnut, and Rambo, that was Andrew.'

'So Lisa was Bonny, then?' Liz said. 'I'm still not making the connection.'

'That's because we read it wrong,' Harry said. 'Remember how faded the writing was? Turns out, it wasn't Bonny at all. It was Bunny.'

Matt shook his head.

'Tenuous at best,' he said.

'Then there's this,' Harry said, holding up Lisa's key ring for everyone to see.

'Hey, that's my rabbit's foot!' Jadyn said. 'No, wait, it can't be, because mine's in my pocket.'

'This is Lisa's,' Harry said. 'Apparently, she's had this since she was a kid.'

'So, she's got a rabbit's foot and was called Bunny as a kid,' said Gordy. 'That doesn't mean she killed Gareth, does it? In fact, it's so far away from anything to do with Gareth that I'm beginning to wonder if all that cheese and cake Matt here has been forcing you to eat hasn't actually damaged your brain!'

'The concert was Lisa's idea though,' Matt said. 'She mentioned that to Jen and me when we interviewed her earlier in the week.'

'So, the only reason Gareth was here at all is because of her,' Harry said. 'See? I'm on to something here, I know I am!'

Liz was reading through her own notes.

'I jotted this down when we were all together as well. Can't remember which day, like, but it was you that said it, Jen, that you thought she had a bit of a crush on Gareth when she was a kid?'

'Actually, Mick said that as well,' Jen said. 'It's why Lisa went into music as a profession, because she was kind of following Gareth. Which is a bit weird I guess.'

'Weird or not, why kill him?' Matt asked. 'Why get him here and do *that* to him? That's what I don't get with this.'

'I honestly don't know,' Harry said, and he really didn't, but there was an itch, a big one, and he was going to scratch it and make it bleed if he had to, just to get to the bottom of what was going on. 'And I know I've not got enough at all to make an arrest. Not by a long shot. But I do have enough to bring her in for questioning, I'm sure I do. So, here we are.'

'Agreed on all that,' said Gordy, 'but why do you need us?'

'Because,' Harry said, 'if I am right, and Lisa, for whatever reason is responsible, then this could go south very quickly. We've all seen how people react to this kind of situation. Some are thoughtful, go in on themselves, some scream and shout and lash out. Others make a run for it, innocent or not, panic taking over.'

'Fight or flight,' Matt said.

'Exactly,' said Harry. 'And with the weather like this, the last thing I want is Lisa running around in the snow because who knows what could happen then, right?'

The team was quiet.

'Fair points, all well made,' Gordy said. 'So, what do you want us to do?'

'Just be ready,' Harry said, turning to make his way over to the house. 'Spread out down the road a bit, see if there's a way round to the back of the house at all, just in case. I'll leave it to you. Just stay low, out of sight. I don't want anyone being spooked.'

'And what are you going to do?' Matt asked.

Harry stopped and turned to look at the detective sergeant, then flashed him his best killer smile.

'Why, be my usual charming self, of course,' he said.

THE KNOCK at the door was loud enough to wake the dead. And that was entirely the point; Harry wanted to make sure that those on the other side of it were in no doubt at all that someone was outside and wanted in and that they had better answer it sharp.

The house remained resolutely silent.

Harry knocked again, no knuckles this time, just a hammer fist against the wood.

'This is DCI Grimm,' he called, then his phone buzzed.

'Grimm!' Harry snarled into his phone.

'It's Sowerby,' came the reply. 'Caught you at a bad time?'

'You could say that, yes,' said Harry, stepping away from the door for a moment, eyeing the house. 'What is it?'

'Your police constable called, asked if I had anything else.'

'And do you?'

'I do,' Sowerby replied, 'but I can call back.'

'No, no, now's as good as any,' Harry said. 'What is it?'

'Rabbit fur,' Sowerby said.

Harry was very quickly growing tired of that particular furry little creature. 'What about it?'

'Mad as this may sound I ran a search on HOLMES.'

'For rabbit fur? You're having a laugh!'

Harry sensed an immediate icy chill from down the line.

'I can assure you, Detective,' Sowerby said, 'that nothing I do is just for a laugh! And if that's what you think, then—'

'No, no, I'm sorry,' Harry said, cutting in. 'What did you find?'

There was still no sound coming from the house, no sense of life at all. Which wasn't just odd, it was downright wrong.

'Well, for fur, not much,' Sowerby said. 'But rabbits was another matter entirely.'

'That news doesn't exactly fill me with glee.' Harry sighed. 'What, so loads of crimes involved rabbits?'

'No,' Sowerby said. 'Well, not exactly. But there's been a few here and there, usually the more bizarre ones involving some kind of animal cruelty, that kind of thing.'

'What kind of thing?' Harry said. 'We're not dealing with a bunny serial killer here, are we?'

'No, you're not,' Sowerby said, 'but something did come up.'

'What?'

'Fatal car crash, three years ago. Down in Kent.'

'You found a report on a car accident caused by a rabbit?'

Harry couldn't believe what he was hearing. Had the world gone mad?

'Hit and run. The driver of the car who caused the collision ran from the scene, and the car itself was found to be stolen.'

'Is there a point to this?'

'Two, actually,' Sowerby said. 'One, that those involved in the accident were Gareth Jones and his wife, Karen. And, as I'm sure you know, Karen died of her injuries not long after.'

There was a sound at the door, a chain being lifted.

'And two?'

'A rabbit's head was found in the car,' Sowerby said. 'Desiccated, mummified pretty much. Amazingly, the remains were still held in evidence and I had them sent up to examine them and—'

Another sound at the door of a key being turned, a latch, distracting Harry as he stared at it, waiting for it to open, but Sowerby was still talking.

'—same DNA.'

'Can you repeat that?' Harry asked, his eyes still on the door. 'Something about DNA? What? What about DNA? Did you get a match?'

The door started to swing open.

'It was the same,' Sowerby said.

'The same as what? What exactly are you saying?'

'I'm saying,' Sowerby replied, as Harry stared at the door, watched it yawn wide into the house behind, 'that the rabbit's head that was found in the car that killed Gareth Jones' wife is from the rabbit that was, for however long, kept in the hole in the wall of the church in Askrigg!'

Harry heard the words but didn't understand them. They made no sense! This was a murder investigation! Why the hell was the pathologist phoning to talk to him about rabbits?

Then Sowerby spoke again, her voice louder this time, firm.

'Grimm! Can you hear me? It's the same rabbit, Harry. The same rabbit!'

But the door was open now and Harry hung up and turned to face the person standing there in front of him.

CHAPTER THIRTY-SEVEN

'LISA,' HARRY SAID, BUT HIS VOICE CAUGHT IN HIS throat for a moment, turning the end of the woman's name into a cough.

'You didn't need to come here,' Lisa said, a smile on her face that managed to curl the corners of her mouth but left her eyes out of it completely, the grimace of the dead. 'We were coming back. I told Dad to tell you that we were coming back.'

'You did, I know,' Harry said, 'but I needed to talk with you. Urgently, actually.'

'Why?'

'Can I come in?'

Lisa, Harry noticed, had the look to her of a cornered animal, frightened and desperate. He was glad he'd made the call to have the team with him, just in case.

'No, I mean, this isn't my house and I need to ask Christopher.'

'I can't see that being a problem, can you? I'll speak to him if you want me to.'

'No!'

She was going to bolt, Harry knew it. But he still had her in the doorway, so that was something. If he could just keep her there, and either persuade her to come quietly, or to go back inside with him for a chat, then that would be fine. For now.

'Look, why don't you just pop back in there and get him for me?' Harry said, keeping his voice calm, if not exactly soft. 'And Mick, too. Then we can all sit together, can't we, and have a little chat? Put the kettle on, that kind of thing?'

'You want to speak to Mick as well?'

'Yes, why not?' Harry said. 'Just a few things I need to go over, that's all, and perhaps Mick will be able to help. So, what do you say?'

Lisa gave no response, just stood in the doorway, staring.

'Lisa?'

'No, you can't come in, I'm sorry. Please, go away!'

She was shutting the door. Harry couldn't let that happen. Neither could he startle her, because another thought was with him now, a darker one. Where were Mick and Christopher? Why was it Lisa who had answered and not the owner of the house himself?

'I need to come in, Lisa,' Harry said. 'Whatever's happened, we just need to talk. You'll be safe, I promise.'

Lisa was shaking her head now, tears starting to bubble up and tumble down.

Harry held up his hands, wide and open.

'See? There's nothing hidden, is there? No handcuffs, nothing like that. It's just me and all I want to do is talk.'

Lisa took a step back.

'I'm not going to hurt you, Lisa,' Harry said, growing desperate now, working hard to keep his voice as gentle as he could. 'That's not why I'm here at all. I just want to talk, find out what really happened. That's all. Do you think you can do that?'

Another step, the door starting to close. Harry needed to take another tack.

'Christopher, are you there?' he shouted, desperate to make sure that anyone who heard him knew the police were here. 'Mick? It's DCI Grimm! I just want to talk with Lisa, with all of you. Can you come to the door?'

'You need to shut up,' Lisa said. 'Please, you just need to stop!'

Harry took a step towards Lisa.

'Christopher? Mick? Is everything okay? It's DCI Grimm!'

'Don't come any closer,' Lisa said. 'You can't! You don't understand!'

With little else that he could think of, bar charging through the door himself, Harry reached into his pocket and took out the photos.

'I've been looking through these, Lisa,' he said, holding the photos up so that she could see them. 'You were happy then, yes? You and all your friends?'

Lisa had paused, was staring at the photographs.

'That's you there, isn't it? Look how young you were!' Harry said. 'I bet you've got some stories to tell, haven't you? I'd love to hear them, you know. I'm a very good listener, Lisa. The best actually. I know my face is a little off-putting, but if you ignore that, then I'm sure we'll be fine.'

'My story isn't very interesting,' Lisa said.

'Oh, now, don't be daft,' Harry said. 'What about those nicknames then, eh? I'd love to hear about those, about how you got yours. Bunny, wasn't it? A lovely nickname, that, isn't it?'

'What?'

Lisa's voice was hard, her eyes wide.

'Your nickname,' Harry said. 'You remember it, right? Bunny? You see, I thought it was Bonny, but I think the writing has faded or smudged, but then your dad told me—'

'I didn't give myself that name,' Lisa said. 'None of us did! None of us! It was his idea, his! Not mine! Not anyone's!'

'Lisa...'

'He called me it! Because I cried, because it was dead and because he still stabbed it! And then he called me Bunny. He said it was affectionate, a pet name. But it wasn't. Not to me! Not to me!'

Harry was suddenly lost. He had no idea what Lisa was talking about, why she was so upset over a childhood nickname, but at least he had her attention again.

'No one's making fun of you,' Harry said. 'I'm not, am I? Like I said, all I want to do is talk. We can look through these photos together, can't we? And you can tell me all about them. With Mick and Christopher as well.'

The house was too quiet, Harry thought. Far too quiet. And something was telling him that he needed to get in there sharpish.

'It was horrible!' Lisa cried. 'And there was thunder and lightning and I was afraid! It wasn't my fault! It was supposed to be fun, like scary fun, you know? But it wasn't. It was just scary and horrid and he stabbed the rabbit! It was dead, but he still stabbed it!'

Harry had managed to get closer still to the house. Just a step more and he would have Lisa and be inside and then he could call in the rest of the team. But if he spooked her now, anything could happen.

'Was the rabbit a pet, Lisa, is that what this is about? Did Gareth hurt your pet rabbit and then make fun of you by giving you that nickname?'

When Lisa spoke again, her voice was a thin thing, choked and desperate.

'You don't understand! You don't! You're not listening!'

'I am, Lisa! I'm really listening. Right here, right now, that's all I'm doing, just listening to you.'

'No, you're not!' Lisa screamed. 'You're listening but you're not hearing! He stabbed the rabbit! He did it and we all had to make a wish and not tell anyone, don't you see? And we didn't tell our wishes, we all kept them secret, like we were supposed to. But only one of us had their wish granted and now he's dead. Gareth's dead!'

'I know he is,' Harry said.

'I loved him,' Lisa said. 'I've always loved him. And now he's gone! Gone because of someone else's secret wish! That's why he's dead! It's why I have to do what he says! I have to! That's why we came over! Or...'

'Or what, Lisa? What? Tell me!'

Lisa's face relaxed suddenly, as though an invisible tap at her chin had just been turned on, draining her completely of all expression.

'Mick...' she said.

Then the door slammed shut.

CHAPTER THIRTY-EIGHT

HARRY CRASHED INTO THE DOOR JUST IN TIME, HIS shoulder impacting with the hard wood just before the latch clicked shut. He tumbled through into the hall on the other side, lost his footing and fell forwards. Instinct took over and he tucked in his head, turned the fall into a roll, and somehow managed to come out of it crouched on his feet. Then a scream sliced through the air and Harry saw Lisa disappear through a door just ahead of him, underneath the stairs.

'Boss?'

Harry looked behind him to see Detective Sergeant Dinsdale standing in the hallway with him.

'She's down there!' Harry said. 'That door! She went through that door!'

'You okay?' Matt asked.

'I'm fine!' Harry snapped back. 'Get that bloody door open! Now!'

Matt was at the door and gave it a hefty kick.

'One more should do it,' he said.

And he was right, the flimsy lock on the other side giving way easily and bouncing off into the thick dark behind.

'Looks like this is the cellar,' Matt said.

'Of course it's the bloody cellar!' Harry sighed, now back up on his feet. 'It's always the cellar, isn't it?'

Harry looked down into the gloom, the stairs at their feet not exactly well lit.

'Lisa?' Harry shouted. 'Lisa! Don't do anything stupid now. Just think, okay? I need you to just think about where you are and what you're doing. Mick has nothing to do with this. Or Christopher. Please, Lisa!'

No answer came.

Harry huffed.

'Bollocks.'

'I'll second that,' Matt said. 'Want me to get the others?'

Harry shook his head.

'No, not right now. We don't know what's down there. She's spooked enough already as it is.'

'What about Mick and Christopher?'

'That's what's worrying me,' Harry said. 'You got a torch?'

Matt slipped a hand into his pocket and pulled out a small, black cylinder. There was the faintest, softest of clicks, and a bright beam of light broke the dark.

'Ready?' Harry asked.

'I'm never anything else,' Matt said.

Harry took point and moved down into the cellar, Matt a couple of paces behind him, the beam of his torch flooding the stairs with light.

The stairs were against a wall, and Harry flattened his back along it to give himself a better view of the cellar as they slipped further down into the darkness.

'We're coming now, Lisa,' Harry said. 'There's no way out now. You just need to come quietly, okay? Come back with us so we can work this out together, before anyone else gets hurt.'

The air was surprisingly warm, Harry noticed, and dry. He could smell oil and laundry and wood.

Something flashed in the dark and Harry threw himself backwards, into Matt. They both fell onto their backs as something slammed into the wall right where Harry's head had been.

Matt pushed himself up.

'What the hell was that?'

Harry leaned forward and saw a hammer on one of the steps.

'Evidence,' he said, and was up on his feet again, only now, he wasn't being careful anymore. Someone had thrown a hammer at his head. And it was that kind of thing that really pissed him off.

'Right, that's it, Lisa, I'm done messing around now!' Harry shouted. 'What you just did? That was easily assault, possibly even attempted murder! So right now, if you wanted me in a bad mood, well that's what you've got!'

Harry was at the bottom of the stairs in a beat, Matt scrabbling to keep up. The cellar was all shelves and shadows and it was huge, stretching off in front of him. He turned to Matt.

'You got pepper spray on you?'

'That I have, boss,' Matt replied.

'If she comes at you, use it. Understand?'

Harry didn't wait for a reply and turned back to head off into the cellar.

Walking down a thin path in the dark, rows of shelving

heading off at right angles away from him, Harry edged forward. The beam from Matt's torch lit the way enough for him to see the end of the cellar just ahead, which meant he was close to wherever it was Lisa was hiding.

'Lisa? You need to give up now. Please. This isn't a game. It's over.'

Harry was lifted off his feet and slammed into the wall. Bright lights burst in his head. Then he was lifted again and brought down onto the floor with such a thump that what wind he had left in his lungs disappeared immediately.

Harry opened his eyes, saw Matt racing to his aid, only to see him levelled by a punch to the face.

'Bastard...'

Harry pushed himself to his feet, steadied himself against the wall, then pushed himself into whoever it was that had just thrown the punch. His momentum was enough to knock them off balance, so he took the advantage and pressed on, pushing with his legs, forcing his assailant to fall back and eventually crash into a stack of shelves.

Pots and jars and bits of wood tumbled out of the dark like hail.

Harry clambered up the shelves, dragging himself upright. Then a thump to his gut sent bile shooting up into the back of his throat. He gagged on it, the acrid burn of the stuff filling his mouth, his nose.

Another thump, but Harry was ready this time, the soldier inside him pushing to the front to take over, the policeman stepping to one side.

Thrusting forward with his elbow and forearm, he created a wedge and stopped the punch, which slid painfully down his arm. Another punch came and he did the same, then Harry turned from defence to attack. He pushed forward, keeping the distance between him and his attacker good and close, throwing his own punches now, short jabs which pressed on, pushed on, knocking the attack further and further back. This was all self-defence because Harry knew that if he didn't drive forward strong and hard then his attacker would be back into him, perhaps even with another weapon, another hammer. He wasn't about to take that chance, not if his life was at risk.

The attacker tried to respond, the bulk of whoever it was almost too much for Harry, but he was into them with his elbows now, striking hard and fast from both sides, not worrying about what he was hitting or where, just pushing and pushing and pushing, never giving the other a chance to think, to get the initiative.

'Boss! Duck!'

Matt's voice crashed out of the dark and into Harry and he dropped to the ground, to his knees, as over his head his DS came in and sent a well-aimed jet of pepper spray into his attacker's face.

A scream ripped through the air and as Harry scrambled out of the way, Matt clambered over him, his light shining bright as he made an arrest. Which was when Harry saw who had attacked him.

'Chris?'

The big man was on the floor, hands now cuffed behind his back. He was spitting and gagging on the pepper spray, a proper mess, but he was breathing and he'd be fine. Though Harry wanted to have another go at him after what he'd just done.

Harry heard another sound then, a whimper in the dark.

Back up on his feet, Harry headed through to the far end of the cellar, took a left and there saw Lisa and Mick.

Lisa stared at Harry through eyes shot to hell with blood and tears. She was kneeling on the ground, Mick's head resting in her lap.

'He said he'd kill Mick if I told you anything! That's what he said! I couldn't let you in!'

'Lisa,' Harry said, approaching her carefully, slowly. 'It's all okay now. It's safe.'

'He did it!' Lisa said, her voice cracked and broken and weak. 'He killed Gareth because he wanted me! He's always wanted me. I was his wish! That's why he wanted us to do it in the first place, all those years ago, when we were kids! The thing with the rabbit in the graveyard! That's why!'

Lisa sobbed, hugged Mick's head tightly.

Harry edged a little closer and then something fell into place.

'You were on holiday,' he said. 'When Gareth and Karen were hit by the car. That was Chris, not you...'

'It was all Chris,' Lisa said. 'All of it. We only came over because he said he wanted to talk about doing something in Gareth's memory and that seemed like such a nice idea, you know? But it was a lie! All of it was a lie! All these years!'

Mick coughed then and Harry saw dark pools on the man's shirt. Then he saw on the ground by his side a pair of scissors.

'Matt? Matt! We need medevac, now!'

Harry had fallen back on a soldiering term, but Matt understood.

'On it, boss,' he said. 'You okay?'

'I'm fine, go!' Harry said. 'Go! Now!'

Matt raced out of the cellar and a moment later other bodies were down there, Jadyn and Jim dealing with Christopher, Gordy and Jen over with Harry, a first aid kit already open as they slid alongside.

'Matt's grab bag,' Jen said. 'I know we carry a police one, but Matt's is just a little bit better.'

Harry pushed himself to his feet and reached over to Lisa.

'Come on,' he said. 'Let's get you outside.'

Lisa resisted, stared back at Mick, as Gordy and Jen got to work on stabilising him.

'He's in the best of hands,' Harry said. 'And there's help on the way.'

Lisa eventually gave in and followed Harry.

Outside, Liz was waiting, armed with a blanket, which she wrapped around Lisa.

'Right, then,' she said, 'let's get you sat down in a nice warm car, shall we? Come on.'

Harry watched them walk away then saw Matt approaching.

'We've an air ambulance en route,' he said.

'That's good,' Harry said.

'How you doing, then?'

'Better than I look, I'm sure,' Harry said, guessing that his face, beyond the old scarring, was a mess of cuts and grazes and fresh bruising.

'Well, you look terrible,' said Matt.

'Thanks.'

'Not a problem.'

Harry leaned back against the bonnet of his Rav4. The aches and pains were coming at him now, setting up little fires all through his body.

'You never did tell me, you know.'

'Tell you what?'

'About Joan,' Harry said. 'Why she was in hospital. Is it serious?'

'It is,' Matt said, 'but she'll be alright, I'm sure. We both will.'

Harry didn't know what to say.

'Look, if you need time off, you just have to ask.'

'Well, not right now, but in a few months, perhaps.'

Harry's heart sank.

'It's that bad? Look, Matt, I'm really sorry. If there's anything I can do...'

Matt stepped round to stand in front of Harry.

'She's pregnant,' he said.

And Harry very nearly punched the man in the head.

CHAPTER THIRTY-NINE

With a month gone since everything that had happened in Askrigg, the snow was now a distant memory, but the air was still knife-sharp with the cold, and Harry ducked out of it and into the welcome embrace of the bar at the Fountain Hotel in Hawes. The place was humming with conversation, a fire roaring in the grate.

'Boss!'

Harry glanced over to the bar and saw Matt waving.

'Pint of Buttertubs,' Harry called back.

Matt responded with a thumbs-up.

'Dressed up for the occasion, I see,' said Gordy, coming over to meet Harry at the door. Anna was with her, though her dog collar wasn't to be seen. 'How is it that you make that tie look like it wished it was anywhere else but around your neck?'

Harry said, 'So, how's Joan, then?'

'Positively glowing,' Anna said. 'And I know it's a cliché, but I think it's true. I mean, just look at her!'

Harry leaned around the two women and there was Joan,

holding court almost from her wheelchair, with the rest of his team around her. She spotted him, sent across a killer smile, and waved.

'I still can't believe Matt didn't just tell me,' Harry said. 'Or any of us. Had me properly worried for a while there.'

'Just being cautious,' Gordy said. 'But I think they're in the clear now.'

'Matt, a dad,' Harry said, shaking his head. 'Is the world ready, I wonder.'

'No, it isn't,' said Gordy. 'Which makes it even more exciting, I think!'

Matt strolled over from the bar and handed Harry a pint.

'Here you go.'

'Very kind,' Harry said. 'And thanks for the invite. To your little party here.'

'Well, we had to celebrate, didn't we?' Matt said. 'And we're pretty sure everything's okay now. Well, as sure as we can be, anyway.'

Harry spotted his brother, Ben. He was over at the darts with Jim, Liz, Jadyn, and Jen. Jadyn was in his uniform, seeing as he was on duty, but had still made time to pop in. And judging by the scores, Jen was, unsurprisingly, thrashing everyone. Ben, Harry noticed, was standing next to Liz, an arm around her waist, and smiling.

'So, how's that going, then?' Matt asked. 'Bit of a surprise, wasn't it?'

'Liz and Ben? You could say that,' Harry said. 'Seems that people around here like to keep secrets from me, don't they?'

He shot a dark look at Matt, who completely ignored it and took a deep gulp from his beer.

'They look happy, though,' Anna said.

'That they do,' Harry agreed, and couldn't stop the smile from slipping across his face.

'How was Swift?'

Harry gave a short shrug. The detective superintendent had been over earlier in the day to once again go over everything that had happened with the Gareth Jones case. There was going to be plenty of paperwork, Harry knew, plus visits to the court and all the rest that went with a case like this, and Swift really did seem to enjoy making the already complicated and long-winded, even more so.

'I had to run through everything again,' Harry said. 'I mean, he's read the file, all the reports, all the notes, but he still likes to go through it all, ask questions. He should've been a secondary school teacher.'

Gordy gasped. 'Dear God, can you imagine?'

'Yes, I can,' Harry said.

Anna excused herself for a moment, leaving Gordy alone with Harry and Matt.

'How's she doing?' Harry asked.

'Well, actually,' Gordy said. 'By which I mean, as well as anyone can be if they're a vicar who had a celebrity murdered in their church tower.'

'She seems nice,' Harry said.

'She's great,' Gordy said.

'So you're—'

'Staying around? For now, yes. Early days, I know, but who knows, right?'

Harry sipped his pint, did his best to not look too relieved.

'Mick's out of the woods,' he said. 'Lisa's dad called, just to let me know. And to thank us all again for what we did.'

'We were just doing our job,' Matt said. 'What about Lisa?'

'She's fine,' Harry said. 'Split up with Mick and she's moved home for the time being.'

Harry fell quiet and stared off into the middle distance.

'You need to move on, you know,' Gordy said.

'From what?'

'From whatever this all is. You've a face on you like the arse-end of a dead chicken.'

'Thanks for the compliment.'

'It wasn't meant as one,' Gordy said. 'And you know exactly what I mean.'

'We got there in time,' Matt said. 'Like you said, Mick's fine now. Chris is going to be spending an awful lot of time locked away, that's for sure. And Lisa will recover.'

'Still though,' said Harry, 'I really thought it was Lisa. I mean, it kind of all pointed to her, didn't it?'

'It did, until it didn't,' said Gordy. 'And that's police work for you. Nothing's ever obvious. And if it is, then it's usually wrong.'

Harry mulled over what he'd learned since Chris's arrest, about how a game Lisa and her friends had played in the churchyard, trying to scare each other, had become something much more serious for one of them. Just a dare, something that had felt dangerous. And then it had become exactly that and two people had been killed. It could have been more.

'He wanted Lisa all to himself,' Harry said. 'When we had a proper look around his house, we found hundreds of photos of her, of Gareth, of their careers. I'm not even sure that he meant to kill Karen when he crashed into them. He'd been following them on and off for years. Taking time off from work, heading down to London, just to watch.'

'That's very, very creepy behaviour,' Gordy said.

'That it is,' Harry said. 'When he found out that Gareth was heading back to Askrigg, one thing led to another. He overheard Lisa coming onto Gareth, outside the pub, and how he stood her up. And I think he just flipped at that point. And after he'd come to the rescue of everyone at the concert, the knight in shining armour, dealing with the gate-crashers? He'd had enough and something just snapped.'

'And he faked being drunk,' Gordy added.

Harry gave a nod. 'That he did. He'd had a few, for sure, but he just played it up and everyone believed it, because drinking wasn't really his thing, what with all that fitness he's into.'

'And he shouldn't have smashed the lock in from the wrong side,' Matt said. 'That was careless.'

'It was,' agreed Harry. 'The damage to the lock matched marks from the hammer he'd taken from Gareth's cottage.'

'And those keys he'd had since he was a kid.'

'Nicked them off their old choirmaster,' Harry said, 'so he could sneak in and check on that rabbit he'd buried behind the wall in the tower. He really believed in what they'd done as kids, that the sacrifice would work and their wishes would be granted.'

'But why?' Gordy asked. 'It makes no sense.'

'Afraid to believe it wouldn't, I think,' said Harry. 'Because if he lost his belief in that, then what hope did he have? And Gareth's wish had been granted, hadn't it? In his mind, anyway. It's why he took up weight training, so he could impress Lisa. But it was already too late, and then she was away to university and he was still here, in the dales. It ate him up inside.'

Anna came back to join the group.

'So, who wants another?' she asked.

'You know, the last time a vicar bought me a drink,' Harry said, but then decided to go no further with the tale, remembering a not entirely appropriate party back in the army, where everyone had been in fancy dress, and he'd discovered that a bouncy castle was never a good idea at two in the morning, particularly when a major from the SBS was involved.

'Well, would you look at that!' Matt said, and pointed out through the window.

Harry leaned in, straining his eyes.

'Snow? You're kidding me!'

'Looks that way,' Matt said. 'Which reminds me...'

'Of what?' Harry asked.

'Come on,' Matt said, draining his glass and leaving it on a table. 'I've something in the car for you. Forgot to give them to you, what with all that was going on, and then the time just went, didn't it? But if this snow stays, then you may as well have them.'

Harry stopped as Matt got to the door.

'Have what, Matt?' he asked.

Matt's grin was wide and wild.

'My spare set of cross-country skis!' he said, then pushed through the door and held it open for Harry to join him.

THE NEXT DCI Harry Grimm crime thriller is only a click away so don't wait to get stuck into Blood Sport

JOIN THE VIP CLUB!

WANT to find out where it all began, and how Harry decided to join the police? <u>Sign up to my newsletter today</u> to get your exclusive copy of the short origin story, 'Homecoming', and to join the DCI Harry Grimm VIP Club. You'll receive regular updates on the series, plus VIP access to a photo gallery of locations from the books, and the chance to win amazing free stuff in some fantastic competitions.

You can also connect with other fans of DCI Grimm and his team on Facebook by joining The Official DCI Harry Grimm Reader Group.

Enjoyed this book? Then please tell others!

The best thing about reviews is they help people like you: other readers. So, if you can spare a few seconds and leave a review, that would be fantastic. I love hearing what readers think about my books, so you can also email me the link to your review at dave@davidjgatward.com.

AUTHOR'S NOTE

My first winter in Wensleydale, in early 1982, was a thing of wonder. We had moved from Gloucestershire, and were used to seeing snow, but nothing had prepared us for what we woke up to one bright, crisp morning.

Outside, the world was bright white, the snow undisturbed by foot or wheel or plough. Indeed, it was so thick across the road, that the snowplough hadn't even bothered. So, after a quickly consumed breakfast, we dressed accordingly and headed out.

The snow was a couple of feet deep. We had to wade through the garden to get to the road. Staring down into Hawes, it was as though the place had been covered in thick meringue, and as we walked through it, the surface cracked and crumbled and crunched.

I remember our winters in the dales very clearly. Days off school because the heating was frozen, or because the busses simply couldn't get through or risk the journey all the way down the dale to Leyburn and back. And if we were in school, those from farming families often not coming in because they were out with their parents, checking on the sheep.

Sledging on the hill, which lay just before the church-yard on the road out of Hawes, was wild and fast and terrifying. And yes, I even had my own skis, though mine weren't cross country ones. You'll remember that Matt mentions to Harry about skiing out on the hills behind Hawes? Well, I did exactly that. Myself and a couple of friends, Adam and Mike, were driven up through the snow and along the old Roman road by my dad. He had been very enthusiastic indeed about having an excuse to drive his ex-military Land Rover through the snow!

Adam and myself had decent skis, Mike was on a pair of old wooden ones. Having been dropped off, we then proceeded to ski down towards Hawes, across the fields, the walls not a problem as most were lost to deep snow drifts. I even remember how, where the snow was thinner on the ground, tall strands of grass stood tall, encased in thick ice, which shattered as we made our way onwards.

We eventually arrived back in Hawes, our adventure over, our smiles wide. Unfortunately, Mike had a bit of an accident with those wooden skis, one of them snapping some-what dramatically as he coasted over a wall and onto his face!

Whatever the weather, the dales hold an enchantment to them, a magic, which is impossible to ignore. In the brightest sunshine, the fields and fells can seem to glow, not just with green, but with purples and yellows, too. When the storms hit, there is a brooding, moody, and haunting beauty to the place, forcing you to hunker down, light a fire in the grate, and maybe grab yourself a mug of tea and some cheese and cake! The rain seems to stir the land, awakening it, filling the air with the rich smell of peat and earth and grass. And when the snow fell, it brought with it such quiet, that it was as though the fells had pulled themselves deep under its blanket to sleep.

If you do ever visit the dales (and you really should!) then my advice would be to not worry about the time of year, but to just go. Yes, the sunshine and warmth of the summer is attractive, but winter, spring and autumn bless the place in their own unique way, and they're quieter months, too, with most of the tourists having headed home.

And if I'm honest, few things can match the taste of a pint of ale in a dales pub, as the rain hammers against the window, autumn drawing to a close and winter creeping in, and as you step back out into the storm, the tang of the approaching snow is in the air...

ABOUT DAVID J. GATWARD

David had his first book published when he was 18 and has written extensively for children and young adults. *Death's Requiem* is his sixth crime novel.

Visit David's website to find out more about him and the DCI Harry Grimm books.

 facebook.com/davidjgatwardauthor

ALSO BY DAVID J. GATWARD

THE DCI HARRY GRIMM SERIES

Welcome to Yorkshire. Where the beer is warm, the scenery beautiful, and the locals have murder on their minds.

Grimm Up North

Best Served Cold

Corpse Road

Shooting Season

Restless Dead

Blood Sport

Cold Sanctuary

One Bad Turn

Blood Trail

Fair Game

Unquiet Bones

The Dark Hours

Silent Ruin

Dead Man's Hands

Dark Harvest

Printed in Great Britain
by Amazon